I AM THE WILD

KARPOV KINRADE

http://KarpovKinrade.com

Copyright © 2019 Karpov Kinrade
Cover Art Copyright © 2019 Karpov Kinrade
Edited by Joseph Nassise

~~~~~

Published by Daring Books

~~~~~

First Edition
ISBN-13: 978-1-939559-53-1

~~~~~

❀ Created with Vellum

To Neil.
My brother.
My best friend.
You called me your North Star.
But I couldn't guide you home.
I hope you've found peace.

~Lux ;

CONTENTS

A poem by Neil Stevens, Lux's little brother who died by suicide July 13, 2018.

Our Memories Are
Like dancing waters in my soul
Like a diamond emerging from a coal
Like hope ere endless flames of pain
Like graceful dances in the rain
Like somber music played in C
Like a distant, alternate vision of me
Like a dream yet fading beyond the mind
Like colors seen by one once blind
Like a conflagration of all profound
Like the ringing of a precious sound
Like lies that tax and take their toll
Like dancing waters in my soul

THE WANTED AD

Being a candle is not easy; in order to give light, one must first burn. ~ Rumi

UNDERWATER, the world doesn't feel like itself anymore. It becomes more like a gateway to another reality. It's an in-between place, water. Same with air. And dreams. They are all in-between places where so much possibility lives.

I often get my best flashes in the water. Some would call them premonitions, but they aren't nearly that defined. It's more of an impulse that has a slight tingle to it. The kind I've learned to listen to.

It's what lead me to turn right instead of left on my way home yesterday, which took me past a homeless person who I gave change to, who then gave me their newspaper as a thank you, which had a strange advertisement for a job, which resulted in a job interview today.

It read:

. . .

Assistant needed for unique firm.

Must be willing to work at night, travel, and live on site.

Strong stomach a perk.

Compensation generous. Will train.

If you're reading this, you're the person we're looking for.

It listed a number but no name. When I called, a woman answered the phone with a chipper, "The Night Firm, how may I direct your call?"

I told her I was calling about an ad in the newspaper for a job. She paused. Became very quiet for a moment, and then said, "Please hold," with less chipperness than before.

When she returned, her voice was nearly robotic. "Be at 333 Alley Lane at 10 p.m. tomorrow," she said, before promptly and unceremoniously hanging up on me!

I sat staring at my phone for several minutes, unsure of what just happened or what I should do.

A quick Google search for The Night Firm revealed only skin care creams and a questionable website that showed women bent over with minimal clothing. I instantly decided I wasn't going to go. It was stupid, possibly dangerous, and surely not worth it.

But then I set my phone down and wandered my two-bedroom apartment, with the secondhand mismatched furniture that smelled like cigarettes and body odor, the carpet that hailed from another epoch, and the couple above who I'm certain are professional dancers who also like to breathe loudly during sex, and I changed my mind.

Rather, my flash changed my mind. I got the tingly feeling, and I knew I had to go.

So here I am, applying one more coat of mascara before heading out the door in a suit I can't afford and will be returning first thing tomorrow, in hopes of landing the most mysterious job ever.

How do you dress when you have no idea what the job is that you're applying for or anything about the company? I figured it would be better to be professionally overdressed than under, thus the blue Prada suit. The woman at the store insisted I wear it, despite my objection that the feather cuffs were a bit much. She assured me it was all the rage and I must confess I do look rather striking in it. My dark hair is pulled into a French twist and I accented my blue eyes with a charcoal powder. Red lips provide the finishing touch.

They can't possibly judge me for my choice of presentation when they didn't give me any hints as to what they are about.

With one last glance in the mirror and a fake smile that I hope looks sincere, confident and competent, I turn off the light in the bathroom and grab my well-worn leather bag as I head to the front door.

I don't open *his* door this time as I pass it, though I do run my hand over the knob briefly, even as my mind unpacks the memories stored there. Memories of before. Memories of us. Always us. "It's us against the world, Evie," he'd always say, his blue eyes, so alike to mine, peering straight into my soul in a way no one else could. My hand lingers a moment longer, then slips off, and I tuck the memories back into their mental box and shove them away.

I'm clearly not over it. Not ready to entirely move on. Still, there's some progress. I think even Jerry—my former therapist—would agree.

Former because we ended up sleeping together and it took me longer than it should to realize how unhealthy that was. He took advantage of me during a low point in my life, and I let him, because I was in too much pain to say no to something that looked enough like love.

His true colors bled into our relationship slowly and by then it was too late. I was already under his thumb.

I don't even cry every night anymore. Not about my brother and not about my therapist/love/ex/asshole.

But when my phone bings, the familiar panic sends a surge of unneeded adrenaline through my bloodstream and my heart quickens as I swallow back bile.

Because I know it's Jerry.

And I'm not wrong.

I'd love to be wrong. Just once.

PLEASE, babe. Give me another chance. We're perfect together. I love you. Isn't that enough?

I SQUEEZE AWAY the tears forming in my eyes as I look around for something to anchor me to the present moment. The silver door knob. The Ansel Adams print hanging in the hall. The spider crawling in the corner of the ceiling. I breathe in. Breathe out. In through the nose for two counts, out through the mouth four counts. I am safe. Whole. One with all. I am safe. Whole. One with all.

As my body settles and my mind calms, I continue my breathing until the panic abates.

It's getting easier to recover from these unexpected contacts. I screenshot the exchange, put it in the file I created specifically for this, and block the number. Again.

The gesture is beginning to feel pointless. He just finds a new number. I think he's got a year's worth of burner phones for the sole purpose of harassing me daily. I've already deleted all my social media and gone dark in every way that I can. My phone number is unlisted and I change it every three months. I would move if I could, but I haven't been able to afford it since Adam died. The authorities are fairly useless. Which leaves me on my own to deal with my ex.

So here we are.

I drop the phone into my bag and let myself out of my apartment, which involves unlocking four separate deadbolts I insisted my landlord install for me. I take a few moments to lock up, suck in my breath, and turn to face my future.

THE SUBWAY this time of night is shockingly less crowded than I would have expected, much to my relief. Rush hour is long past, but still, New York is overcrowded at any time, day or night. Yet our train is only moderately full, mostly of people who look to be heading out for a good time or coming home from one.

I find a seat as far from everyone else as I can, pull out my sketchbook and pencils, and look around for the perfect subject.

I'm about to settle on a beautiful older male couple holding hands and talking quietly with their heads close together when I see him.

My body's response to him is physical, visceral and immediate. It takes me a moment to remember how to breathe. It's as if all the oxygen has been sucked from me, and when it returns I gasp, then cough to cover up the sound.

He hasn't noticed me—the god-like specimen across the train—and I'd like to keep it that way.

Never have I seen someone so perfect, so symmetrical, so angular in all the right ways, so handsome but also devilishly sexy at the same time. I feel a tightening in my gut as I study him, an awakening of something dormant within, something I haven't felt in a very long time. I shove that feeling aside and focus on the art as my fingers work quickly to sketch his form.

He's tall, maybe 6'4" or 6'5", broad shouldered, tapered waist, all wrapped in a suit that looks custom-tailored just for his body. His dark hair is wild, falls past his collar and compliments his forest green eyes, and I have to look away quickly before he catches me staring. A viral energy emanates from him and he fills the train with a kind of magic that belies his expensive suit.

The woman to his left can't take her eyes off of him, and is practically straining to get closer even as the man she's with wraps his arms around her possessively while he shoots dark looks at the stranger. Two college girls give up their seats to stand closer to him. Even the men respond, some with anger and fear, their bodies betraying their desire to get as far away from him as possible.

It's not just his attractiveness or the wealth he oozes

with every detail of his bearing and clothing. He doesn't look as if he belongs on a New York subway. In fact, he doesn't look as if he belongs in the beautiful but grungy city of New York at all. He looks like a photoshopped magazine cover come to life, but whether that magazine is GQ or National Geographic is hard to say.

I watch, amazed, as some people on the train scoot away from him even as I'm fighting every instinct in me to move closer, as if he has a force field around him repelling and attracting, pushing and pulling. He's drawing me in without even knowing it. I could be invisible to him, but suddenly he's become the only thing I can focus on.

I work almost mindlessly, letting the art and inspiration flow through me. This has always been my release, my way of connecting to the creative movements of life. I minored in art after my college boyfriend convinced me an art major wouldn't be worth the paper my degree was printed on.

I chose a more practical route and kept my art a side hobby, a passion, a secret obsession at times.

I don't completely regret the choice. It turns out I'm damn good at what I do. Sometimes, I even like it. Though finding joy in anything for the last few years has been hard. Even my art has been more therapy than pleasure.

My fingers are smudged black by the time I complete the portrait. I stare at it for a moment, happy to discover I caught that undefinable energy he has, even while standing still. It's like he's always in motion, almost imperceptible, but it's there. A kind of hunger that drives him. I normally like to put stories to the people I draw on the subway, but he seems to defy my silly storytelling. He's telling his own story with every breath, every movement of his head, every glance at his overpriced watch.

I'm completely lost in my drawing when a baritone voice in a British accent shocks me back to the present.

"That's an incredible likeness."

I look up and into his forest eyes—and I feel suddenly lost in sensations of the wind and earth and tall trees and wilderness. My flash is buzzing like a trapped bee in my gut. I'm flustered, which isn't like me. "Thanks," I manage to mutter, though I can't seem to pull my gaze from his.

"You just drew this? In the last few minutes?" he asks, pushing the reluctant conversation forward as he takes the seat beside me. I move my bag to give him more room, and now our thighs are touching and I suck in air like I'll never have the option again.

I nod in answer to his question, my jaw locked stubbornly in place. Come on, get your shit together. Stop acting like a tongue-tied teenager.

"Yes. It's a hobby of mine while on the subway. To draw people I find interesting in some way." There. A complete sentence. We're making progress.

His lips form a smirky little smile. "And what did you find interesting about me?"

I manage to pull my gaze away from his to glance down at my drawing as I consider his question. Obviously he's smoking hot, but I actually see a lot of sexy men in New York, and yet they generally bore me as subjects for my work. It's not his incredible good looks that drew me in. "You seem juxtaposed against life," I say, as if that makes any sense to anyone but me.

He raises an eyebrow. "Do tell," he says.

Great. Okay, how to explain. "You stand out. Most people fade into the fabric of life. They are colors blended into the whole, washed out by the pulse around them. You...you don't blend in. You stand out in sharp contrast, like you don't entirely belong, or maybe you're the only one who truly does belong and everyone else is just faking it. If...if that makes any sense." My mouth is dry now and I reach desperately into my bag for my water.

I pull it out and suck down half the contents just as our train lurches to a halt. My hands, sweaty from stress, can't maintain purchase on the plastic and it slips from my grasp. For a split second I'm aware that my entire sketchbook—and my lap—is about to take a bath it won't recover from.

I'm about to decide that this fiasco ends any chance of me attending my job interview when the stranger next to me reaches out and catches the water bottle before it spills even a single drop.

The movement is so fast I don't even see it. I only see the aftereffect of him holding the bottle that a fraction of a moment ago slipped from my hands.

My eyes widen. "You have quite the reflexes," I say, taking the water back from him and slipping it into my purse after making sure the lid is secured. "Thanks."

He nods but says nothing, just continues staring at me. "You're an unusual woman."

I shrug. "I get that a lot."

"Where are you headed?"

"A job interview," I say.

"Something in art, I hope?" he says.

I chuckle. "No. Haven't you heard? There's no money in art."

He frowns, but doesn't say anything, so I continue. "Business," I say. "I chose business, and that's what the interview is for. Though it's far from what I really want to be doing, to be honest."

I have no idea why I'm telling a total stranger this, but again, here we are.

"Don't settle," he says, "Trust me when I say you don't want to get stuck in a life you hate." His gaze settles on me, his eyes mining mine for secrets. "Hold fast to dreams, For if dreams die, Life is a broken-winged bird That cannot fly."

"Hold fast to dreams," I say, finishing the poem, "For when dreams go, Life is a barren field Frozen with snow."

He raises an eyebrow. "You know your poetry. Are you a fan of Lansgton Hughes?"

"I actually don't read much poetry anymore," I say. "But I took a class in college and I have a good memory."

"Better than good, I would say."

The train slows, and I realize we're at my stop. I stand, regretting the break of contact with his thigh, and he stands with me.

"Looks like we're both getting off here," he says.

I nod and grab my bag, then walk through the doors with him just a step behind me. I can feel him with every movement. My own body actually seems to be orienting itself to his movements, which annoys me, so I take an extra large step to the left and let him catch up to me as we walk up the stairs and into the chill night air.

It's an awkward moment. I don't want to leave him, but I can't be late to my interview.

He nods. "Good luck," he says, turning away from me.

I can't help myself. I call out before he walks too far. "Wait!"

I run up to him as I tear the portrait out of my sketchbook. "For you. I usually give my subjects their portraits when I'm done."

He takes it from my hand, studying it and then studying me. "You always give your art away? Without compensation or recognition?"

I cock my head. "I don't do it for money or recognition," I say. "I do it because it drives my soul in a way nothing else does. And I give it away because it brings joy to people. It brightens their day to know someone has truly seen them, even if just for fifteen or twenty minutes during a subway commute. Everyone has a light to give to the world, and that's mine. *In lumen et lumen.*"

"What did you just say?" he asks.

"*In lumen et lumen.* It's Latin for *In the light, of the light.* Something my dad used to say to me and my brother, that we should always strive to live in the light and be of the light. It's always been a kind of guiding mantra for me."

I cock my head and smile. "You never told me your name," I say, holding out a hand. "I'm Eve."

"Sebastian," he says automatically, bringing his hand to mine.

When our palms touch, a shock of electricity shoots through my arm and into me, and my eyes widen. So do his, or I'm imagining it.

"Well, Sebastian, it was a pleasure meeting you tonight. I just have one more question for you before we part ways."

"And what's that, Eve?"

"What's your light? Do you know?"

11

* * *

HE MIGHT STILL BE BACK THERE, PONDERING my question, or watching me walk away. I don't know, because I refuse to look. Back straight, chest up, I am confident and smart and I am not blowing a potential job for a cute face. Besides, no way am I ready to date after the last shitfest of a relationship. I'm happy enough single.

I stick to my resolve. I don't look back.

But I won't lie, my fingers are itching to draw him again.

And to touch him.

But I shove that inappropriate thought aside and continue on.

On the way to the office, a meow interrupts my thoughts, and I pause and kneel to give an orange tabby some love. The cat pushes against my hand, purring and demanding affection, which I'm happy to accommodate. I always have time for cats, and they always seem to have time for me.

I arrive at my destination after a five-minute walk, the tabby following me until I reach the front door. It's a tall glass and steel office building with no sign out front other than the address and blacked out windows. Very mysterious.

When I walk in, the mystery only deepens. The front lobby is a blend of modern and zen. Clean lines, minimalistic décor, everything in beige and white. The wall behind the receptionist's desk flows with an indoor waterfall over stone. A man and woman, both unnaturally beautiful, both dressed in black, sit behind the desk typing on sleek computers. They look up simultaneously when I walk over, and I'm struck by their matching hazel eyes set against their dark amber skin. Even their bone structure is similar, and before I can stop myself I blurt out, "Are you twins?"

They each nod once, briefly, and then the woman asks, "How can I help you?"

I recognize her voice from the phone call. "I'm Eve Oliver. I have an interview right now."

I don't give more details because I don't have more details to give.

She frowns, then taps a small silver device on her ear. "She's here." She nods. "Have a seat. They will be with you shortly."

I pick a spot close to the front desk so I can do some sleuthing and see if I can find out more about this company. It also occurs to me I should try asking. "Excuse me?"

The two look up in unison and my heart lurches at the familiarity of that in synch connection one can only have with a twin.

"What does this company do exactly? What position am I applying for?" I feel stupid asking, but I'll feel even more stupid going into the meeting knowing nothing.

"They will tell you what you need to know during the interview," the woman says. I still haven't heard the guy speak.

"You can't give me any info?" I ask, perplexed. "A brochure, maybe? Website URL? Anything?"

She gives one curt shake of her head and then returns to her computer.

I sigh, give up, and pull out my sketchbook. I take a deep breath and quiet my mind, closing my eyes, letting stress and worry flow off of me like water. It doesn't take long for my attention to return to Sebastian. I envision every detail that I can recall. The different shades of green in his eyes. The aristocratic slope of his nose. His smooth brow and sharp cheekbones. I don't open my eyes as I sketch. I find sometimes drawing blind helps me hold the vision.

I don't know how long it takes me to finish, but when I open my eyes, I'm staring into his. Well, not really his, but his likeness on my paper. Even in charcoal and pencil he's breathtaking, and I'm ridiculous, lusting after my own drawing. I close my sketchbook and check the time, shocked to see I've already been here over an hour.

"Excuse me," I say, drawing the attention of two sets of impatient hazel eyes. "My interview was some time ago. Do you know how much longer I'll be waiting?"

"Until they call you up," she says, unhelpfully.

"Great. Thanks."

It's after midnight, and I've played more Candy Crush on my phone than I'm willing to admit, when the woman finally leaves her desk and gestures for me to follow.

She says nothing as we walk through marbled halls featuring modern paintings and I'm led to a boardroom. "Sit. They will join you shortly."

Lovely, more waiting. I take a seat at the long, mahogany table and stare out the window overlooking the New York harbor.

When I hear the click of the door, I stand, straightening my skirt suit and wiping my sweaty palm against my jacket. Taking a deep breath, I put on my best professional smile as the door opens.

My smile falters when I see the man standing there. The man whose eyes have haunted me since the subway.

"Sebastian?"

My pulse quickens and I feel a sinking in my stomach. I wanted to see him again, it's true. But not here. Not like this.

Not after I just confessed that I don't really want the job I am here applying for.

A job… apparently… with his company.

THE INTERVIEW

Though my soul may set in darkness, it will rise in perfect light;
I have loved the stars too fondly to be fearful of the night. ~
Sarah Williams

ANOTHER MAN PUSHES past him into the room, turning to face Sebastian, then glancing at me. "You two know each other?" he asks. He has the same British accent as Sebastian.

"No," Sebastian says, pulling his eyes away from mine and taking a seat as far from me as possible.

It takes me a moment to really see the other man, but when I finally look at him, I have to do a double take.

I might be in a room with the two sexiest men that have ever lived. And I'm not even exaggerating.

Man #2 is just as tall as Sebastian, though his build is leaner. His hair is a lighter brown and shorter, cut stylishly, and his eyes are ocean blue rather than the forest green of Sebastian's, but the two men share the same sharp cheekbones and nose.

He smiles at me, and I'm dazzled by his charm and his dimpled chin as he introduces himself. "I'm Derek Night," he says, as he takes my hand to shake it. The moment we touch, I'm lost in his eyes, adrift in an endless ocean, nearly drowning in him. I can almost smell the salty spray of the ocean.

I realize I'm holding my breath and I suck in air as my head spins.

He pauses a moment, staring into my eyes as if he also feels this connection. Cocking his head, he releases my hand. "Curious," he says under his breath, before taking a seat near me. "This is my brother, Sebastian, but you seem to already know his name?"

I nod, returning to my seat. "We briefly met in the subway a few hours ago." Brothers. That makes sense. Damn, they come from good genes, though.

Derek raises an eyebrow at his brother. "You took the subway?"

Sebastian shrugs and still doesn't look at me. He seems pissed, and I'm assuming it's because he thinks he's wasting his time interviewing someone who doesn't even want the job.

But I do *need* the job. And I can probably do the job, once I figure out what the job is.

Derek sighs as if he's used to his brother's mercurial moods. He returns his focus to me. "Once our other brothers arrive, we can begin. I apologize for the long wait. We had an emergency with a client that took longer than expected."

My heart hammers hard in my chest at the thought

that there are more of them. Isn't two enough? "What kind of business is this that it handles client concerns in the middle of the night?" I ask.

But before my question can be answered, the door opens and two more men walk in. The air around me cracks with unseen electricity and I wonder if I'm the only one who can feel it. The four of them together overwhelm my senses and I brace myself against the table, my flash buzzing under my skin and in my head, making me dizzy.

Derek stands, smiling at the new arrivals. "Everything go okay?"

The tall blond with eyes such a pale blue they're almost white nods. "It's handled." He looks my way. "You must be Miss Oliver?"

I nod.

"I'm Elijah Night." He doesn't offer to shake my hand, and I'm equal measures disappointed and relieved. He's taller than the others, lean, and his light blond hair is longer and pulled back into a tie at the base of his neck. He's pale with a face that looks carved from marble. He pours himself into the chair with ease and grace, like a wild animal settling in.

In fact, all four brothers have an animalistic energy to them. Wild and untamed, despite the expensive suits and polished exterior.

The last brother steps forward and extends his hand, a small frown on his face. "I'm Liam Night," he says. "Welcome to The Night Firm."

He studies me with golden eyes that look like twin suns as we shake hands. He's shorter than his brothers, but only by an inch or so, which still makes him quite tall, and he has wild, dark auburn hair that is stylishly disheveled. When we touch, it's like touching fire but without the pain. A deep burning in my soul, a warmth that spreads through me. I'm melting under the heat of it, under the heat of him.

I pull my hand away as graciously as I can. "Nice to meet you."

He holds my eyes a moment longer, then takes a seat.

Four sets of eyes are on me, and I sit back down, trying not to fidget. The collective stare of the Night brothers is disconcerting. Each of them is entirely unique. Entirely original. And yet, I can feel their connection to each other. I can see the family resemblance. I can feel it in their intensity and power.

"We realize this is a bit of an unusual interview," Derek says, smiling. "Thank you for agreeing to come."

I nod. "I'm certainly intrigued. Do I now get to find out what kind of job I'm applying for?"

Once again, the most critical question I need answered is interrupted when the door opens, and a woman pushing a cart walks through. She is tiny, standing not much taller than four feet if that, with long silver hair pulled back into a braid that rides down her spine. She wears a white robe tied around her waist with a knotted sash. Her face is lined with age and softened by kindness. Her silver eyes are clear and piercing. When she sees me, she smiles as if she's been expecting me—like we are old friends becoming reacquainted. She leaves her cart to take my hand in hers. Her skin is thin and soft, like aged crepe paper.

"It's such a pleasure to finally meet you, my dear," she says in a different accent than the brothers. More Irish than British. "I'm Matilda Night, the grandmother of these boys. If they give you any trouble, you just let me know. I brought snacks and drinks for everyone."

She gives a pointed look at her grandsons before passing out drinks. The brothers have glasses of what look like red wine. An odd choice for a job interview. She hands me a cup of tea and a plate of cookies.

"Thank you," I say, my curiosity about this job and this family ever growing.

Matilda pats my hand and shuffles out the door with the cart, closing it behind her, but not before she gives me a mischievous wink.

I pick up the tea, grateful for something to keep my hands occupied, and blow on it, then sip, surprised to discover it's chai, my favorite, with just the right amount of cream and sugar. Interesting.

"Your grandmother is sweet," I say to the silent room. The brothers exchange secret glances that clearly hold hidden layers of meaning I'm not privy to—the kind of sibling communication I used to have not so long ago— and the pang of seeing it still alive in others causes something in my gut to clench. I squeeze my eyes closed a moment, putting Adam out of my mind.

"To address your question," Derek says, "the role you're applying for here is a bit unusual."

Well, there's a shocker.

"We need someone to manage schedules, help with clients, and assist with any investigations, emergencies or events that arise."

I nod. "Okay. I mean, I'm definitely capable of doing that, but... " I pull out my resume from my bag and place it before me while he continues speaking.

"And we're not an ordinary firm. You'd be working from sundown to sunup, and our location frequently changes, so it's something of a live-in position."

"Live-in? I'd have to live here? In an office building?"

"No. You'd live in our home. With us."

"Just the four of you?"

"And our grandmother and other staff," he says.

My nerves tingle, and my flash hits me with a wave of light that makes me almost vomit. "Where is your home?" I ask, trying to mask the effects of my gift. That's what Adam always called it. A gift. "We're secret superheroes," he would whisper to me when I would cry myself to sleep every night after our father's death. "No one can hurt us."

"That's also complicated," he says.

"This is a waste of time," Sebastian says, speaking for the first time since this meeting began.

Derek looks at him. "What do you mean?"

"She doesn't even want to be here. She doesn't want this job. She told me herself. She's wasting our time. She's not qualified."

My face burns red as blood rushes to it, and that mental barrier that's supposed to keep people from blurting out what's on their mind at inappropriate times snaps in half. So I blurt. "Not qualified? What could you possibly know about my qualifications? Or anything about me at all? You haven't asked about my work history or seen my resume. You have no idea what I'm capable of." I stand, to the surprise of all four of them, and walk to Sebastian, shoving my resume in his face. "I'll have you know I'm more than qualified to work for you. In fact, I'm overqualified. I graduated from Harvard's MBA program with honors. I was Managing

21

Director of the last company I worked for. I'm probably more qualified than you to run your business, whatever the hell it is. You should be working for me." As soon as the words are out I regret them, but it's too late. Words, once spoken, cannot be reined in. They take on their own life, which is why it's so important we choose with care which ideas or words we give birth to. My father tried to teach me that, but I'm clearly still learning the lesson.

Sebastian shoves the resume aside. "And where did you get your law degree?" he asks with ice in his voice.

"What?" I ask, confused.

"If you're more qualified than me to run my business, you must have a law degree. After all, we are a law firm. Where did you get your law degree? I don't see it on your resume."

"This is a law firm?" I ask, more confused than ever. "What kind of law firm does interviews at midnight?"

Derek shoots Sebastian a stern look and takes the resume from him. "We offer our services to a niche clientele. One you will have to become familiar with, should you choose to accept this job."

"Who are your clients? Vampires?" I say with a laugh, but none of them smile. Sebastian smirks and leans back in his chair. I want to smack that grin off his beautiful, perfect face. Derek narrows his lips and glances at the others. This is too weird. "It was a joke. I obviously don't think your clients are vampires. Sheesh. Tough crowd."

Still, nothing but uncomfortable stares and awkward silences.

"She's not the one," Sebastian says again, and I'm stung by his rejection of me, despite my qualifications, despite the connection I thought we had on the train, and despite the fact that I'm not even sure I want this stupid job.

I ignore my flash that's pushing me to stay and glare at Sebastian. "You're right. I'm not the one. This would be a huge step down in my career. Perhaps if your creepy receptionist gave me an inkling of what this interview was for, I could have spared us all the waste of time. Good day."

I grab my bag and make my way to the door, pulling it open in one harsh movement, but then I stop and glance back at Sebastian, leveling him with my stare. "Harvard," I say.

He narrows his eyes at me, confused.

"My law degree," I clarify. "It's from Harvard as well. I didn't put it on my resume because I didn't take the Bar, and I was never told what kind of firm this was." And with those closing words, I storm out and slam the door behind me.

The moment I do, tension builds inside me, buzzing on my skin, in my head, like spiders hatching within my body. I've felt this before, in the past, when I ignored my flash, but it will go away. I just need to get out of this soulless building and away from these men who make me crazy in too many ways.

But the tension doesn't go away as I walk the halls. It builds. It builds so much it scares me. I search for a bathroom and see a door ajar down the hall. My brain feels like it's swelling and tears prick my eyes at what's to come. This hasn't happened in so long. Not since…not since that day. I thought this was under control.

I knock gently on the door and it opens slowly. I expect to see any number of things—a broom closet, a standard office or waiting room, but what I find is nothing that should exist in this building.

It's as if I've been transported to a castle in an age of magic and wizards. The room is windowless and covered on one wall with floor to ceiling shelves filled with leather-bound books that look like they should be under glass at an important library. Another wall has shelves full of jars filled with different colored powders, roots, and other strange objects. In a corner sits a round table carved from jade and etched in ancient symbols. A fire burns in the center, though I see no source to feed the flames. And the flames are blue, rather than the standard red or orange. While I know blue flames can occur in nature - for example, wood saturated with sea salt can produce blue flames - I don't know of any that can dance atop solid stone like that. Must be a chemistry trick, though why it would be in a law office is beyond me.

The room smells of spices and wood and earth. Against another wall is a desk covered with scrolls, with books and jars lined above it on shelves. A large chair sits in the center of the room in front of a blazing stone fireplace with a strong fire burning within. There's no chimney, no way for any of this to work.

"Hello there, dear, can I help you?"

I jump at the sound and turn to see Matilda standing in the doorway.

The pressure in my brain is building. I don't have much time to find somewhere private. Damnit.

Black spots appear in my vision. Light dances before my eyes as pain explodes in my head. I only have time to say, "Help, please!" my eyes filling with tears as I grip my skull and sink to my knees, a sob escaping my throat.

Matilda rushes over. "Oh, my dear, it's all right, love. Come now." She rests a cool hand on my forehead. "You're burning up!"

I know. I always do when these hit.

And it's not over yet. It's just starting.

She helps me to the chair, supporting my body weight as sweat slicks my skin, and I shiver as if cold. I am both cold and hot. The pain hasn't reached its climax yet and I'm not looking forward to when it does. I won't be able to stop what happens next, and that terrifies me.

"I have to leave," I say between breaths, grinding the words out through the pain.

"Of course you can't leave. Not in this condition."

I reach for my bag, knowing I don't have enough time to get out of here, hoping I still have the leather strip I used to carry just in case. I fumble, my sketchbook falling out, still opened to the page of Sebastian's sketch. Matilda notices it but says nothing as I find what I'm looking for and stick it into my mouth to keep from screaming.

Just in time, too.

The pain breaks my skull open, shattering my mind into a million pieces, undoing me, removing from my consciousness any memory of who I am or where I am. All I know is pain. And I bite down, moaning, muffled screams escaping through the leather.

My body convulses, and I experience a moment of a flash, and a vision so dark and terrifying fills my mind that I let the scream burst forth, spitting out the leather strip in the process, my body thrashing.

Something is pressed against my lips. Hot liquid pours into my mouth, a trickle at a time. It's bitter. Vile. I cough and try to spit it out, but a hand holds my head, and a soft voice soothes me. "This will help, my dear. Drink it all. It will help, I promise. You poor thing."

As more of the liquid makes its way down my throat, I feel its effects. The vision fades. The pain ebbs. The vice-like grip on my brain eases. And I slip into the darkness.

* * *

HE IS ALWAYS THERE, in my dreams. In my sleep. In my mind.

This time we are children. Nine or ten years old. I'm in bed, sweat beading on my forehead, the pain in my small body building. Adam is laying next to me, holding my hand, his face contorted in pain as well, but it's not his pain he's feeling. It's mine. "Why is this happening?" he asks our father, his voice a scared whine.

My father places a cool washcloth on my forehead and tenderly brushes away the wet hair clinging to skin. "Every superhero has to go through hardships to come into their powers," my father says, his smile sad, untold secrets living in his dark brown eyes. Eyes my twin and I do not share. We have our mother's eyes.

"When will I go through my hardship?" Adam asks, with equal mixture of fear and excitement.

Adam wanted to be a superhero more than anything. And he felt sure we were meant to be just that.

Our father's smile slips, but he catches it in time and pastes it back onto his face. "Someday, my boy. Someday you, too, will go through your own transformation. *In lumen et lumen*. Always remember to stay in the light."

* * *

I TRY to cling to the vision of my brother and my father—two men now lost to me forever—to the memories that feel more real than the present sometimes, but consciousness steals him from me once again. When I come to, my head is still pounding, but it's no longer splintering into jagged edges. It's just a normal headache. My mouth is dry and bitter tasting, and I am curled up on a huge chair in front of a fire. It takes a moment for the preceding events to flow back into my mind. When they do, I shift my body and move to stand, but a wave of dizziness forces me back into the chair. Okay then. I have to take this slower.

I've never been hit with a headache that bad before. I'm dreading the recovery length of this one. I don't have time to be laid up. Moving slowly, cautiously, I lift myself upright, using the back of the chair as support. A wave of nausea passes through me, then recedes. I got this. I inch forward on the chair, my nails digging into the leather upholstery.

Voices in the hall give me pause. I strain my ears to listen, then slowly lift myself to standing and creep towards the door, retrieving my bag along the way.

"She's a mundane. She'll never fit into this world. It's not worth the risk!" That sounds like Sebastian, his voice deep and commanding. A voice that leads armies, that men and women will follow into battle and die for.

"She's exactly what we need—did you see who wrote her letter of recommendation? Do you want to tell Richard Dwarvas that his protege isn't good enough for us?" Derek pauses dramatically, and I almost laugh. Rick would have laughed.

"Even if she weren't," he continues, "we are out of time. He'll be expecting us by week's end."

"She is hot-tempered and ill-suited to this world." I think that one is Liam.

"You're one to call someone out for being hot-tempered," Derek says haughtily. "And if any of you have a better idea, now's the time to give it voice. We need her. You know we do."

"The four of you need to pipe down," Matilda's voice interjects. "The girl passed out and is in my office."

"What?" Sebastian says with a fierce growl.

"Oh, calm yourself, boy. She'll be fine. I gave her some tea to help. Poor thing. She'll feel it when she wakes up though."

I don't need to hear more. I just need to get the hell out of this office of horrors. Coming here was a giant mistake, one I intend to immediately remedy.

Slipping out of the office quietly, I head down the hall in the opposite direction of their voices. I see the shadows they cast from around the corner, but can't see them, so unless they have eyes in their shadows, they can't see me either.

I do my best to move confidently through the halls, but I haven't recovered from my episode, and I really need to be at home in bed right now.

I'm forced to pass through an open office space with cubicles, where people in suits are busily working on what looks like important matters. There are law books open, phone calls being made, frantic typing on sleek, modern computers that match the space in which they dwell. I'm at least dressed the part, though my face must look ashen and my eyes sunken. Likely my makeup is smeared as well. I try to touch up my eyes with the pad of my index finger as I walk, avoiding eye contact with anyone who might glance my way.

I wonder what will happen when Matilda and the Night brothers discover I've left. Maybe nothing. I'm surely not special in the grand scheme of things, despite my impressive letter of recommendation. As I walk down another hall trying to find a stairway or elevator to take me back to the first floor, I notice a glass meeting room with what looks like clients and their attorneys. At first my glance is just that, a casual noticing, but then I turn back, slowing my step to reassure my brain I didn't just see what I think I did.

My breathing quickens as I try to stay casual and totally normal. Inside the room, one woman stands apart from the rest, and no one seems to acknowledge her presence. It takes me a moment to register what I'm seeing. She has long silver hair down to her feet, styled into hundreds of tiny braids. Her skin is a deep black, dark as midnight, with freckles on her prominent cheekbones that glow silver like stars in the night sky. Her eyes are wide and large and are entirely silver. And on her forehead is a delicate silver horn.

I know the moment she sees me. The moment we see each other. Her presence washes over me like a waterfall on a warm day, inviting and cool and so refreshing. I hear the soft whisper of my name carried on the faintest drift of air, or maybe it's in my head, I can't tell. But as my name enters me, I feel peace even through the pain.

A tear rolls down my cheek and she smiles, revealing large white teeth, and in my mind's eye I see her in a brilliant emerald glade, prancing through the thick grass, but her body is not that of a woman, but a unicorn.

I walk as if in a daze, somehow finding the elevator and making my way to the first floor. The twins both stare as I walk out and hail a cab, my mind spinning with all that I saw, but my heart is full from that brief glimpse of the woman with silver eyes.

THE OFFER

I am not yours, not lost in you,
  Not lost, although I long to be
  Lost as a candle lit at noon,
  Lost as a snowflake in the sea.
  ~ Sara Teasdale

I MAKE a quick stop at the grocery store, tipping the cabbie generously with money I can ill afford to spend, so that she'll wait as I pick up the necessary supplies for my evening plan. It should be sleep, since it's almost two in the morning at this point, but this is New York, a city that's always awake. And I don't sleep much at any rate.

When the cab pulls up to my apartment, I tip once again, mentally counting down how much—or rather how little—money I have left. I slink into the building, hoping the manager isn't around. It was a nice place once upon a time, and the architecture is still breathtaking, but lack of care has worn it down. You can feel the spirit within has given up the fight. Even still, the rooms weren't cheap to come by. New York is New York, no matter what neighborhood you live in.

At my old job the cost was no big deal. In fact, I had my sights set on something much grander once upon a time.

Now...

I'm just about to make it to the elevator when I hear his voice. "Miss Oliver, I was hoping to run into you. Can we talk privately in my office a moment?" he asks, while placing his hand at my elbow and giving me a pointed stare.

It's not a question, it's a command, and I resent him and myself for the fact that I feel like a misbehaving child as he leads me to his office and closes the door. He sits behind his desk, and I stand, giving me a good view of the balding spot on his head, the light bulb overhead flashing against pale skin. Roger Lemon's parents own this building, which is his only qualification for managing an apartment complex. He's got a skinny mustache across a thin lip that makes him look Hitleresque but without the gravitas to lead a country.

"Miss Oliver, your payments are now several months past due. You have gotten my notices, I trust?"

"Every single one of them," I say, through gritted teeth.

"Then you know this cannot be allowed to go on. We will have to take, dare I say it, drastic measures if you do not get your account in compliance."

Compliance. I've always hated that word.

"I should have the money to you soon. I had a job interview today that looks promising."

His thin lips pinch together, forming a crease between

his eyebrows. "I sympathize with what you've been through, but I think we've been patient long enough."

"I'll get you your money," I say. "I just need a bit more time."

His dark beady eyes bore into me. "You have until the end of the week, Miss Oliver. If you are not caught up on all your payments—including interest, you will be locked out of your apartment and all of your belongings will be confiscated and sold to pay your balance."

I seethe with rage boiling inside me, but I can't act on it. Not yet. "I'll get you your money by the end of the week," I say, then I turn to leave, but he grabs my arm, and when I turn to face him, he licks his lips.

He hands me an envelope with a red "PAST DUE" stamp on it. "There are other ways you could work off what you owe," he says.

It's not the first time he's pulled this shit, and it likely won't be the last. I yank my arm out of his grip, knowing his fingers will leave bruises. "I'll get you your money."

I can feel his eyes watching me as I go, and I force myself not to shiver.

Once in my apartment, I triple lock the door behind me, draw the curtains, and head to my bedroom. It only takes me ten minutes to change into my pajamas, scrub my face, and warm up a blanket in the dryer. While the blanket warms, I dig through my bag of goodies and pull out my current romantic threesome. Ben & Jerry. My rebound guys. Always here for me. Never disappointing. I grab a spoon and fill a glass generously with red wine, then head to the couch.

But the past due envelope snags my attention, and I rip

it open in frustration, my eyes burning when I read it through once, then twice.

That bastard is charging an insane amount of interest. I owe twice what I thought, which was already more than I know how to get.

Not only will I lose my home, I'll lose everything in it.

Once I have my blanket, I tuck in for a night of watching horror movies as I try to mentally process what I saw, heard, and now suspect about my job interview, and what I'm going to do about this new deadline.

I would move out, if I could. But I don't have the money for a first, last, and deposit. Hell, I don't have the money for boxes to pack my shit. And after the last year, my credit is shot. The only way I don't become homeless in a week is to find a job that will give me an advance large enough to get caught up on my payments.

I think back to The Night Firm. We never got around to talking salary. Even if I was willing to work for them. Which I'm not.

I try to remember why I'm not, but my thoughts are muddled. It's becoming harder and harder to pull out the details of my exchange. I blame it on the wine, the sugar, the haunting soundtrack of the movie I'm watching. My massive breakdown earlier. Speaking of, I should be feeling much worse right now. I don't understand how I recovered so quickly.

Halfway through the movie and the bottle of wine, I've nearly got myself convinced that my mind was playing tricks on me. I've been under tremendous stress for over a year now. I'm exhausted. I'm probably malnourished. That can do things to the brain. I just need to move on. Tomorrow, I decide, refilling my glass, tomorrow I'll go online, search for more jobs, find more interviews. I'll stick to 9-5 listings only!

With that decided, I give all my attention to the movie, and am mildly disappointed when I try to pour more wine and only a reluctant drop comes out. But I planned for this and bought two bottles.

A bit wobbly, I head back to the kitchen to uncork the other bottle, when I'm interrupted by a knock at my door and a ringing of the doorbell.

This shocks me almost more than anything else that evening.

No one comes to visit here, certainly not in the middle of the night. If it's Roger, that slimy bastard, I'm going to sue his ass for harassment.

In my alcohol-muddled mind, it doesn't take me long to convince myself that's exactly who's behind the door. Roger thinks if I'm desperate enough he can have me. He doesn't seem to get I would literally rather be homeless than let him touch me.

I school my face into one of a fierce warrior, then I march to the door and swing it open, ready for battle.

"You can go shove it up your ass if you think I'm going to—"

"Hello, Eve," Sebastian Night says, standing in my hallway with a pissy expression on his god-like face. "I see your outburst in the office isn't a one-off."

"I thought you were someone else," I say, my wine-addled brain sluggish. "What are you doing here?" I cross my arms over my chest, feeling suddenly self-conscious in my cat slippers and matching robe.

He hands me an envelope. "I was sent to give you this."

"What is it?" I ask, taking the envelope. As I do, our

fingers touch, and that sense of an earthquake rocking my insides overwhelms me again, though not unpleasantly. It's just intense. Passionate. Buried passion. He flinches at the touch, so I assume he feels something, too, but isn't thrilled with it.

"It's a job offer," he says, ignoring whatever is going on between us.

"Are you serious?" I ask, completely shocked. "After that interview, why would I work for you, and why would you want me to?"

He shrugs, avoiding my eyes. "It wasn't my decision." He turns to walk away, then pauses, glancing at me over his shoulder. "But if I were you, I'd burn that paper and pretend you never heard of The Night Firm. Stick to the light like your father said."

I watch until he disappears around the corner, then close my door, locking up once again. Back on the couch, I stare at the thick cream envelope, stamped with a wax seal. How pretentious, but kinda cool, too. I break open the seal and unfold the letter. It's handwritten in calligraphy, so formal it feels like a summons from a king, not a job offer from a law firm.

THE NIGHT FIRM would like to offer Miss Eve Oliver the job of Manager of Operations, to begin immediately, or as soon as Miss Oliver can avail herself of the position. It is a full time, live-in position, with generous compensation and benefits. We await your decision.

IT'S SIGNED with each of the four brothers' names and

signatures and stamped with an "N" matching the wax seal.

There's a second page, this one indicating a generous signing bonus, salary, benefits and spending budget for wardrobe, food, and more.

The numbers make me gasp.

I sit there in a daze, staring at the letter to make sure it's real and not something I'm imagining.

This is enough to get caught up on my payments and then some. Though I realize that since it's a live-in position, I wouldn't actually need this place anymore.

Tears burn my eyes. This job could save me from bankruptcy and homelessness.

Two years ago, if you'd told me this is what my life would look like right now, I never would have believed you.

I was happy, at the top of my career, in love with who I thought was a great man, living in a luxury apartment in the heart of New York's posh neighborhood. I had it all.

Then I lost it all the day my brother called with the news.

I didn't know it at the time. Not yet.

But certain events in life have the ability to strip you of everything so slowly you don't realize it's happening until it's too late.

Now I'm single, deeply in debt, unemployed, and as unhappy as I've ever been in my life.

I glance down at the thick parchment, shaking my head. This could solve all my problems.

I can't even believe I'm considering it. That place was insane. Even if I was only imagining parts of it.

After all, the strange things I saw did happen after my

explosive headache. I've never had one that bad, but even in the past I've had moments of seeing things that aren't there. This might have felt more real, but that's likely due to the severity of the episode.

So, what's really the problem with taking the job? I reach for my wine glass but realize I never finished opening the new bottle. Damn.

The worst thing is a few of the brothers clearly don't want me there. Especially Sebastian.

So what? I climbed to the top at my last job despite men like that, not because of them. I could do it again. Would do it again.

I consider waiting until morning, but I realize this is now my new work day, if I really am going to do this. Am I really going to do this?

Apparently I am.

I dial before I change my mind. The female twin answers. "This is Eve. May I please speak with Derek?"

I decide to use his first name since Mr. Night would bring all the boys running, and I only want to talk to the one who actually fought for me to be there.

"Hello, Eve," his warm voice says a moment later.

"I'll take the job," I say hurriedly, before my liquid courage fades.

"I'm delighted to hear that. Can we expect you to start tomorrow evening?"

"You said this requires a live-in situation, yes?"

"Yes."

"I might need a few days to get my belongings packed and my things in order. But I have... a favor to ask."

"What might that be?"

I bite my lip, hating that I have to ask this. "Is it possible to get my signing bonus now?"

"Of course, that can be arranged." He pauses, and I hear some clicking in the background. "The money has been transferred into your account. You should see it there now. Is there anything else I can do for you?"

I'm dumbfounded. I set my phone to speaker and click open my banking app and check. Sure enough, the deposit was made. "But, I didn't give you my account information."

He chuckles. "You will find we have significant resources at our disposal. You don't think we offered this job to you without doing a thorough investigation into your life, do you?"

"That's... that's invasive!" I feel vulnerable and violated, but not enough to take back my acceptance of the job. I can't totally blame them. I always encouraged background checks on new employees. Of course, they would look into me, especially if I'll be handling sensitive client information or dealing with large amounts of money. And if I'm living with them, then that's a whole other deal. They'd certainly want to know the person they were bringing into their home.

I should be so diligent, but I can't seem to find anything about this company or this family online, which is just strange, and I don't know what it means. How do you run a business, a successful one by the looks of it, without having some online presence these days?

"I apologize for the personal intrusion, but given the sensitive nature of our work, I fear we had no choice but to be thorough. As for your relocation, I can send a moving team to your apartment tomorrow to help you pack and move whatever you want. I can provide a storage, or if you'd rather, I can arrange for whatever you'd like to be sold and the money sent to your account."

"Um. Thanks. Yeah, I guess that would be helpful."

"Very good. Can I expect to see you Thursday evening, then?"

"Yes, that should be enough time."

"Wonderful. We look forward to having you as part of our family. I'll send a driver for you and your belongings at seven p.m. Anything you'd like sent to our home, please let the movers know tomorrow and it will be here waiting for you."

"Can I ask you one more thing?" I rush the words before I lose my nerve. This may be a bad idea, but what the hell. I'm full of those tonight.

"Anything," he says.

I explain to him what I need and I can hear the smile in his voice. "It would be my pleasure to assist in this."

He ends the call, and I sit staring at my phone. Have I completely lost my mind? I kind of feel like I have.

I yawn, and the adrenaline rush of seeing Sebastian and making that call crashes through me, leaving me weak and tired and ready for bed.

I abandon the second bottle of wine and retire to my bedroom, falling onto my mattress like the drunk, exhausted woman I am.

That night my dreams take me to a grove of trees near a stream. The moon is full and reflects off the water. A woman shrouded in a robe stands in front of a blazing fire, her long, dark, hair - wild and curly - whips in the wind as she raises her arms.

"I am the woman in the wild!" she screams into the

shrieking wind. As she speaks, the wind thrashes, the water becomes brackish, the fire blazes, and the trees seem to bend into her.

"I am the blood sister of the moon! I am the call of the night and her secrets. The radiance left from a star. I am all that you need and more than you know. I am the hidden that shall now be found. Tell my story. Set me free. I am the magic that you seek. I am the wild!"

As her robes fall off, she stands naked, her face covered by her hair, the flames dancing off her pale skin, moving around her. She controls the flames, sending them forward. Sending them into me in a flash of heat and searing pain.

My heart slams against my ribs as I wake with a start, gasping for breath, clutching my chest.

I lay in my bed, staring at the ceiling, replaying my dream. It felt so real. So visceral. Like I was standing in the clearing with her. I could feel the heat of the flames, the splash of the water from the stream. I could smell the wood burning and the mulch from the forest. I could feel her power flowing in and around me.

My breathing slows and I check the time. It's not even seven in the morning yet, but I know I won't be getting anymore sleep.

I slide out of bed and am about to head to the shower, but I decide to take a run instead, despite my hangover, either from the bottle of wine or the headache, likely both. Still, it's been too long since I worked out. I need this.

On my way out the door, I pause outside my brother's room and take a deep breath. Some days are easier than others. All days are hard. I push it away most of the time, but when I'm home, I allow myself a moment to our memories. Just a moment.

Then I leave the building and begin running.

With music blasting in my ear, and the pounding of the pavement under my feet, I don't pay too much attention to where I'm going, so I'm a little surprised when I end up at The Night Firm.

But I'm not nearly as surprised as when I poke my head in and see it's empty. Not just no one at the front desk, but totally empty. No sign. No furniture. No cool zen decorations. No fountain overflowing.

I pull out my phone and call the office number. The creepy twin whose name I should probably learn answers. "The Night Firm."

"Derek, please, it's Eve."

She puts me on hold without a word. As usual. If I were them I'd put someone more personable up front as the first contact, but that's just me.

"Derek Night here," he says in a distracted voice.

"Hi, it's Eve," I say. "I'm um. I'm confused."

"About what, Eve?"

"I'm at the office, only The Night Firm no longer exists here. Is this some kind of scam?" I ask.

"How could this be a scam?" he asks. "I've sent you money. Isn't a scam usually the other way around?"

He's got a point there.

"So you relocated in the few hours I slept?" I ask. "How's that even possible?"

"With the right motivation, anything is possible."

I don't know what to say in response to that.

"And we did make clear that this job was live-in and involved travel. We go where our clients need us."

"That's a highly unusual way for a law firm to do business," I say, which is honestly the biggest understatement in the history of understatements.

"We are a highly unusual firm, Miss Oliver, as I'm sure you've noticed. But I am glad you called. The movers will be at your house in two hours. They should have everything done by noon."

That seems unlikely, but I don't say as much. After all, anything is possible according to this guy.

We end the call, and I run back to my apartment and shower before the movers arrive.

If they really are on their way, I need to hurry.

I pause in front of my brother's room, my hand resting on the cool, metal doorknob. I haven't entered his room since the day he died. I know that sounds foolish, but it's like Schrödinger's cat. There's a box with a cat in it, and the cat has an equal chance of being alive or dead. But once you open the box, it's over, the truth staring at you. As long as I keep the door closed, I can pretend my brother yet lives. At least in my own mind. Once I open the door and face the emptiness, it'll be over.

Still.

It's time.

I twist the knob and close my eyes, then push the door open.

His scent—cinnamon and honey—hits me first, and it shocks me so much I crumble to my knees with a whimper. It's as if he was just here. How is that possible?

I open my eyes and see that the room is empty, as expected. It looks exactly as it did when he was alive, minus the hospital bed we rented for him. Now, in lieu of a bed, there are deep grooves in the carpets where the wheels had pressed in. But everything else is untouched. The bottles of medication on the side table. The open book lying face down, holding his page as if he might come back to it at any moment. His favorite socks folded just so next to his shoes.

A breeze catches the curtains of his window, blowing through the room gently, carrying more of his scent to me. I could have sworn the window had been locked. It always was.

Adam and I fought about it constantly. He needed fresh air, but he refused to let me leave the windows open. "I don't want to stink up the rest of the world with the scent of my death," he said.

And so his scent grew stronger in our home, turning from the beloved and comforting and familiar, to a mutated version of itself, similar enough to inspire a fresh wave of grief, but more rancid and laced with rot. A reminder of what was to come.

I suck in my breath and cross the room in ten steps, stopping in front of the window. When I touch it, I feel the pull of a flash, but it fades before I can follow the thread. The window slams shut quite suddenly, and without my aid, or the aid of anyone as far as I can see.

It must have been the wind.

I turn towards the bedroom, to face what remains of my brother. There are some things I cannot let someone else pack, or even touch. Not until I am done.

And so I begin one item at a time, savoring the memory each of his belongings brings up in me, even as it slices a fresh wound in my already eviscerated heart.

A sweet torture.

In the end, I only keep one thing.

His ring.

He always wore it. To the very end.

I had given it to him the day we both graduated college.

I slip it onto my middle finger and then leave his bedroom for the last time.

I DON'T KNOW how it happens, but Derek wasn't wrong. The movers have everything cleared out by noon. I am left in an empty apartment, save my personal items. I've decided not to store anything, and to take only what I truly need and a few keepsakes.

A fresh start, as it were.

Letting them into my brother's room was the hardest part, but I know it's time to move on. He would want me to if nothing else.

When the movers leave, I take out my checkbook and march down to Roger's office. He grins when he sees me. "I see you've come to your senses and are ready to discuss my terms," he says, his smile a lascivious sneer.

He licks his lips and I shudder. I clench my fist around my checkbook, then smile. "Why, that's so sweet, but you see I've come to pay off what I owe."

His face pales. "Well, that's great news, but surely you don't need to spend all that money when there are other ways to satisfy the debt."

I slap the check onto his desk. "Here is my payment in full, plus interest."

He looks at it and the sides of his lips curl up. "It seems you're several thousand dollars short."

"About that," I say, shoving a letter into his hands featuring The Night Firm letterhead. "It seems it wasn't contractually legal for you to hike the interest after we'd signed an agreement. I've paid what was originally agreed upon. Nothing more. It's also not legal to extort sexual favors as payment for a debt, you miserable sleaze-ball. If you have any questions, you can contact my lawyer."

I let myself gloat as I walk out of his office, leaving him gaping.

I owe Derek a big thanks for that one.

* * *

TOMORROW MY NEW LIFE BEGINS. Today, I'm going to pamper myself and use my new expense card to make sure I have the right wardrobe for this job.

I want to enjoy the shopping, the makeover—god I've needed a new haircut for ages—the pampering. But my mind keeps turning back to Sebastian and his brothers. They mesmerize me even as they confound me. And I still don't really know what this bloody job is. My life feels entirely too surreal.

Back in my hotel for the night, I push myself to stay awake until morning. It's time to get used to my new sleep schedule.

I spend the night sketching Sebastian in different poses. Tired of my obsession, I move on to other subjects. First, I sketch Matilda leaning over that strange table with the fire. Then I sketch the scene that dances in my mind like a dream, of eyes glowing silver in a face of midnight, that delicate horn in the center of her forehead.

I manage three hours of sleep before waking in the

afternoon. I realize I'm ready to go. This is too much waiting. I pass the time exercising in the hotel gym, taking a bath, eating, watching movies. Finally, it's time. I check out with all my belongings and wait in front of the hotel for the driver Derek promised. It's been awhile since I've owned a car, and I've never had a driver. This is quite a change of status for me.

A limo pulls up at precisely seven pm and a perky young woman bounces out and smiles widely at me. "I'm Lily. I'll be your driver from now on."

Lily has pink punk rock hair, multiple facial piercings, and wears a driver uniform that's bright neon colors mixed with tie die. It's quite the combination and it stands out starkly against her ebony skin. I'm instantly drawn to her sparkly personality.

"I get a driver all the time?" I ask.

She laughs. "Of course, silly. You're part of the family now."

I don't know what she means by that, but she opens the door for me to get in, and then proceeds to pack my luggage into the trunk.

Once we're both settled, she asks if I want the middle window up or down. "It's sound proof. You'll have complete privacy."

"No, I like talking to you," I say, as I study the limo. I've been in one before, but this is especially nice. "Where are we going?"

"I don't know," she says sheepishly.

"You don't know where we're going? Then how will we get there?"

"The GPS is programmed with the current address," she says.

"Current address? They have several homes?"

"No, well, yes, but that's not what I meant. The home changes locations as needed for security or work."

A shock of horror fills me. "Am I going to be living in a mobile home?" I ask.

She laughs. "No way. Wait till you see it. It's not that kind of mobile. It's…really hard to explain. You'll have to wait to get there and see for yourself. It's going to blow your mind."

She snaps her mouth shut. "But I'm not supposed to say too much. They want to tell you everything themselves."

"Everything like what?" I ask, hoping I can get more out of her.

"I'm sorry, I can't!" She squeezes her lips together and shakes her head.

I sigh, letting her off the hook. I don't want her to get in trouble.

"Can you at least tell me if they're a good family to work for?"

She smiles broadly. "Oh, yes. Granny Night rescued me when I was little. I was practically raised with the Nights. The brothers are like my uncles. They can seem a bit gruff at first, but they each have a soft spot worth searching for. Don't give up on them."

It's good to hear someone speak well of them. It makes me feel less nervous about relocating my life into theirs with so little warning.

I resign myself to my own thoughts and wonder idly who Roger's next victim will be. A thought occurs to me, and I call Derek.

"Hello, Miss Oliver, I trust your driver is taking good care of you and that the movers were helpful?"

"Oh, yes, to both. And call me Eve. I... have another favor—and it's... unusual."

"Oh, I'm intrigued," Derek says.

"My former landlord is a sleaze to women. I'd hate to imagine another woman getting that apartment and being harassed by him. Is there anything you can do to...I don't know, make sure that doesn't happen?" I don't even know what I'm asking, and I feel like a moron. "Maybe somehow ensure it gets rented to a big, buff dude or something?"

Derek chuckles. "I like your style, Miss...Eve. You'll fit right in, I think. I can definitely handle that. Anything else?"

"Um, I don't think so. You've already been more than generous."

When we hang up, I check my bank account again to make sure my eyes weren't deceiving me before, but the money is all there. I know the check I wrote will clear soon, but that still leaves a comfortable savings and a decent buffer fund should this job go south fast. That gives me a little room to breathe. I worked so hard to build a stable financial structure, never imagining that one year of medical expenses could wipe it all out so quickly.

Cancer kills in more ways than one.

It destroys everything about a person's life.

I shake my head, unwilling to dwell on that now. I'm turning things around. Making progress with my life. I think.

I hope.

I close my eyes and let myself try to doze until I feel the limo slowing.

"Are we there already?" I ask, surprised the drive went by so fast.

"Not exactly," Lily says. "We have one more passenger to pick up." She says this sheepishly, and I realize why when the door opens and Sebastian slides into the back, newspaper in hand.

The look of irritation doesn't appear on his face until he sees me.

Naturally.

Seriously though, what did I do to piss this guy off?

THE DRIVE

We grow accustomed to the Dark—
  When Light is put away—
  ~ Emily Dickinson

I SIGH as he picks a seat as far from me as he possibly can. Fortunately, there's plenty of room back here, and we don't have to sit too close to each other.

Not that my body isn't craving being just a little bit closer to this insanely attractive man. But my brain knows better, and I'm sticking with my brain for now.

He gives me a curt nod. "I hope you do not mind, since we are both going to the same location."

"It's fine," I say. "I mean, obviously. This is your car and driver. I just appreciate the ride. And the job." I add, almost as an afterthought.

He grunts and opens his newspaper to begin reading.

"You don't find it tedious to read the news that way?" I ask, as Lily starts the limo and gets us back on the road.

"No. I do not."

"You can find all that and more online," I say, holding up my smart phone.

He sighs in exasperation and lowers the paper to glare at me. "I prefer analogue to digital. Call me old-fashioned."

Lily giggles at that and doesn't seem the least bit intimidated when Sebastian casts his standard glare at her. She just laughs harder. "Oh, Uncle Seb, stop being such a brat."

I'm surprised to hear her teasing him like that, but not as surprised as I am when his face lights up in a smile and he laughs in return. It's the first time I've heard him laugh, and it's deep and husky, and makes his face even more handsome. Damn him.

The moment passes, however, and when he returns his focus to me, his energy shifts.

And not for the better.

"Look," I say, ready to settle this between us once and for all. "I know you think I'm not serious about this job because of what I told you on the subway, but I am. I don't even think I'd want to do art for my career. If I had to worry about drawing for others, for money, I might not get the joy from it I do now. I meant what I said during the interview: I'm smart, educated and resource-ful. Granted, I'm still not entirely clear what my job is, or how your law firm even operates effectively if it's only open at night, but I can promise you I will learn every-thing I need to, and quickly. I work hard, study hard, and always excel at what I do. Always. So, if you'll just give me a chance, you'll find that I'm an excellent employee."

I say this all in one breath, and when I'm done I slump back into my seat, emotionally spent.

He stares for a moment and then says, "Do not presume to know my thoughts, Miss Oliver." And with that he finds the next page of his newspaper and turns away from me once more.

I've clearly been dismissed.

Determined to make some use out of what is proving to be a long car ride with an unpleasant companion, I pull out my sketchbook and close my eyes. I take a deep breath and mentally count backwards from ten. As I do, I follow a staircase in my mind down, down, down until I'm standing before a large red door. Opening it, I step through into a secret garden where I instantly connect to my muse. She glows within a swaying willow tree, her form moving through the bark and branches, her hair falling around her in waves of green. Her voice echoes in the wind and the rustling of leaves.

She sings to me a song. I catch it and smile. Then open my eyes and draw.

I don't think too hard about what I'm drawing. I just let my muse's voice speak through the charcoal and pencil.

Everything around me is silent as I work, and I don't realize until the drawing is complete that Sebastian is staring at me.

Or rather, at my drawing.

I study it myself, now that my focus is returning to normal and my head is clearing. Four men—clearly the Night brothers—stand back to back, forming a circle around a woman, surrounded by a dark and menacing wood, with trees that look alive and hungry in the worst possible way. The brothers hold drawn swords, steel glinting in the moonlight.

I am the woman they are guarding.

We're all standing in the center of a pentagram burned into the grass beneath our feet.

Sebastian is still staring, and I quickly close my sketchbook and slip it into my bag, embarrassed that my boss saw what I drew. Embarrassed that my subconscious pulled that image out of my mind for this exercise.

And more than a little unnerved at what that image might mean.

"How did you learn to do that?" Sebastian asks.

"Do what? Draw?"

"Well, yes, that, too. But how did you learn to induce a trance state so easily?"

"Um. I taught myself. Both things. As a kid I loved drawing, and the obsession never went away. I drew on anything I could with anything I could. By the time I was ten I was selling my drawings to the neighbors. My brother was my business partner and marketer," I say with a smile. "He could sell shoes to a shoemaker. He'd go door to door, and by the time he came back all my art had sold. I didn't learn until much later that he was the one buying most of it, because he didn't want me to give up on my dreams." I suck in a breath to keep myself from rambling even more. He doesn't need to hear about my childhood. And I don't need to dive into stories about my brother right now.

Instead, I turn to his original question. "As for the trance, it's just a silly self-hypnosis trick. It helps put me in a more creative mindset. It's nothing, really. Anyone can do it. Just google a YouTube video."

He scoffs at that. "Trust me, it is not "nothing" as you say. And I do not watch the YouTube."

I snort-laugh at that in a very unladylike way. "What are you ninety years old? *The* YouTube? Oh dear. You have so much to learn."

"No offense, but I highly doubt there's anything you could possibly teach me," he says, and then he snaps up his newspaper and proceeds to ignore me again.

"How could I possibly find that offensive?" I ask, with a sharp dose of sarcasm before I turn away from him, folding my arms firmly across my chest to reinforce my point.

I press my lips together, biting my tongue to avoid saying something hot-headed and stupid to my new boss who already doesn't like me. The boss I now have to live with.

What have I gotten myself into? I wonder, not for the first time and very likely not for the last.

The minutes tick by slowly, and the exhaustion of the last couple of days seeps into my bones. Just as I'm about to doze off, my flash buzzes in my head. My eyes blink open just as my body slams forward. My seat belt tightens around my waist and chest, digging into my skin even through my clothes, pushing out all the breath in me.

And then my world is spinning. Spinning wildly, toppling end over end, crunching and slamming and crashing into itself.

Pain bites into me, but I can't tell where on my body it specifically hurts. My nerves dance, lit up like current pouring through live wires. I feel everything and it becomes a kind of nothing.

When I can think clearly again, I find I'm hanging

from my seatbelt, upside down in what's left of the car, my head spinning and my breathing coming in short gasps.

There's a voice, but I can't find the face it belongs to.

He's saying my name.

"Eve. Eve, focus on me. Eve. Stay with me."

I blink. Something thick drips into my eyes, stinging. The face in question comes into focus, and though my mind is sluggish, and words and names come reluctantly, as if being dragged through tar, the visceral response of my body is instant. Warmth floods me, and I feel myself sinking into him, like into quicksand.

"Sebastian." My throat croaks. "What happened?"

"We hit a deer. The limo flipped. I need to get you out of here. I'm going to unbuckle you, but I need you to hold onto me. Can you do that?"

I lick my parched lips and nod. His words sound like they're coming from underwater, but I think I understand.

He reaches for me, one hand wrapping behind my back, the other hand over my waist. "Are you ready?" he asks.

I nod, then mumble, "Yes."

My heart quickens - in fear? anticipation? - as he unlatches the seatbelt. Gravity takes over and I fall unceremoniously into his arms. The removal of pressure causes blood to rush into my extremities, leading to pain.

A whole lot of pain.

I look down and see a metal rod sticking out of my right leg. "Holy shit!" I scream, as my leg spasms.

I reach to pull the rod out, but Sebastian stops me.

"It's safer to leave it for now."

I'm fighting to breathe, my ribs aching with the effort to move oxygen through my body.

I bury my face in his chest, closing my eyes against whatever is happening outside his embrace. Fear pulses through me, tainting my body with the sour smell of it.

Everything slows, and there's an unearthly quiet outside for a moment, before a loud WHUMP comes from somewhere behind us and heat begins penetrating the back seat, filling it with smoke.

For a moment I contemplate my own death, that this might be my last moment on earth. I find I'm not as scared as I always expected I would be. I will be with my parents and my brother. With my family.

But I don't die. Not now, anyways.

Sebastian holds me close to him, crouching in the ruined limo.

"I need you to trust me," he says, his mouth pressed against my ear.

I nod.

"Good. I'm going to set you down so I can pry the door open. Stay close to me."

I nod, ignoring the panic rising in my chest and the pain spreading through me.

My lungs fill with smoke and I choke as he puts me on the floor – actually, the ceiling since we're upside down - beside him, my head pounding, my vision dancing with specks of light.

I glance toward the front of the limo, where Lily was, but she's not there. Did she get thrown out of the car when we crashed?

Sebastian grunts, pulling my attention back to him, as he uses his muscular legs to kick the door. I'm about to tell him that's not going to work, but my mouth clamps shut when the door flies off the hinges and into the street.

I stare in confused wonder and awe, the pain from my injuries subsiding at the distraction of seeing Sebastian perform superhuman feats of strength. I've read stories about this. About the adrenaline surge that can happen during a life or death crisis. How it can give ordinary people extraordinary strength for a few moments to accomplish the impossible. And Sebastian certainly isn't ordinary. He's anything but.

Before I can process much more, he's lifting me up into his arms. I grab my bag and clutch it to my chest as he extracts us from the wreckage of the burning limo. And then he runs. I expect to be jolted around like a sack of potatoes, but the motion is smooth, seemingly effort-less, which is mind-boggling.

"Wait! Lily! We can't leave her. We have to go back!"

"Lily got away," he says, showing no sign of weariness. "She knows what to do. We have to get out of here." His pace does not slow, and I'm beginning to worry he's going to try to run all the way to our final destination.

Whereas his adrenaline may be everlasting, mine, alas, is not. It crashes, leaving me writhing in pain.

I scream as I feel the deep wound of the metal bar plunged into my leg.

Sebastian glances down at me, his brow furrowed. "You are not dying. I know it hurts, but you will live. Help is coming."

As if on cue, I hear the sound of an approaching vehicle and glance around to see a black sedan pull up beside us. Sebastian nods to it and somehow opens the back door, laying me gently in the backseat. I expect him to take the front seat, but he surprises me by scooting in next to me, careful not to bump my injured leg.

I'm shocked to see that Lily is the driver. She somehow got away completely unscathed and found us a new car. There's definitely more to her than meets the eye.

Lily hands Sebastian a small black bag, flinching when she gets a good look at me.

"Is it that bad?" I ask. I feel beat up, bloody and miserable, so yes, it probably is.

"You'll be okay," she says, with an encouraging smile.

Sebastian pulls a jar of green goo and a strip of leather out of the bag. "This will hurt. A lot. But then it will be better." He hands me the leather and then gently pulls my injured leg onto his lap. "Bite on this."

Still somewhat dazed, I do what I'm told, taking the leather and placing it between my teeth, thinking, is this really necessary?

It only takes a moment to realize...It's necessary.

My teeth dig new grooves into the leather as Sebastian pulls the rod out of my leg and proceeds to smear the putrid-smelling green goo over it.

The sensation vacillates from fire to ice as the ointment is absorbed into my flesh and blood. I feel infected. Feverish. The pain is so fierce I lose sense of anything else.

He brushes my hair to the side and rubs more of the ointment into my head wound. The smell is nauseating, and my headache, already a level ten, ramps up until I have to close my eyes to keep from vomiting and passing out.

I fade in and out of consciousness for some unknowable amount of time, until finally the pain eases and then disappears entirely.

With its departure I come back to myself and open my eyes. I let out a deep sigh of relief and tentatively test sitting up on my own. Nothing terrible happens. Yay.

I extricate my leg from the delicious lap of Sebastian Night and am stunned to see that the gaping wound that was there just a few moments ago has now knitted itself back together.

"How?" I ask, my words failing me.

"You'll find out soon enough," he says, though he doesn't sound happy about it.

"That's all you have to say? I'll find out soon enough?" I respond, incredulous.

"Why did you take this job, Eve?" he asks, deflecting.

"You answer my question first," I counter.

And then I wait. Silently. Eyes on him as he weighs what he wants more.

"There's a lot I'm not telling you, though not by my choice. There is risk with this job. We make enemies. And our latest client is something of a high-profile celebrity in certain circles, and that comes with additional risk."

"Who's the client?"

"You'll find out soon enough. Your turn, Eve. A deal's a deal"

I nod. "That it is. Very well. I took the job because everything about who I am changed the night my brother died."

"From cancer. I was sorry to hear that. My condolences."

I clear my throat and continue. "He didn't die of cancer. Not officially," I say, the words alive in my throat, like bees demanding to be let out. Words I have never spoken to another living person. But words I tell myself every single day.

"My brother, Adam, had cancer, yes. But it was in remission. We were happy. Celebrating. Planning for the future. Or so I thought. I got the call at 4:34 am on Friday the thirteen. No joke. On Friday the thirteen, of all days, I got the call that my brother had died by suicide. He'd gotten the results from his latest scan. The cancer was back. He left me a note explaining it all. How he knew this had already wiped me out financially. How I'd put my career on hold to stay home and take care of him. How my health was going to shit and I needed to take better care of myself." At this I can't stop the tears. They flow, and the emotion sticks in my throat as I speak. "As if losing my twin, my best friend, my other half, as if losing him would ever make my life easier in any way at all."

What I don't say is that I already knew he was dead when the call came in. I had the worst flash of my life that morning. And I knew.

Sebastian doesn't look away from my grief when our eyes meet, and I can see in his eyes that he's known his share, too.

I wipe my tears and calm my breathing, centering myself before I continue. "After that, going back to the life I had before, well, it just seemed pointless. And painful. My brother is everywhere in my old life. There was no aspect of our lives that didn't intersect in some way. I needed something different."

Sebastian lets out a sudden humorless laugh. "You definitely got different."

Our car slows and Lily turns to look at us. "We're here."

I've been so caught up in my story, and in Sebastian, that I failed to notice the scenery around us changing.

We are in the middle of the country, surrounded by the ocean on one side and forest on the other, and there is a house—nay an estate — lit by thousands of candles, with a manicured topiary garden lining the path to the front of an actual castle made of white stone and complete with four towers and several turrets. In the center, above the drawbridge, is a jaw-dropping rose window made of stained glass that shimmers even in the darkness. The castle is surrounded by a moat with koi splashing within.

"This looks like something you'd find in Europe on a tourist to-do list," I say through breathy excitement, momentarily forgetting about my freshly healed leg and Sebastian's evasiveness. "Is this where I'll be living?"

"It is," Lily says, when Sebastian doesn't answer. "Welcome to your new home, Eve. Welcome to the family."

THE NIGHT ESTATE

There are darknesses in life and there are lights, and you are one of the lights, the light of all lights.
    ~ Bram Stoker

MY SPINE TINGLES the closer we come to the castle. Lily pulls the limo up to the front and Sebastian lets himself out before the car has hardly had a chance to park. As an afterthought he glances back at me. "Lily will take care of you." Then he leaves, rushing across the small bridge over the moat as if his pants are on fire.

I let myself out as well, and Lily rests her hands on her hips and frowns. "Hey, that's my job!"

"Sorry. I'm not used to people opening doors for me."

"You'd better get used to it in your position."

"What? As glorified secretary?" I ask with a not-so-subtle snark in my voice.

Her eyes widen. "You think you're a glorified secretary? Wow, they really haven't told you anything, have they? I'm surprised you took the job with what you know."

"You and me both," I say. "But I needed the money."

She nods. "I get it. Oh, your stuff arrived earlier today. It's all been taken to your suite."

"I have a suite?" I ask.

She giggles. "You have no idea what you have!"

The door opens as we approach and Matilda comes out to greet us, arms held open for an embrace. Tears burn my eyes when she wraps her surprisingly strong arms around me. I have to lean over to hug her, but it's worth it. Her hug makes me feel like I'm being hugged by the universe. Unconditional love flows through me and I instantly love this old woman I already knew I liked.

She wipes a tear from my cheek and pats my hand. "Don't worry, dear. You're home now. With family. I'm so glad you decided to trust yourself and come, despite everything."

Her words are layered with double meaning and I get a strong sense she knows more about my life than I realized, even factoring in the extensive background check. "I hope you and I can be friends," I say, surprising myself.

"We already are, and have always been," she says kindly. "I heard what happened on the way here. That's certainly not an ideal first day on the job, is it?"

I half laugh through brimming tears and shake my head.

Lily is glancing worriedly from me to Matilda, bouncing on her tip-toes. The girl can never seem to stay still for long. I put her in her mid-20s, though she looks younger.

"Lily, dear, you handled the situation perfectly. We're all very proud of you and grateful."

Lily beams, and her eyes practically glow with the joy the compliment inspires.

"Would you mind showing Eve to her room? I've got to meet with the boys," Matilda says to Lily, then she looks to me. "I suspect you'll want a few minutes to get settled and orient yourself. The boys are in a meeting but will speak with you when it ends. They wanted to be here to greet you themselves, but on top of discussing what happened on the way here, we're meeting with a big client tomorrow and they have a lot of work to do. So will you, once you familiarize yourself with your job."

"About that," I say. "When will I learn more about what my job entails?"

"Tonight. I promise many of your questions will be answered tonight. I hope you like your suite. I designed it myself just for you."

I thank her and follow Lily into an entryway that's larger than some apartments in New York. Two grand staircases wind up to a second floor, meeting in the middle. There's a door to the right, a door to the left, and a hall beneath the stairs that leads to another part of the castle. Lily leads me upstairs and down several hallways. I try to memorize the path, but quickly lose track. I feel like I should be leaving bread crumbs to find my way back.

We stop at a door that looks the same as several others we've passed. "This is your suite. Just ring the bell if you need help. It's a big place and easy to get lost in when you're new."

"Do you live here, too?" I ask.

She nods. "You're going to love it."

She walks away, leaving me with my bags, but turns back to face me before I enter the room. "We're all really glad you're here, Eve. You're just who they need."

She leaves for real this time and I wipe my palms on my pants and turn the knob, letting myself in.

I expect to walk into a bedroom, but I actually step into a sitting room with a loveseat and chair positioned in front of a fire with a coffee table between them. There's a patio with a cream-colored silk curtain dancing in the wind coming in from the open glass door. There's a desk with my some of my books stacked on it and the rest are lined up on the shelves next to it. My personal items have been dispersed through the room just as I would have placed them, including a sketch I drew of my brother framed on the fireplace mantel, right next to my brother's urn.

Seeing it brings more tears to my eyes. I place my bags down and walk over to it, running a finger down the side of the urn, my heart contracting with the grief that daily threatens to overwhelm me. It still doesn't seem real, and yet it's altogether too real at the same time. Grief is like that, I've learned. It lives on the impossible edge between real and unreal. Between waking and dreaming. And that makes it all the more crushing. Not understanding what happened to the brother I knew. How his body, the fullness of his life, could be reduced to a handful of ashes.

I turn away from his remains and focus on exploring the rest of the room. The hand-painted tile flooring is partially covered by thick rugs to take the chill off, and the blazing fire in the hearth warms the space. A large bookshelf covers one wall and is filled with books, some of them mine, some new. Well, old, actually, but new to me. Mine stand out as the only ones without leather covers.

In another corner is a two-person table with a bowl of fruit and a jug of juice or wine atop it. There's another jug with water, and a bar with stronger drinks to the side. I step through a door and into my bedroom, which boasts another lit fire with two comfortable leather chairs in front of it, and a huge four-poster canopy bed carved from a beautiful light wood and decorated with cherry blossoms. A thick purple velvet comforter covers it and I push my hand into the bed and sigh at how luxurious it feels. Way better than the bed I just sold. There's a large wardrobe that reveals all my clothes unpacked when I open it, plus other clothes, very fancy dresses and suits, that I've never seen before but are all in my size with matching shoes. The new clothes are gothic and Renaissance in style, which is unusual, but beautiful and clearly expensively, made with the finest craftsmanship and fabrics.

I've been well off in the past, comfortable enough to live in a nice neighborhood in New York, buy nice clothes, and go to restaurants when I wanted. Granted I had to sell anything of value to help pay Adam's medical expenses and relocate to a much cheaper apartment, but I still remember that life. But as I look around I realize this is a whole other level of wealth that most people can only dream about.

The bathroom is spacious, with a huge tub in the center of the room. One wall in the bathroom is made of stone and hides the shower behind it. There's no door, just stone walls and floor with a window overlooking the grounds, though I'm high enough up that I don't think anyone can see me from here. It's not immediately clear how to operate the shower or tub, and I make a mental note to ask someone how to work all of this.

I return to my bedroom and realize there's one box under the bed that hasn't been unpacked. I pull it out and find a note on it, written in formal writing. "I thought you might want to unpack this one yourself, so I had the movers leave it." It's signed Sebastian. I open the box and discover that it contains my brother's belongings. I pull out his old college hoodie. A sob chokes my throat as I put it on, hugging it around me. His scent has surely faded after all this time, but I can still smell him. Maybe it's in my mind, but I cling to it, nonetheless.

"Oh, Adam. You were too young. This shouldn't have happened."

There's another balcony door in my bedroom, and I step out and realize the balconies are connected into one large one, with a small table and two chairs outside, and several beautiful plants adding an earthiness to the space. It's dark, but the sky is full of moonlight and the stars are bright. I take a deep breath of the crisp late fall air and close my eyes, listening to the sounds of the night creatures. I always loved the night, the darkness, the eye of the moon on me. It never occurred to me I would end up in a job that required me to live in the night, but I'm finding myself excited by the prospect. The moon holds the secrets the sun cannot see. But I want to see.

I want to know all the secrets the moon holds.

I want to see the wild woman again. I want to feel the power she held.

And, I realize, I also want to get to know my new home.

Slipping my phone into my pocket, and grabbing my sketchbook, I leave my room and hope I'll be able to find my way back. I keep track of where I'm going by drawing a map as I go. Most of the rooms I try are just guest suites or bedrooms, and I worry I will come across someone's lived in quarters but I always knock first, and so far they've all been empty.

The place is huge, and I use more and more pages of my sketchbook to map it, making notes when I find bedrooms, bathrooms, random meeting rooms, storage rooms. I'm sticking to upstairs at the moment, but I know there will be so much more to explore downstairs. The dark, windowless halls are lit by torches on the walls, though they are not flames but rather some kind of strange bulb. At least, I assume it's a bulb. There's no actual evidence of one. Just a ball of pale blue light that is cool rather than warm.

There's a flurry of activity happening near one suite. It sounds like several people are working, but when I glance in, I see only Matilda. "Is someone else coming?" I ask, since she is clearly preparing this suite for someone who doesn't already live here.

"He arrives tomorrow. We must prepare." She is distracted and looks around as if trying to find help.

"Who's he?"

"No time to explain. We'll talk later, dear." She rushes off, so I keep exploring, turning corners, studying portraits and paintings that line the walls, until I find myself in a hall that has no doors or windows, though it's very long. At the very end is one red door, intricately carved. I reach to turn the knob, forgetting my own rule about knocking, when a voice barks at me.

"Do not open that door! This wing isn't meant for you." I turn to face Liam, and his eyes are alight with simmering rage. Dude has issues.

"I'm sorry. I was just trying to get my bearings here. What's in the room?" I ask.

"None of your business."

"Is it like your sex dungeon or something? The red room of pain?" I laugh, but he doesn't. Again. Tough crowd.

"That would be a different red door," another voice chimes in. Derek arrives, with Sebastian and Elijah following. "It seems our meeting has started without us."

"She has no business being here," Liam says harshly. "This is a mistake. She could ruin everything. She's a mundane."

"I've heard that twice. Mundane. What does that mean?"

Derek sighs. "We have to tell her sometime. It's not like we can keep this a secret for long. Not with him coming tomorrow."

Sebastian crosses his arms over his chest but says nothing.

Elijah nods. "The decision is made, now we must make the best of it."

Liam looks furious, but says nothing as Derek pulls a key out of his pocket and opens the door. "There's something you should know about us, and this company, Eve." He steps into the room, and I can't help but stare.

"Do you also run a funeral parlor?" I ask, because there are four beautiful coffins side by side in the darkened and windowless room. "Or this really is your sex room and y'all are super kinky? I mean, I'm not judging, to each their own, but I don't really think I need to know about this part of your life. We can have some secrets, don't you think?"

Sebastian laughs, but it's more of a disappointed sound as he shakes his head. "You don't get it, Eve. This isn't a funeral parlor. We weren't drinking wine at your job interview, and there's a reason we only work at night."

"Are you... ?" I swallow, thinking through the ramifications of it all. Realization finally sets in, but it's a hard pill to swallow. "Okay, I get it. You're really deep into the lifestyle. I mean clearly, solidly committed. Structuring your law firm around it is pretty intense, but it's cool. I've met some people with vampire and bite kinks. None who took it quite this far, but enough that I know it's pretty serious for some. Is this why you need me? Because you want to stick to your role? No going out in daylight and all that? I'm down with going along, to an extent. I don't want to, like, participate though. If you catch my drift." I show my teeth. "No bitey bitey on me and we're all good."

Sebastian throws his hands in the air and turns away, sighing. Elijah presses his lips together, and Derek frowns.

But not Liam. He clenches his fist, and what happens next is too fast for me to do anything to prevent.

Before I realize what's happening, my body slams into the wall, knocking the breath out of my lungs, and Liam is pressed against me, his rock-hard form crushing my breasts, his hands gripping my wrists tightly, pushing them against the wall. A guttural growl, inhumane in its sound, emanates from him, and I see his teeth are elongated far beyond what's normal or natural. Then his mouth is at my neck.

I feel pain, fire burning in me, through me, as his teeth sink into my flesh, then a kind of strange bliss washes through me, even as fear leeches into me, trying to find purchase in all the confusion.

There's no time for panic to take me. My heart slows as my blood is drained, my head spins, and my body feels disconnected from my mind, unable to support itself. Liam is holding me up at this point. If he pulls away, I will crumble to the ground, a pale, bloodless ghost.

My thoughts flicker to random moments in my life. My last fight with Jerry. My last hug from my father. My last long talk with my brother. So many lasts. We seldom know what moment will be the last of something. We celebrate the firsts, but we don't think of the lasts. They are the memories that stick when all else is gone. Those final footprints in the snow, covering all others. The last words, last laughs, last tears. It's only in hindsight that we see how precious those moments were.

I close my eyes and give into this moment. Savoring it. Savoring my life, what little is left. Will I see my brother soon? My parents? That won't be so bad. Death is the ultimate last and first, all at once. It encompasses it all.

Someone shouts, and Liam is pulled away amidst argument and fights. My body crumbles to the ground, but strong arms catch me and lift me. My head rests against a muscular chest. His breathing is heavy, his anger solid and intense.

Sebastian.

"Why?" I ask, with the airy breathlessness reserved for those whose life is leaking out of them. "Why are you always angry at me?"

I pry my eyes open to meet his, staring at me, his jaw clenched, his face conflicted.

I hear more arguing, and someone shouts, "Get her out of here. Take care of her. We'll handle Liam."

Sebastian grunts and we begin to move. My body is limp, like carrying noodles, but Sebastian doesn't seem to have any trouble managing it.

He takes me to a room with a fire and lays me on a bed. It's not my room or my bed, but I'm too out of it to care.

I feel his hands on my body, on my neck. Water, something cold, then something that stings. Then his wrist is at my mouth, and he forces thick, viscous liquid down my throat. I gag and try to spit it out but he doesn't let me.

"Drink. You need this. Trust me. Drink."

My eyes flicker open and closed, the world swirling in a confusing array of light and color.

A cool cloth on my forehead.

A gentle hand brushing away my hair from my face.

A body next to mine in the bed.

"It's not you I'm always angry at," I hear, as my mind drifts away and my thoughts scatter into dreams.

THE NIGHT BROTHERS

I am a forest, and a night of dark trees: but he who is not afraid of my darkness, will find banks full of roses under my cypresses.
  ~ Friedrich Nietzsche

"SHE NEEDS TO LEARN. Do you think *he* will be as gentle if she mocks him the way she mocked us?"

The voice wakes me from my sleep, but I don't stir or open my eyes. I don't want anyone to know I'm conscious. I hope to glean more feigning sleep than I've managed to learn thus far while awake. Though pieces of the mystery are starting to fall into place, I still can't make sense of any of it. Nothing I've experienced with this family makes sense, actually.

"She wasn't mocking." That's Derek. I appreciate how he always defends me. He seems to be the only one really on my side since I was interviewed and subsequently hired to this job I'm beginning to regret.

There's a deep ache in my neck, and my brain is still

trying to put it all together in a way that doesn't make me sound crazy.

"It's to be expected," Derek continues, "that she would have trouble embracing the truth immediately. We have to give her time, not attack her and make her fear us. You nearly killed her!"

"That's nonsense," says the first voice. Liam.

Flashes penetrate the fog in my brain and cut through the pain in my throat.

Liam, his teeth unnaturally long.

Liam pinning me against the wall with superhuman strength.

Liam's teeth sinking into my neck.

Blood.

I feel nauseous and quickly sit up, afraid of choking should I vomit. I see a water basin on the dresser by the bedside and grab it, leaning over it to retch, though there's little in my stomach to empty. Still, my body convulses, and I feel bad for whoever has to deal with my mess.

My head spins, my throat burns and aches, like my muscles are tearing, and I close my eyes, moaning in pain as the hell continues.

Cool hands touch my face, and I open my eyes to find Sebastian standing beside the bed.

"Eve," he says, gently, but I recoil from his touch, scrambling away from him until I'm pushed up against the headboard, as far from him as I can get without leaving the bed.

"Don't touch me!" I tell him, the memories of what Liam did to me still fresh in my mind. Layered over other memories of abuse. Pain. Betrayal.

I glance toward the door, wondering if I can cross the

distance to it before Sebastian can catch me, and he seems to read my mind.

"It's okay, Eve. I'm not going to hurt you."

"Right," I tell him, as anger slowly begins to replace my fear. "And you expect me to believe that after what Liam did to me?"

He frowns. "I am not Liam."

"No, but you're a vampire just like he is!" I respond hotly, realizing even as I say it that I've given a name to the elephant in the room.

There's no denying the truth of my statement and, thankfully, he doesn't try. It would just have been embarrassing for him if he had.

He sighs and mentally seems to be counting to ten. Then, "What Liam did was wrong, and I apologize for it. It shouldn't have happened. I've brought you something to help with the...after effects." He hands me a glass of something purple and fizzy. "Drink this. You'll thank me."

I pause. "Why should I trust you?"

"Because I only wish to help."

Carefully, I take the drink and sniff at the contents. The sweet smell has me nearly drooling despite myself, so I guzzle it in one shot—and nearly puke it back up. How can something that smells so good taste so very awful? I gag, but force the vile brew down my throat, at the quiet promptings of Sebastian, who takes the cup from me when I'm done and hands me a cold rag for my head.

Eyeing him cautiously, I lay back down.

He hesitates, then gestures at the space next to me on the bed. "May I?"

I'm still ticked, but nothing's going to be gained by staying mad at him. He's right; he's not Liam. Only today he saved my life, in fact. Never have I had a twenty-four hour period where my life was in such peril with such frequency. Still, I nod and stiffen only a little bit as he climbs into the bed next to me.

He doesn't speak for several minutes, and I close my eyes and enjoy the silence, and, I'll admit, the feeling of his body so close to mine.

It happens in a wave, like water washing over me, and as it does, my body buzzes with energy. The pain recedes, the aches dissipate, and I feel a kind of euphoria that leaves me relaxed and grateful for the relief.

"You are feeling better." It's a statement, not a question.

I nod with my eyes still closed, a small smile on my face. "Thank you," I whisper.

His thumb gently rubs against my temple, all the way down to the line of my jaw, tracing it to my collarbone. His touch leaves a trail of fire in its wake, and I sigh at the contact, though my heart and body are confused by his on again, off again attentions. And my brain is trying to convince me that whatever these feelings are that I'm having for my boss, they need to shut the hell down right away. I'm done with unhealthy power dynamic relationships. They've already messed up my head too much.

The euphoria I was feeling wears off too quickly and I'm left with my doubts and confusion. I sit up quickly and instantly regret it, my head spinning a bit as I look around. "Where are they?" I ask.

"Who?" Sebastian says.

"Your brothers. Their voices woke me. I heard them talking."

Sebastian frowns. "They're in the right wing where I

77

left them. This is my room, in the left wing. There's no way you could have heard them talking," he says.

"Huh. It must have been a dream." I twist to face him, and our bodies are so close—and in his bed, no less—that it's driving me to distraction, but I ignore it, or try to. "What's going on? Maybe those voices were a dream, but the rest of it isn't, is it?"

"No. It's not."

"So, it wasn't the adrenaline..."

Sebastian frowned. "Sorry?"

"After the accident. The door was jammed shut by the crash. You not only kicked it open, but sent it flying off its hinges. At the time I thought it was due to a sudden, massive burst of adrenaline, but it wasn't, was it?"

A slight shake of his head. "No."

"And then you ran with me, carrying me miles, as if I weighed nothing."

He nods again.

"You have coffins in a locked room."

His gaze bores into mine.

"Liam drank my blood."

"Yes. All of this true. Which is why you should have turned down the job. Why you still should. It's not too late. Not yet. You can leave now. I can help you."

"What do you mean it's not too late yet? When will it be too late?"

Before Sebastian can answer, the door slams open and Elijah stands there, an intensity to his eyes. "He's on his way right now!"

Sebastian straightens at that. "What? He's not due to arrive until tomorrow."

Elijah shrugs. "Seems he's come early."

"Bloody hell," Sebastian says. "She doesn't even know everything yet."

Elijah looks at me, then back at Sebastian. "You'd better fill her in fast. He'll be here in twenty."

Elijah leaves, closing the door behind him, and I turn to face Sebastian. "Who's coming? What's going on?"

"We have a new client," he says. "An important client. When you meet him, it's critical you are careful. He's very... dynamic. And dangerous."

"Who's the client?"

"If I told you, you wouldn't believe me. You're having a hard enough time believing what you've seen with your own eyes."

"What I've seen is impossible," I say.

"There are more things in heaven and earth than are dreamt of in your philosophy," he says, quoting Shakespeare.

"Funny, you don't strike me as the Shakespeare reading type," I say, deflecting the seriousness of the situation.

"There's a lot about me you might be surprised by, Eve," he says, and I can't help but love how my name sounds on his lips. "We both need to get ready for his arrival, but first, let's be absolutely clear about what's going on here. You are correct; we - my brothers and I - are vampires. And The Night Firm isn't just any firm. It's a law firm for paranormal creatures. We have our own justice system and court of law. Humans could never keep us in check, so we do it ourselves."

"Paranormal creatures," I say, in a breathy whisper. "So there are more than just vampires?"

He nods. "But you knew that already. You saw others when you left your interview, did you not?"

It's my turn to nod, as I remember the woman I saw as I left the building that night.

"They were real. Just as I am real. This is a dangerous place for you, Eve. You asked before why I'm always mad at you. I'm not. I'm mad you're here, because I worry you will not be safe. Especially now."

Everything he's said and done since we met is suddenly seen in a new light, and all the attraction and pent up desire I feel surfaces. My eyes fall to his lips, and I can see by the way his body tenses, he feels the energy in the room shift as well.

Our hands are touching, skin brushing against skin on the silky sheets. My hip is pressed against him.

Panic wells in me and I pull back. "The accident wasn't an accident was it?" It's all starting to click into place.

"No, it wasn't," he says, regaining his composure quickly. "We make enemies. Our clients make enemies. Especially the client you're about to meet. You will be in constant danger if you stay."

It's clear he wants me to leave. But... where would I go? I have nothing left to return to.

I slide off the bed and adjust my clothes. "I think I'll take my chances," I say, though I have a million questions. "And I should probably get ready, if he's on his way." I need an excuse to leave, because I can't stay in the room with him any longer and not act on the desires building up in me.

Before I leave the room, I turn, a question on my mind. "Why do you have coffins if you also have a regular bedroom?" I ask.

"We don't regularly sleep in the coffins," he says. "It's for emergencies. If we have to travel during the day or heal from serious injury. They are filled with dirt from our homeland, from before our vampire lives."

I nod, processing that, and he doesn't speak to stop me as I turn to leave.

I wander around the mansion trying to find my room until I bump into Lily, who's wide-eyed and jittery. "I've been looking everywhere for you. We have to get you dressed. Come on!"

She practically drags me to my room, and once there, opens my closet and starts pulling out dresses. "It needs to be perfect. This is a big deal."

I can't tell if she's excited or nervous or both. I'm not sure how to feel. The Night brothers seem pretty powerful. Who could they possibly be this jumpy about seeing?

My mind is still reeling from my conversation with Sebastian, and now I'm supposed to play dress up? I sit on the bed as Lily fusses with my hair.

"Is it true?" I ask Lily. I assume she knows everything. How could she not?

"Is what true?" she asks, twisting my hair expertly into a Dutch braid any hair stylist in New York would be jealous of.

"You're all vampires."

She freezes, and then moves to stand so we are face to face. "Not all of us."

A blink.

The pink hair is gone. The dark complexion changed.

The being that stands before me is naked, skin a deep-moss-green. Hair thick like vines, adorned with white flowers and auburn branches. Eyes like emeralds.

The smell of spring's first rain overtakes me.

And as quickly as it appeared, the vision is gone.

Lily smiles across from me, rosy hair falling over her shoulder. "Now let's add some make-up."

I nod, unsure of what I just witnessed, curiosity and fear mixing within me. "What about Matilda? Is she a vampire? Or is she... like you?"

Lily retrieves a blue eyeshadow and begins applying it to my face, pursing her lips. "Granny Matilda is something else, but that's her story to tell, not mine."

"Is it rude to ask what you are? I don't mean to be impolite. This is all just so new to me."

She smiles, and I see a shadow of the wild woodland creature she truly is.

"I'm a dryad," she says, simply. "A creature of the forest, the soul of a tree."

I'm not sure if I should be relieved or worried. Everything poses more questions than answers. "Am I safe here?"

She narrows her eyes. "The Nights won't let anything happen to you."

I scoff at that. "Liam just tried to kill me."

She rolls her eyes. "Liam can be a giant ass sometimes. He's hotheaded, impulsive and prone to reckless acts. But if he wanted to kill you, you'd be dead. That much is certain. No, what he did, it was a warning."

"Nothing like getting into a near deadly car accident on my way to my first day, then getting attacked and bitten by my boss." The snark is strong in my voice.

Lily sighs. "I know it doesn't make sense, and it's a crap way to start your work here, but I promise it will get better. Give them a chance."

I don't know how to respond, so I stay silent as she finishes helping me dress in a sapphire blue gown that matches my eyes and is cinched at my waist and flared at my hips, cascading down my legs in layers.

When she's done, she pulls back to admire her handi-work. "You look incredible. And you have such perfect porcelain skin. You could pass for a vampire if you smelled different," she says, wrinkling her nose.

"Uh, thanks?"

She laughs. "I'm so glad you finally know. It's been agony waiting for those dummies to tell you everything."

"I hardly think they've told me everything," I say, slip-ping my feet into a pair of heels that match my dress.

"It's a lot for some people to take," she says. "Some-times it's easier to get it in pieces than all at once."

As Lily leads me out my room and through the labyrinth of halls and towards the library, I ask a question that's been prickling my mind since discovering the truth. "Why did they hire me?"

Lily shrugs. "Your resume impressed them, I guess?"

"I don't mean me specifically. Why did they hire a human? Why not stick with vampires or...whatever else. Keep it in the family so to speak. Why expose this world to an outsider for no reason?"

She stops and turns to frown at me. "I could tell the moment we met that you belong here. If I can feel it, they can definitely feel it. And besides, you wouldn't have even heard about the job if you weren't the right person."

With that she continues to walk, but once again I'm left with more questions. "What do you mean? I would have seen it in the paper like everyone else."

She laughs. "That's funny."

When she realizes I'm not laughing she stops again. "You're serious. Oh dear. There's just so much you don't know. Granny spelled the job advertisement so that only the perfect candidate for the job would find it. In fact, they're the only one who would even be able to see it. You had the job the moment you called the number. You were the only candidate."

We're walking again, and I try not to stumble over my dress as I work to keep pace with Lily's power walk. "She spelled it? Like with magic?"

"Yup. She's got all kinds of spells up her sleeves. She even showed me how to make a potion that changes my hair color, which is really fun for when I'm out clubbing."

I don't have time to unpack that statement as we have finally arrived at the library where the Night brothers and Matilda are waiting. Sebastian gives me a brief nod and a slight smile of encouragement. Liam doesn't make eye contact with me. Coward. Elijah's eyes hold mine for a long moment, and it's as if a cool breeze dances against my skin when he looks at me like that. I feel an uncomfortable stirring in my body as I consider the quietest of the four brothers. Elijah always seems more contemplative. I can practically see his mind working even as he locks eyes with me.

Derek heads to the bar, pours a drink and walks over to me. "For your nerves," he says, handing me the glass. "You look beautiful."

"Thank you," I say, for the drink and the compliment. A glance at the bottle he poured from shows this is an expensive whiskey. I savor each sip, enjoying the way it burns as I swallow.

"I had hoped to have more time to explain everything," Derek says, his smile faltering. "This has all happened faster than we expected. I wanted to apologize for my brother. He will never do that again. I give you my word."

Despite his promise, or perhaps because of it, the anger bubbling inside me spills out. I'm not just upset, I realize. I'm royally pissed. "Damn straight he won't or I'll shove a wooden chair leg through his heart faster than he can blink!"

Derek stares at me wide-eyed, jaw slack.

Before he can say anything, I turn and glare in Liam's direction.

He's studiously ignoring me.

That won't do.

Won't do at all.

Downing the rest of my drink, I set the finely etched crystal glass on the table slowly and deliberately and then head straight to over to Liam, getting right in his face so he can't avoid my gaze anymore.

I can feel everyone in the room staring at us.

I stab my finger into his ridiculously muscled chest as I speak with all the authority and rage I can muster. "You had no right to do that, and you will never, ever touch me like that again, am I clear? If you so much as think about doing that again, I will stake your ass so fast you will wish you'd never been born...er...unborn. Or made undead. Whatever. You get my point. Do. Not. Do. That. Again." I say, pushing my fingernail harder against his chest with each word. "Also, you owe me an apology. Or I walk. I'm not working here without one."

He blinks. I don't. I wait. Eyes focused. Heart pounding. My neck is completely healed, not even a scratch, but the memory of the pain still haunts me.

"I apologize," he says, breaking the silence in the room.

One of his brothers makes a sound of surprise, but I don't look away from Liam to find out who.

His eyes burn with heat and his muscular chest probably did more damage to my finger than I did to it.

"Why did you do it?" I ask, in almost a whisper. For that moment, as his gaze pulls me in, it feels as if we are the only two people in the room.

"To show you the danger you're in. Be careful, Miss Oliver. We're the good guys, and even we aren't that good."

He turns away just as Matilda enters the room. The look on her face is more serious than any I've seen so far. Addressing the brothers, she says. "Your guest has arrived. Shall I show him in?"

"Please," Derek replies. He glances at me quickly, winking flirtatiously before turning his attention back to the library entrance.

The tension in the room ramps up. I have no idea what to expect, since everyone here is so damn tight lipped, but I know it's something big.

My palms are suddenly sweaty, but I can't wipe them on my dress, they'll stain. I consider surreptitiously wiping them on the nearby chair, but I can feel Sebastian's gaze upon me and I do my best to resist. A moment later he passes me his handkerchief.

"Take a deep breath," he says. "We have our reasons to be worried, but you needn't fear for anything," he whispers as I gratefully wipe my hands dry.

And then all eyes are on the doorway as Matilda returns, our guest in tow. "May I present the eminent Count Dracula," she says solemnly.

THE GUEST

It was in my flaws,
I found a much deeper truth—
and it is from them,
I bloom: a black rose.
~ Segovia Amil

THE BROTHERS GIVE CURT BOWS, while I stand in shock as a tall, lithe man walks into the library.

The man—Dracula—wears a tuxedo reminiscent of older times. A long cape, coal-black on the outside, crimson on the inside, drags behind his leather boots. His pitch-black hair is slicked back, though one strand falls lose over his eyes, which are almost as dark as his hair. His skin is the palest cream, and though unlined by years, he feels ancient, powerful, and his presence fills the room.

It's almost suffocating, being in the same space with him. I take a step back instinctively, which is a mistake, as his eyes jump to me, devouring me in one glance.

I feel naked.

Uncomfortable.

And way too exposed in a room full of vampires.

Derek steps forward first, taking the lead. "Vlad, welcome to our home."

He nods. "If only this visit were under better circumstances," he says, his accent Slavic and his voice deep.

"We will sort out all that," Derek says with confidence, though I can sense a flicker of unease in him, despite his valiant attempts to hide it.

"And who is she?" Dracula asks.

Derek gestures for me to step forward. "This is our new associate, Miss Eve Oliver. Eve comes highly recommended by Richard Dwarvas and has both an MBA in business and a law degree from Harvard University."

I'm not entirely sure why he's trying so hard to sell my credentials to this guy—to Dracula — but I do appreciate the reminder to everyone else in this room that I am damn well qualified to be here. Aside from me being super frail and human. And I suppose, mundane.

Still. I can hold my own.

I put my hand forward to shake his, but he brings it up to his lips and brushes it with a soft kiss. "A pleasure to make your acquaintance. It seems my sons have certainly done well for themselves."

"Sons?" I say, my eyes flickering to Sebastian, who grits his teeth and clenches his fists.

"We aren't your sons," Liam says, stepping forward, his anger on full display.

Dracula shrugs. "Your birth father gave life to you. I gave you immortality and power beyond measure. Which one sounds like more of a father?"

Click. Pieces falling into place. Dracula turned the Night brothers. I'm having a serious holy shit moment. I feel a bit as if I'm in a farce, playing the part of the only person who doesn't know the joke's on them.

But that bite on my neck. That was real.

I glance at Liam, who looks toward me, as if he knows I'm thinking about him, then he returns his attention to Dracula. "We are paying our debt to you now. We will keep you from being buried alive for all eternity, and you will leave us the hell alone. Forever."

The tension is so thick in the room I can barely breathe. Everyone is frozen, breaths abated, waiting for what will happen next.

"If you deliver justice," Dracula says, "then our blood debt will be cleared. You will be free of the sire bond."

The brothers exchange glances and everyone nods. Well, nearly everyone.

"I need to hear him say it, first," Liam says. "I need to him to look me in the eyes and tell me he didn't do it." Liam walks over to Dracula and stands inches from him, their eyes deadlocked. "Tell me you didn't kill Mary. Convince me of your innocence."

Dracula's face changes, morphing from calm and collected, to monstrous in his rage. And I realize I'm seeing Vlad the Impaler right now. He lifts Liam by the cuff of his shirt and pushes him forward, slamming him against the wall in much the same way Liam did to me earlier. I can't help but feel a little bit gloaty about that.

But when I see the crack in the stone from the impact of Liam's body, I cringe. Ouch, that's gotta hurt.

Dracula growls at Liam, his teeth elongated, full on vampire mode. "I did not kill my wife. I would never harm her. She was my heart and my soul. I am nothing without her."

With those words, the anger and rage seems to drain from Dracula, and he drops Liam to the ground and sways back on his heels before righting himself. He seems to come back to the awareness that he is not alone, and his face, previously so full of raw emotion, clamps down instantly, the mask so effective it's tempting to think I just imagined anything but the haughty, cold, measured way he assesses everyone and everything.

Dracula looks at all four of the Night brothers. "Prove my innocence, and you will get what you want. Fail, and I will not be the only one suffering an eternity of torture. You have my word on that."

Dracula turns to me and bows. "Miss Oliver, a pleasure." He shifts to Matilda. "Madam Night, good evening." And then with a click of his heels, he turns and marches out.

Apparently, he knows his way around the castle.

As soon as he's out of earshot, the room seems to exhale the breath it has been holding for far too long.

"This was a mistake," Liam says. "We will either be freeing the monster who murdered Mary, or we will be at war with Dracula himself. Neither option is optimal."

"We have no choice," Derek says with a shrug. "He pulls our strings until he breaks our sire bond. Until then, we are beholden."

"Is that how it works?" I ask, breaking everyone's focus. Four sets of eyes move to meet mine, as if just realizing I am still here. "If you turn someone, you can control them?"

"Not entirely," Derek says. "But close. It's a compulsion

that's hard to resist. And if you resist too long, it can cause serious pain. But it takes energy from both parties, so it's not used as often as you might imagine."

"But he's using it now? For this?"

Derek nods. "He's been formally charged with murdering his wife and unborn child and draining them both of blood."

I gasp. "Why would he do that? Why would anyone do that?"

The silence that greets my question tells me all I need to know.

"If he's been charged, that means there will be a trial. Are you defending him?"

"Yes," Elijah says.

"What if he's guilty? Will you really work to prove his innocence to save yourself?"

Liam glares at me. "We have no choice. It's not the pain that's the problem. Eventually the compulsion will work. No one is strong enough to resist, especially not when it's Dracula himself. And besides, it's not our job to determine guilt or innocence. After all, who are we to judge?"

"Then let's get to work," I say. "I need to bone up on my knowledge of your legal system. Where do I start?"

They all stare at me, and a flicker of a smile appears on Matilda's face. "Elijah, dear, why don't you take Eve to your study and give her an overview, then direct her to the right books so she can get started."

Elijah nods. "Would you like to change first?"

I look down at my formal gown and nod. "Yes. I would, actually. Thank you."

It doesn't take more than ten minutes for me to change and find my way to Elijah's office. It's a cozy room with wall-to-wall books and a few comfortable chairs in the center near the fireplace. There's a desk to one side piled with more books, and ladders to reach the highest books.

I take the seat offered, and Elijah brings over a pile of books and places them next to me. "Our kind are tried similarly to the American justice system, by a jury of our peers, with a proper defense and prosecution, and a judge to oversee it. The biggest differences are the laws—what's illegal and what's not—and the punishments. Out of necessity, given the power many of us have, the punishments are harsh and often permanent."

I nod, "That makes sense, I suppose."

He raises an eyebrow. "The punishments can seem medieval and even inhumane to someone not used to our ways," he elaborates.

"Yeah, I get it. Like Dracula will be put to ground while still alive, presumably in a way he can't escape, for all of eternity."

He nods. "Amongst other things, yes, that is one example. Though other punishments are much more gruesome, and often the guilty do not live through the experience. Paranormals tend to liken themselves to the gods of old and are just as capricious with our punishments."

I shudder at the images that come to mind, but then I shake it off. This is my life now. Better acclimate fast. "Gotcha. What else?"

He leans forward, studying me. "You surprise me, Miss Oliver."

"Just Eve is fine, thanks."

"Eve, then. You're not what I expected."

"What did you expect?"

"Not you," he says, a smile playing at his lips.

My heart skips a beat at the look he's giving me right now.

"You have a sharp mind," he says. "That much is clear. And courage, for standing up to Liam like that. That hothead is going to get himself killed someday if he's not careful."

"He needs balancing," I say. "Too much fire. He needs water to cool his engines. Earth to ground him."

"What did you just say?"

"The elements? You know, how we all have these qualities in us, and if they get out of balance it can create an excess of certain personality traits. Honestly, you guys should check out Google more often. You might learn a few useful things about the 21st century."

"Yes, of course. Well, you do have a keen eye, Miss Oliver, er, Eve. But I'm afraid I must retire. Sunrise is upon us, and contrary to popular media, we do not function during the daylight hours. Not in this world."

"Oh, right." I stand as he does. "Um, is it okay if I stay and read? I have a lot to learn and not a lot of time in which to learn it."

Elijah nods. "As you wish. Until this evening, then." He touches my arm gently, letting his fingers slide over my skin, before walking away.

My skin tingles where he made contact, and it takes my body a beat to settle down from the effects of his attention.

These Night brothers might be the death of me, in more ways than one.

I attempt to read, to study the pile of texts left for me, but my mind keeps returning to the enigmatic Elijah, his clear blue eyes holding keen intelligence and secret knowledge. Giving up, I pull out my sketchbook, which I take with me everywhere, and begin to draw from memory the eyes that I can't put out of my mind. I draw him as I saw him when I entered his study, sitting at his desk, a book before him, his expression one of lost reflection as he looks up at the noise of me entering his space.

When I'm done, I study it and smile. It's as if he's sitting before me, mid-interruption, just before he's about to speak. I tuck the sketchbook back into my bag and refocus my attentions.

For the rest of the morning, I read. And let me just set the record straight, in case there was any confusion about this, reading law books is about as exciting as watching paint dry. Paranormal law books are no exception, though a few of their laws raised my eyebrows.

For example, there's a law that werewolves aren't allowed to leave their clothing on private property not belonging to them, or on public lands, during full moon shifts, unless they request a special permit, which has to be signed by a judge. The penalty for breaking this law is one full moon cycle locked up in silver chains.

I make good work on the books. One of the ways I was able to graduate with both my MBA and law degree so fast was my ability to speed read and retain the vast majority of the material I take in when I do. When I told the Night brothers that I'm smart, I wasn't being vain or exaggerating. I'm a member of Mensa, after all.

At around three in the afternoon, I'm in the middle of a thick book on court procedures when I get a flash that I'm needed in the topiary garden. I have no idea by whom or for what, but there's no resisting the sensation. I decide to take a stroll outside to enjoy some sunshine and Vitamin D before my planned slumber.

There's a gentle breeze that carries the scent of wild flowers, and the sun is so warm and bright that I feel sorry for vampires who can no longer feel the kiss of daylight on their skin. What a sad existence that must be, to be forced into darkness, never again experiencing nature's light.

I make my way through the garden, passing bushes molded into fantastical beasts straight from fairy tales, following my instincts and marveling at the artistry that went into creating the landscape around the castle as I go, until I hear something coming from one of the bushes. A meowing, tiny and faint, but there.

I squat down to peer into the bush, and stuck there between two branches is a tiny black kitten with big yellow eyes staring at me plaintively. It meows again and looks at the end of its rope. Careful not to hurt the fur ball, I maneuver it out of the bramble and scoop it into a pouch I make of my sweatshirt. I give the kitten a quick exam to see if there are any obvious injuries.

"You look in one piece," I say. "And it seems you're a boy."

He holds eye contact with me and purrs each time I pet him. He looks at me with such love and devotion my heart melts, and I'm determined I will keep him. Hopefully I don't have to go battle with the brothers over this, but I will if I must.

I head back to the castle and I find Lily, bringing her into my plan. After a high-pitched squeal of delight, she goes off in search of food and supplies to care for him.

I bring him back to my room and take a warm cloth to

his fur, brushing away bits of stick and dirt. He purrs the whole time.

When I'm done, I hold his face up to mine, nuzzling him with my nose. "You're going to need a name," I say. "What shall we call you?"

Lily comes in, carrying a bowl of food and one with water, and I ask her the name of the bush he got stuck in.

"It's called a Moonweed," she says. "Though it's not really a weed. And it can only be grown with magic."

I look into the kitten's eyes again, studying him. "I'm not going to name you Weed. But I like the name Moon. What do you think?"

He purrs and licks my nose. I laugh. "I think we have a winner. Lily, meet Moon."

She claps and then sits next to me and gives him some love. "I don't think we've ever had a pet in the castle before. Especially not a cat. This is going to be so fun!"

"Do you think the brothers will give me a hard time about it?" I ask.

Lily shrugs. "Who cares? What are they going to do to stop you? Take him to Granny first. Once she's on board, they're powerless. Everyone thinks they run things around here, but it's really Granny. Always has been."

I yawn, the day, or rather night, catching up with me. Lily nods sympathetically. "It's a hard schedule to get used to," she says. "My kind are drawn to the sun, but fortunately we also don't need much sleep. But humans do. Get some rest. Tonight is going to be a busy day."

I laugh at that and nod, my body suddenly feeling as if weights have been added to my arms and legs.

Lily pulls the curtains in my room, sending it into complete darkness, and stokes the fire to ward off the constant chill in the castle. I always dreamed of living in a castle when I was a little girl, but I never realized how drafty they could be.

Before Lily leaves the room I call after her. "How do I use the plumbing in the bathroom?"

I'm looking forward to a long bath once I'm not so exhausted.

She smiles. "It's not plumbing, it's magic." She makes a series of symbols in the air. "Use those and you'll be fine."

I practice a few times and she nods. "You've got it. Goodnight, Eve."

She closes the door softly and I crawl into bed with Moon, who curls up on my shoulder in the crook of my neck and purrs contentedly.

It only takes moment for me to fall asleep after my head hits the pillow.

That night my dreams turn dark. I'm in the woods, alone at night. Naked. Bleeding. Scared. Moon is trapped in barbed vines and I can't get to him. He's crying, meowing to get out, but every time he moves he gets cut.

My hands and arms are covered in bloody gashes, but I've made no progress in getting him freed.

Then a tall man walks up to me, black cape flowing behind him. It's Dracula, his pale face shining in the moonlight.

He walks with a black ebony cane tipped with jade at the handle, his dark eyes taking everything in.

When he reaches me, he smiles, but his eyes remain hard, cold, calculating. Taking another step, he places himself between me and Moon, then leans in, sniffing me. "You smell different," he says. "How have they not noticed?"

Then he pulls my body towards him, his pupils dilating as he brings my bloody hands up to his mouth. His tongue flicks out, licking one of the wounds, and he smiles. "Ah, now I understand."

He laughs, dropping my arm, and reaches into the vines to pull out Moon. He does not get cut, but rather seems to repel the barbed plants away. I reach for Moon, grateful he's okay, when Dracula clutches the kitten around the neck. He stares at me for a moment. "Never trust us," he says, then he snaps Moon's neck.

I wake with a scream, and Moon startles from my shoulder, meowing and stretching as I jerk up in bed. I see him grooming himself and relief floods me. It was just a dream. But my flash is screaming at me, buzzing under my skin in a way I can't ignore.

Dracula is dangerous.

That much I know.

The question is how dangerous? Dangerous enough to kill and drain his wife and unborn child?

Dangerous enough to be a threat to the Nights and to me and Moon?

That's the question I need answered.

And soon.

THE LEGEND

If you want the moon, do not hide from the night. If you want a rose, do not run from the thorns. If you want love, do not hide from yourself. ~ Rumi

THAT NIGHT I wake from a restless sleep full of strange dreams as my subconscious tries to process all that I've learned.

Moon is off exploring our suite, and the fire in my bedroom is dying down, leaving the room with a deep chill. I decide it's time to test the magical plumbing and take a bath.

I handle my morning business then stand before the large bathtub and draw the symbols into the air that Lily showed me. Immediately, hot steaming water begins to fill the tub. I test it with my hand and sigh at the warmth, then quickly strip and step in. It's a heady experience, playing with magic.

The heat fills me, penetrating a layer of chill I thought

would never leave. I add scented oils to the bath and scrub my body with a soft sponge, then lay back with my eyes closed, enjoying the peace. My relaxation is brought to an end when I hear Moon hissing at something in the other room. I step out of the water that stayed hot the entire bath—much to my surprise—and wrap a thick robe around myself before making my way to my kitten to see what's upsetting him.

There's nothing obvious out of the ordinary, but the bed is made and the fire is stoked, bringing heat back into the space. This wouldn't seem that odd in and of itself, except that last night I locked the door to my suit from the inside, and it's still locked.

No one could have gotten in to do these things, and Moon is still hissing at something that I can't see.

I pick up the angry kitten and soothe him as I dress, then the two of us make our way to the dining room for breakfast.

Matilda, Lily, and the four Night brothers are already seated around the large table. The brothers each have a goblet of crimson liquid. Blood, presumably. I shiver at the thought and wonder where it came from. And though they don't eat real food, the center of the table is filled with platters of bacon, fruit, yogurt, granola, eggs, pancakes and biscuits, a pitcher of orange juice and a pot of freshly brewed tea.

"Are we the only people who live here?" I ask, marveling at the plethora of choices before me.

"Dracula's a temporary guest as well, but generally yes, why?" Lily asks.

"Were any of you in my room earlier?" I ask.

Everyone says no and continues with their conversations.

While Moon sleeps in the pocket of my cardigan, I get a cup of tea and dish up some fruit, yogurt and granola before taking a seat between Matilda and Elijah, my mind still on the mystery of my made bed and stoked fire.

Elijah smiles at me. "I saw you put the books I gave you back. Give up? They can be very dry."

I shake my head, swallowing a bite before answering. "No. I mean, yes, they're dry for sure. Dear god they're dry. But no, I finished them all and am ready for more."

His eyes widen. "What do you mean you finished them?"

"I mean finished them. You know, read them."

"All of them?"

"Of course, all of them. Hopefully I put them back in the right places." I shrug. "Anyway, I need more." I'm saying all this in between bites because I realized with all the excitement last night, I never got dinner and I am starving.

"How's that possible?" he asks.

At this point, everyone else at the table is paying attention as well, so I explain about my speed-reading and my near photographic memory. "Didn't you wonder how I got so many degrees at such a young age?" I ask.

And I realize no one at the table even considered the fact that I actually am the age I look. I have not lived multiple lifetimes. Just the one.

"So in twenty-five years—and you started as an infant, yes?" Elijah asks, in all seriousness.

I laugh so hard I spit tea out and turn bright red as I

clean it up. "Yes. Of course. You don't get around humans very often, do you?"

"It has been awhile," he says with a soft smile. "So, in that time, you had to grow to adulthood and you still got your degrees?" he asks, again, clarifying.

"Yes," I say, smiling at the strangeness of this conversation.

He gives me an appreciative appraisal. "You really are quite a find, Miss Eve Oliver. Quite a find. But I have a hard time believing you retained any of that knowledge. That would be—extraordinary."

"Try me," I say. This was my favorite game in college and grad school. My roommate and I would go to college bars and start talking about our classes. Inevitably some know it all mansplaining dude would come up and try to instruct us on what so-and-so meant when they wrote this or did that. We would then challenge him to a duel of knowledge. We'd find a book, (or he'd provide one, which usually made him even more confident), I would read through it, then our friends would quiz us on the content. I would quote complete passages. He would muddle through. I would win $100. He would walk away calling me a bitch.

Good times.

Elijah takes me up on my offer and begins to quiz me on the history and laws of the paranormal community.

Lily leaves the table first. Impressed, but bored. Then Matilda, who kisses my head and whispers something in another language in my ear.

Liam and Derek are quick to follow. Sebastian stays the longest, surprisingly. He's studying me as I recite and give my opinion on entire passages in their complex law and history books. But even he eventually gets bored and leaves.

At last, Elijah pauses, cocking his head. "Extraordinary. It's been many, many years since I met anyone with a mind like yours."

That perks my attention. "Really, who was the last one?" I ask.

"Al," he says. "Al had a brilliant mind. I begged him to let me turn him before he died, but he refused, insisting that all life must cycle from dust to dust. Such a waste though."

"Al?" I ask.

"Albert, actually. He hated when I called him Al. Albert Einstein."

My mouth drops. "You knew Albert Einstein?"

He smiles. "Yes."

I don't know what's giving me the full body buzz right now. The fact that I'm sitting in a house with beings who have lived with some of the most amazing talents and minds our world has ever seen, or the fact that he just favorably compared me to Albert Einstein.

I feel giddy either way, and it's nice.

Just then, my phone rings, and I answer on instinct, though the number isn't one I recognize.

"This is Eve," I say, holding a finger up to Elijah, who nods.

"You finally answered."

Jerry.

Though I've only been in my new life a few days, already my old life feels light years away. Like an old dream I struggle to remember but find the details fuzzy at best.

"You need to stop calling me," I say. "Whose number is this?"

"It doesn't matter. You keep blocking me, so I had to find a way to get through. I went to your apartment, but they said you moved. That's an extreme reaction, one propelled by grief. One you will regret in time. I spoke to the manager of the building. He and I agreed it would be best if you came back. He will return your money and you can keep your apartment. We can get you better, Eve. Have you had any more episodes?"

I frown, anger bubbling in me. "How dare you! How dare you show up at my place! How dare you speak to anyone on my behalf or imply I'm not stable enough to make my own decisions. I didn't report you to spare you your career, but there's still time to change that, Jerry. The statute of limitations hasn't expired. I do have a law degree, if you'll recall. I know my rights and I know what would happen to you if everyone found out what you've been doing with your patients." I let my threat hang in the air, lingering there like a bad scent. I want him to feel uncomfortable in the silence. I want him to imagine what his life would be like if I followed through on my threat.

"Eve, you don't want to do that," he says, his anger brimming to the surface. I know what would happen if I was there.

Explosive anger. He would attack, verbally and physically. Afterwards he'd apologize, justify, tell stories about his abusive childhood, anything to avoid facing what he'd done and who is he. He could never handle looking at his true reflection and seeing the monster he was underneath the handsome exterior.

"I'm hanging up now and blocking this number. Do

not contact me again. I will call the police if you do." I end the call and block the number, but not before taking screenshots. My hands are shaking and my breathing is labored.

I nearly jump out of my skin when Elijah puts a hand on mine.

"It's all right," he says in a calm soothing voice, like a gentle breeze on a warm night. "You're safe."

My panic attack settles into something more manageable as I use the tools I learned—ironically from Jerry himself. I find something to look at. The wood pattern of the dining room table, with its variation and imperfections that make it all the more perfect. Something to listen to. The clicking of the grandfather clock in the next room. Something to feel. I grip Elijah's hand more tightly, noticing how soft his skin is, and how long and elegant his fingers are. Something to smell. I inhale and am rewarded with the scent of fresh coffee brewing in the kitchen. And something to think about—my happy place. My sanctuary.

With Elijah's hand still in mine, I dive into my mind, controlling my breathing as the winding staircase comes into focus. I follow it down, down, down, so far down, until the red door appears. I open it and smile, relaxing into the beautiful environment I now find myself in. Nature. Running water. Birds chirping. The sun shining. Flowers swaying in the gentle breeze. And her. My Muse.

She reaches for me with a long-branched arm, leaves for fingers, and brushes them against my face gently. The wind rustles in her branches and I hear a message for me in them, but I cannot make out the specific words. It's just a feeling. I settle into that feeling, and then open my eyes.

Elijah is waiting patiently, his hand still holding mine, his eyes seeking out my own. "You are very skilled at that," he says.

"I went through a bad spell," I say. "This helped. Still does."

"And that man who called?" he frowns, worry lines forming on his smooth face.

"My ex. And former therapist."

"Does he need to be dealt with?" Elijah asks.

"Who needs to be dealt with?" Sebastian asks, returning to the dining room, his eyes seeking mine the moment he enters.

"Eve's ex is bothering her," Elijah says, with clear malice.

Sebastian's face hardens and his eyes lock onto mine. "In what way is he bothering you?" His words are slow and controlled, but there's a power behind them and I almost want to laugh at the pickle Jerry would find himself in if I unleashed the Night brothers on him.

"He just called. It's not a big deal."

Elijah flashes me a look and frowns. "It sent you into a state of panic. Did he hurt you?"

Of the four brothers, Elijah is in many ways the easiest to talk to. He has a calmness and gentleness to him that is missing in the others, but it doesn't take away from the raw force of his charisma or power. He's just as mesmerizing, and just as dangerous, I'm sure. I certainly see that danger in his eyes now, and even though it's not directed at me, it still makes me shudder.

Sebastian puts a hand on my shoulder, and his stability and solidness center me. I lean into him, relishing the touch, closing my eyes as I think back to memories I'd rather not revisit.

"I met him while my brother was sick. I was having panic attacks and they were interfering with my work and life enough to worry Adam. He convinced me to go see a therapist, thinking it would help. At first it did. Jerry was good at his job. We talked about medication, but I was able to manage it with some self-hypnosis tricks I learned online and tools he taught me to center myself back into my body and into the present moment. I should have stopped seeing him then, once my panic was under control," I say.

Elijah's hand tightens around mine and Sebastian squeezes my shoulder in support.

"But things were so hard. I was constantly cutting my hours to the point that I had to take a leave of absence as Adam got worse. My bank account was drained, but the bills weren't slowing. I thought having someone to talk to would be helpful. He took advantage of that. I see that now. He preyed on my vulnerability and need for someone—anyone —to step in and help bear some of the load I was carrying. It started innocently enough. A run-in at the coffee shop which lead to lunch at the cafe next door, which led to another plan for dinner the following week. Slowly it built, until I was convinced everything I was feeling was real and that I'd found my prince charming. Then it turned dark."

I suck in a breath, take a sip of orange juice, and continue. "He would lash out at the smallest things, then apologize and make it up to me with lavish gifts he couldn't afford. Then the money stress would create another cycle of abuse. He'd choke me, belittle me, twist my fingers until they almost broke. He never full on hit me though. So I didn't think it was abuse. At least, at first."

There's a low growl emanating from Sebastian, and Derek and Liam return, but I continue.

"But Adam walked in once when...when we were fighting, and he lost his shit over what was happening. Nearly beat Jerry to death. He ended up in the hospital with stitches—Jerry, not my brother—and I cut him from life from that point on. When Adam died, I almost caved and called him back. I was so lonely and Adam had been my only real friend. But I resisted, knowing Adam would have been so pissed if I'd done that. But now Jerry won't leave me alone. Though the solution is easy enough at this point."

I surprise them all by standing and tossing my phone to the floor, then stomping it with my feet. I expect a dramatic spraying of glass and metal as the phone explodes, but I'm disappointed. Nothing happens. Not even a crack.

"Seriously?" I ask, picking it up and examining it. "I dropped my last phone on my bed and it sustained more damage than this."

Liam holds out his hand. "May I?" he asks.

I hand it to him, and to my utter shock and astonishment, his hand lights on fire, flames peeling out from his palm and engulfing the phone in dancing golden flames. The phone melts in his hand, and he drops it onto the table and takes a napkin to wipe his palm.

I'm staring bug-eyed at Liam, but no one else seems phased. "This is something you can do? Shoot fire out of your hand?"

Liam glances up at me, but it's not him who answers.

In fact, it's not any of the Night brothers. It's Dracula himself, but today he's dressed in jeans and a band t-shirt and I do a double take because it's so incongruous with his appearance yesterday that I can scarcely picture him as the same man.

Dracula steals the room with just his entrance. His voice commands attention. "Have they not told you? They always were too modest with their gifts."

He walks closer to me, delicately sniffing the air as he does. I nervously wonder if I remembered deodorant. And then I wonder why I care what this prick thinks. And then I go back to being nervous. This is exhausting.

But I won't be baited. Not by him. I don't give him the satisfaction of asking what he means. He laid the trap, but I won't walk into it. I long ago learned the value of silence.

I keep my mouth shut and I wait.

After several moments during which I have to frequently give a gentle shake of a head to warn one of the brothers away from breaking the silence first, Dracula raises an eyebrow and continues. "You're quite a treasure," he says, with a gleam in his eye that makes me uncomfortable.

"An often underestimated one," I say, deliberately catching the gaze of each of the brothers.

"Quite so," Dracula says. "Very well, then. The Night brothers are not just ordinary vampires. No. There is nothing about this clan that is ordinary."

Liam growls under his throat, his muscles contracting and his stance shifting to attack mode. Elijah lays a hand on his brother's shoulder and leans to whisper something in his ear. This seems to take Liam's rage down a notch or two, which eases some of the tension for everyone. But it's clear that the brothers do not want Dracula to tell me whatever he's going to tell me.

It's equally clear Dracula doesn't give a shit and is going to tell me anyway.

So I wait.

"The Night brothers," he continues, his long, elegant finger raised to rest contemplatively against his chin, "were once Sacred Druids of the Holy Order, a secret sect devoted to the higher calling of the gods of nature. But they were banished from the Order and cursed with the Unforgivable Curse. They were each branded with the darkest, most evil aspects of the elements they held in such reverence - earth, air, fire and water - dooming them to a life of pain and hurting all those they had sworn soul vows to help. The inner conflict of their new demons drove them mad!"

Sebastian flinches at his words, his hands clenched to his sides.

"They made a suicide pact and did what they could to end their lives. I found them just before the last vestiges of life had left their bodies. I saved them. Turned them. Made them practically immortal, though they could still be killed under the right circumstances. I didn't want them falling to their basest instincts and attempting self-destruction again, so I compelled them to never attempt anything that could lead to suicide or imminent and fore-seeable death. I compelled them to live."

Derek glances away, his shoulders slumped. Liam refuses to make eye contact with anyone. Elijah is studying a book in his lap, though I suspect he isn't actually reading it.

Only Sebastian looks me in the eyes, with a small nod of the head. He wants me to know the truth. He doesn't want to hide from me anymore.

The implications of what he's said settle into me in layers. The first is that they are under constant compulsion, which to my understanding is a drain on everyone. I can't imagine having a compulsion running 24/7 for like, ever. That's gotta create some serious baggage.

Second, that the brothers are magical ancient Druids. So they have magic. Maybe not all they possessed before, but something.

And Dracula collected them like dolls and ordered them to stay alive even when their lives had turned into their worst nightmares day in and day out.

What pain must they be in? And how long have they endured this?

In a flash, their personalities come into focus, and I can see the wounds hidden beneath the anger in Liam, the stubbornness in Sebastian, the stoic intellectualism in Elijah, and the flirtatious charisma of Derek.

They each carry their sorrows in their own way.

And I wonder if part of my job is to help lighten those sorrows.

If only I understood how.

THE IMPALER

Look at how a single candle can both defy and define the darkness. ~ Anne Frank

THE ATMOSPHERE IS uncomfortable in the dining room as Dracula finishes outing the brothers and their secret past.

I'm wrapping my mind around the Druid part. If they each represent an element, then Liam is obviously fire. I study the other three, wondering what they each are. My eyes land on Sebastian and I flash to the drawing I did of him when we first met, with a mountain range behind him. He must be earth, with his stubbornness and inflexibility. And Elijah is the thinker, the intellectual, full of ideas…that would make him air. Which leaves water for Derek. I wonder how those all manifest negatively. With fire and earth it's easy enough to see, but water and air? I'll have to pay more attention to the four of them. As if my thoughts aren't entirely consumed by them already.

Derek clears his throat and walks to the entrance of

the dining room. "Shall we all retire to the library where we can discuss the case and get started? The trial will be starting soon. We need to be ready."

We all quietly shuffle out the door and follow Derek to the library. That's when Moon wakes up and begins meowing in my pocket. Everyone turns to stare at me.

"Are you aware that your sweater is meowing?" Elijah asks.

"Yes, uh, about that." I pull out the kitten, who hisses at the brothers fiercely. "I rescued him yesterday from the Moonweed bush. I'm keeping him."

I stare at each of them, daring them to challenge me.

None do.

"Very well," Derek says. "But he has to stay in your room while we're working. Cats don't like vampires."

I exhale, relieved it was that easy, and use a bell in the library to summon Lily, who is more than happy to take the kitten and keep an eye on him for the evening.

Matilda comes in pushing a tray of goblets filled with blood and a pitcher of tea with cream and sugar for me, then winks at me as she leaves.

We each take a seat—I choose a chair that gives me a good view of everyone without being in the way—and I pull out a legal pad and pen, ready to take notes.

Derek pulls out a file and places it on the coffee table between him and Dracula. "This is the police report," he says. "At 2:23 a.m. on November 4, your wife, Mary, was found dead in your home. She was drained of blood. The child—a boy—was beheaded and also drained of blood. Mary was still alive when all this happened. She died last."

The gruesomeness of it startles me, and I study the faces of the men in the room, looking for emotional cues.

Dracula's jaw is clenched. Liam is full of thinly veiled rage. Derek and Elijah are all business. Sebastian is… well, Sebastian. Brooding.

"You are being charged with two counts of murder, two counts of unlawful draining of blood, and two counts of violating the Non-Violent Vampire Act," Derek says.

I'm already rattled by my mental image of this crime, but then he pulls out a crystal and says something in Latin. Before my eyes, an image, like a holograph, appears and begins to move. It's a bedroom covered in blood, with the corpse of a woman and the beheaded infant she recently gave birth to laying in the center of it all.

I find the nearest trash bin and empty my stomach.

As if on cue, Matilda arrives with a cold washcloth and a new trash bin. I raise an eyebrow at her, and the men in the room are all locked in some kind of power play staring contest and don't even seem to notice I'm over here losing my breakfast.

"I'm going to ask you one more time, Vlad. Did you kill her?" Derek says.

"I did not kill my wife and child," he replies through gritted teeth, his eyes fixated on the projected image. "But I will make the person who did this pay. They will feel the wrath of Vlad the Impaler as no one has ever felt it, and they will know pain before I let them die. *If* I let them die."

There's a cruel gleam in his eyes that sends shivers up my spine. It's not hard to imagine him being responsible for the deaths of tens of thousands of people, as history says he was in Romania in 1462. Whether he was defending his home region or a truly sadistic monster, history can't agree, but looking at him now, I can imagine both. He may have been fighting for a greater cause, but he also reveled in the bloodshed, savored ripping the heads off his enemies and drinking their blood as it poured out of their skulls. He enjoyed it, and still does.

"Then tell us what happened," Elijah says, flicking off the crystal. "How did someone manage to kill your family in your own home and leave without you knowing or seeing them?"

Dracula's spine stiffens. "The night that it happened, I had left to find someone to feed on—within the rules and bylaws established, of course—and when I returned, I found them dead. My butler didn't see or hear anything, and no leads have turned up since. I am the only suspect as far as I can tell."

"We will need a list of your enemies," Derek says, making a note on his legal pad.

Dracula laughs. "That's going to be a longer list than we have time to investigate," he says.

Derek sighs. "If you don't cooperate in your own defense, we can't help you. I need a list of anyone who might have such a grudge against you, or Mary, that they would do this. A list of anyone who worked for you at that time. Household staff. Anyone who had access to Mary or your home."

The count sighs and digs into the briefcase at his side. He hands Derek a file.

"That should have everything you need."

Derek flips it open and scans the contents, then nods and closes the file. "We will begin our investigation first by talking to the coroners and visiting the crime scene. We need the name and contact information of the person or persons you fed off of that night as well as anyone who can provide an alibi or character testimony on your behalf."

Dracula shakes his head. "I have no alibi, not anyone useful at any rate. I was hunting for blood. I didn't ask for their name and number. I fed, wiped their memory and left. They will be no help."

Sebastian shifts in his seat. "We still need to know where you were. An accounting of every minute. Other people could have seen you that night and they may be able to vouch for your whereabouts."

"Can you bring human witnesses into your courts?" I ask, speaking for the first time.

All eyes shift to me. Elijah answers. "Not specifically, no. But we can use a Memory Catcher—like the one you just saw—to capture their memory of the night in question, and that's admissible as eyewitness testimony."

I'm torn between being impressed and dismayed. "So you steal memories from people without their knowledge or consent?"

"Not exactly," Elijah says. "It's more like we are picking up the impression of the memory that's left. If it's strong enough, it will give us a clear indication of what happened." He gestures to the crystal they just activated a moment ago. "That memory was lifted from one of the Enforcers who first responded to the murder."

"Then can't you do that with Dracula? Catch his memories to prove what happened?"

"Paranormals can tamper with memory imprints, so they are not admissible in court unless they are expert testimony used to establish the facts of the case, such as an Enforcer or coroner's memory," Derek says. "Otherwise only human memories can be used. We will do a

Memory Catch of the crime scene, but it's unlikely to yield anything useful since we don't have any non-paranormal memory prints to pull."

"This is your whole plan?" Dracula asks. "Throw some magic around and hope for the best?"

Derek scowls at his sire. "We will do everything we can to win this case. We want to be freed of you as much as you want to be freed of this mess. Maybe more. But we have to work with what we have, which, at the moment, isn't much."

"Very well," Dracula says, standing. "I will find you a character witness. In the meantime, you will find the evidence that proves me innocent and identifies the murderer." This is a statement, not a question, and with a sharp turn he walks out of the library.

Derek stands. "Elijah, you and I will work on the paperwork we have to file for court." He looks to Liam next. "Put your ear to the ground, brother. See if any of our sources know anything about the murder or the nature of their relationship."

Liam nods. "I'll report back later," he says, leaving the room.

Derek looks to me and Sebastian. "I need you two to talk with the coroners and examine the crime scene for anything the Enforcers might have missed."

Sebastian glances my way, but his face is impartial, and I can't get a read on his emotions. I, for one, am nervous and excited to be assigned fieldwork. I assumed I'd be stuck in an office all day doing paralegal grunt work.

Elijah leaves and Derek approaches me with a frown on his face.

"Are you comfortable doing this?" he asks. "I know

you're getting thrown in head first. It can be over-whelming."

"It can be," I admit. "But I'm ready. I want to go."

I'm about to turn away, when I pause. "Is there any chance we can make a detour on the way back? I need a new cell phone since Liam melted mine. And I'll need a new number, so Jerry can't call me again."

"About that," Derek says. "We will be moving, and where we're going, you won't need a cell phone."

"We're moving? Now? I don't understand."

Derek glances at Sebastian. "You'll see what I mean shortly. Is there anything else I can do for you? I am, as always, at your disposal."

"No, I'm good." Answers. All I want is more answers. But I feel as if I've found a magic lamp with a genie who is granting me all my wishes, and though this new life comes with a heavy dose of danger and mystery, it's kinda worth it. Something about all of this crazy fits. I feel like this is where I belong.

Derek reaches for my hand, and the touch sends a shiver up my spine. "Never hesitate to let me know if you need anything at all." His gaze holds mine for too long, and I look away first, blood rising to my cheeks.

"Thank you," I say sincerely, forcing myself to look him in the eyes. "For everything you've done for me. I appreciate it. I...I've been worried that you'll regret hiring me. Because I'm...mundane."

He frowns. "It is...unusual, especially since we work within the legal system of our community. But it's not unheard of. There's a precedent if I need to justify your presence. I know Lily told you about the spell on the ad. You shouldn't have been able to see it at all as a human, but you did. That's significant. You're meant to be here, Eve Oliver. That much is clear."

He says this with such conviction and authority that I know he believes in what he's saying and will fight for me. I can hear it in his voice. See it in the hard set of his jaw. He really believes I belong here.

I smile and squeeze his hand. "If you're sure."

He nods. "I'm absolutely sure, Eve."

Sebastian approaches us, hands in his pockets. "Ready?" he says, though he looks none too happy to be doing this, whether because I'm going or because of where we're going I can't say. Either way, being with mister grump is going to be less than awesome if he's going to be in a bad mood all day.

I link my arm through his and smile my most charming smile at him as he leads us out the library. "Come now, you can't spend your whole life growling and grimacing at everyone. You really need to lighten up and enjoy life more."

He snorts at that. "Lighten up? That's your advice for me while we're investigating the highest profile murder case in the paranormal community?"

I nod. "That's exactly my advice. There will always be something that gives us an excuse to be miserable. Our job is to find the reasons to be happy. To make joy and gratitude more of a habit than misery and excessive amounts of stress and worry."

He looks down at me, his face unreadable. "You're very wise for such a young human," he says.

I make an exaggerated scrunched face. "I'm not that young. Sheesh. You old guys think everyone is young."

"Old guys?" he asks, his stern facing cracking into a small smile despite himself.

"You are male, yes?" I give him an appraising look with a bit of a flirtatious edge.

He rolls his eyes. "Yes, I am male."

"And you are old, yes?"

He glares at me a moment, but then nods. "I suppose by some standards you could consider me aged."

"Some standards? By whose standards would you not be considered ancient?" I ask.

"Dragons," he says without hesitancy. "To them everyone is young."

I nearly choke on my tongue at that. "There are dragons?" I ask.

He nods. "There are dragons, yes, and so many other creatures. Was that not in the books Elijah gave you?"

I shake my head. "Nope. It was just dry, boring, law books."

"I have a book for you. If you'd like to read it." He says this almost shyly, and I'm intrigued.

"Definitely. I most definitely want to read it. Thank you."

He nods and leads me down a corridor I haven't seen before. An archway lined with moss and branches and vines climbing up the walls. Lily joins us, though I don't see her arrive or what direction she comes from.

"Aren't we going to the limo?" I ask.

He shakes his head. "It's time to move the castle."

"Move the… castle?" I remember Lily mentioning something about their home changing location. "Is this what Derek meant when he said we are moving?" I ask.

He grunts, as if that tells me all I need to know.

I roll my eyes. "Lily? Care to elaborate?"

"Sure, bosswoman," she says eagerly. "My uncles have clients all over the globe. We go where needed. And right now, we're needed in the Otherworld."

"The Otherworld?"

"It's where I was born. Where most paranormals are born these days." She pauses, losing her chirpy composure for a moment. "My tree was still young in the dryad grove when a land-bound mermaid with a penchant for arson started a fire that would burn for a fortnight. My home was destroyed in the blaze, killing my family and nearly killing me. But Granny Matilda saved a seed from my tree, a seed of my soul. She saved *me*. And when she planted the seed in the castle, it flourished, and so did I." She finishes with her natural spunk and pulls open a heavy wooden door.

My next question catches in my throat at the sight before us. A massive tree grows at the center of the room; bark white as snow, roots digging into the glass floor, spreading out endlessly into the darkness below. Leaves of all colors, emerald and crimson, burnt-orange and deep purple, reach toward the ceiling, except there is no roof, but a whirlpool of stars and clouds swirling above.

I am frozen. Transfixed by the impossible imagery.

Sebastian squeezes my hands and steps forward onto the glass floor, which stays firm beneath his heavy body. "It will be all right," he says.

I nod with a smile and join him in the room. From here, I cannot see where the world ends, and I feel suspended, floating in the night sky, the tree glowing like the moon.

"It takes a great deal of energy to move an object the

size of the Night Castle and surrounding property," says Sebastian, leading me to the base of the trunk. "Lily's tree provides the fuel."

I look at her compassionately. "Is that difficult?"

She shakes her head. "Dryad magic is meant to be used. Traveling is like a rollercoaster ride for me. But I suppose I would get tired if my tree teleported a bunch of times in a short while."

"So how does it work?" I ask. "Do we need to do anything special or…"

"Lily's the only one who needs to be here. But if you lay your hand on the bark, you can feel the power," Sebastian says, placing his palm flat against the tree. I do the same, and when I touch the wood, a sense of easy comfort fills me, like drinking warm tea by the fire on a cold night.

"You both ready?" asks Lily, her hands scrunched up, her face bursting with anticipation.

Sebastian nods.

"Ready," I say.

The dryad places her hand on the tree, and the stars above begin to swirl around us, covering my vision with blinding light.

I close my eyes.

And a flash comes over me.

Three figures stand on a cliff. Their faces hidden in darkness. I can barely make out their forms in the night, until lightning strikes, and they look like shadows, hungry and cruel. Rain falls heavy and thick, and a stormy sea swirls below them.

I can't breathe.

I can barely think.

I am here. Standing on the shore at the base of the cliff.

One of the figures leaps down, cape billowing in the angry wind. They land before me, and for a spilt moment lightning strikes, and I see their face, their beautiful face. Blood red lips. Eyes like the ocean. Hair dark as night. It is a woman, I realize, and she reaches forward and grabs me by the throat. Her nails rip into my flesh. "You should have died with your mother."

I scream.

And strong arms reach around me, holding me close.

A soothing voice whispers to me.

"Shh… you're safe. You're safe, Eve. No one is going to hurt you."

He grips me firmly, my head is against his chest. My tears stain his shirt.

I try to adjust my breathing to match his. Slowing it, steadying it.

A warmth flows through me and my head fills with images of the mountains and tall trees reaching for the sky. I feel my body settle into the earth, like my soul is being grounded, tethered gently to something strong and sturdy, something immovable.

Eventually my shaking stops, my breathing normalizes, and the panic subsides, leaving in its wake a massive headache.

I open my eyes and see that I am laying in Sebastian's arms at the base of the dryad tree. The swirl of stars is gone. Lily stands uncomfortably to the side.

Now that I'm feeling a bit better, embarrassment floods me and I pull away from Sebastian and wipe my eyes. "I'm…sorry about that. I get panic attacks from time to time, though they seem to be coming in more frequency recently. I think the lights triggered something—"

"You have nothing to apologize for. This isn't your world. And it's dangerous. You're smart to be scared."

I frown, looking at both of them. "That's just it. I'm not scared. Of any of this. I know I should be. And I keep waiting for it to hit, but so far, nothing. If anything, this feels like home. Like I've finally come home after being gone for far too long."

I look at the endless darkness below me, at the roots reaching into nothing. "Adam and I never felt like we belonged anywhere. Our father did his best to make us feel special, since we weren't very normal. But after he died, it was hard. Foster homes and other people's agendas and expectations of us. And then Adam died and it was like the last tether I had was cut. I was floating away until I found this job. This life."

"Your father sounds like he was a special man," Sebastian says softly. "Foster care must have been hard."

"He was," I say. "And most of the foster parents weren't bad people. But they didn't understand us or our relationship. They didn't understand why we never fit in."

I look over at him again, our eyes locking. "Is it weird that this is the place I finally feel like I belong?" I ask.

He shrugs. "Who's to say what's weird or not? Life is full of impossible dreams, often wrapped in the ordinary."

"You're very wise for such an old vampire," I say, teasing him with his own words.

A quiet laugh escapes his mouth. Reluctantly, I think. "Touché," he says.

I chuckle and stand, smoothing out my clothes with my hands. "So did we do it? Did the castle travel?"

Lily beams. "See for yourself." With a spring to her step, she leads us out the door we came, and out the front entrance of the castle. When we step outside, I gasp.

Green lights dance across a dark sky. Shimmering and coiling like a snake. "The northern lights," I whisper.

"Perhaps," says Sebastian. "Here we call it the Dragon's Breath."

I study the shapes in the sky, like green fire amongst the stars. "Are we near the northern hemisphere, or the southern? It doesn't seem too cold."

Sebastian shrugs. "No one knows, save the dragons. They created the Otherworld as a safe haven for all paranormals of the earth. Elijah suspects we are near the Antarctic."

"And you?"

He shakes his head. "Personally, I believe we are in a different world altogether. The sky here never changes. It is always like this, both darkness and light. A place where both creatures of the night and creatures of the sun can live in balance."

He guides me forward. Where once stood a driveway, now the land is covered in cobbled streets, and instead of a black limo, a dark carriage awaits us. And not just any carriage, but one fit for a man of Sebastian's wealth, with sleek lines and a polished mahogany frame that's pulled by a team of four horses. Something about the majestic beasts doesn't look right, however, and when I step closer I understand what it is.

The horses have six legs each and manes of glistening silver and gold hair!

Past the moat, golden lights drift in the sky like fire-flies. They are lanterns, I realize, illuminating buildings torn from a different century. Manors that belong in medieval France. Villas reminiscent of Spain. Gothic cathedrals with sharp angles and stained glass.

The sky turns moist and rain begins to fall, soaking us, but I don't care. I'm too entranced by what I'm seeing.

Lily opens the carriage door, and Sebastian helps me in.

"Ready to experience the Otherworld?" he asks with a wink.

I nod, my mind exploding with the possibilities of what my life has become.

THE MORGUE

Death, be not proud, though some have called thee
  Mighty and dreadful, for thou art so;
  ~ John Donne

LILY GIVES a sharp cry from the driver's seat outside and the carriage shifts into motion with barely a jolt.

Sebastian is quiet as we travel through cobbled roads, and I don't disturb his silence with the million questions buzzing through my mind. Instead, I stare out the carriage window, marveling as we leave the Night brothers' estate behind and enter the town proper. The northern lights, or Dragon's Breath as they call it, casts rays of color against the rain-slicked streets. The buildings around us resemble something straight out of a Bavarian village, with peaked roofs and colorful shutters. They're pushed up close to the edge of the cobblestone streets, leaving narrow walkways on either side for pedestrians.

And, despite the late hour, there are people making use of them, too. We pass several couples headed in the opposite direction we are, as if coming back from an evening event. They're dressed in a style that reminds me of the fashions of Victorian England; formal vests, coats and hats for the men, narrow-waisted skirts and bonnets for the women. Many of them look as human as I do, but when I examine them more closely I can see evidence of their supernatural heritage, from the twitch of a tail that peeks out from beneath one man's topcoat to the gleam of vertical pupils in the yellow eyes of a woman who looks up at me as we speed past.

It is almost too much to take in.

I sit back and run a hand through my damp hair, shivering a bit as I attempt to wrap my mind around the new world I'm now inexplicably a part of.

"Everyone lives together peacefully?" I ask, finally breaking my silence.

"As peacefully as humans do," Sebastian replies.

"Right. So that's a no, then."

"We have our justice system, as you know," he says, finally turning to look at me. "And there are communities of paranormals here, with their own rules and laws. Overall it works. But we do have our conflicts and occasional wars, sometimes between different races, sometimes amongst our own ranks. If it's an internal conflict, the dragons usually leave the community to handle their own as long as it doesn't spill into the rest of the Otherworld. If it's between factions, the dragons will get involved and arbitrate before things get too out of hand."

"Dragons. Those are judges, right? And they're like, real dragons? Big flying dragons?"

"Yes. Big flying dragons. There are six. One born of each of the elements that shape this world."

I shift in the carriage as we go over a bump and my hip hits a sharp edge of wood. That's going to leave a bruise. "I thought there were only four elements? Earth, air, fire and water?"

"In our world there are two more. Light and darkness. Vampires are born of darkness."

"Makes sense," I say. "So, the dragons rule all?"

"They created this world. They came together to create a place that would protect paranormals and humans alike."

"Like from the witch trials? That kind of thing?"

He smirks. "You caught no real witches during your massacre," he said. "All of those killed were human. Witches are too powerful to get caught up in such a human mess."

"Right. Well, I'm anti-witch hunt, just for the record."

He nods. "The witches will be glad to know it."

The carriage slows and then comes to a stop in front of a cemetery. The rain has slowed to a slight misting of the air, and fog hugs the earth around the ancient-looking tombstones, setting a sinister tone.

Lily opens my carriage door and offers her hand to steady me as I climb out. I'm about to tell her I can manage without aid, but then I slip and nearly land on my ass in the mud. She rescues me with a strong arm around my waist, surprising me anew with her dexterity and strength.

"Thanks," I say, with a smile.

"It takes some getting used to," she says, and I don't

know if she means carriage riding or magical other-worlds, or both. I'm going with both.

"Why are we at a graveyard?" I ask. "I thought we were going to the coroner's office?"

"We are," Sebastian says, without further comment as he begins walking.

I follow, but Lily stays behind with the carriage, giving a little wave and wink as we walk away. "Don't be scared," she says. "They're harmless."

"Well that's not ominous at all," I say under my breath. I catch up to Sebastian and grab his arm. "What am I not supposed to be scared about?" I ask. "Who's harmless?"

"You'll see soon enough."

Ugh. If I get that answer from one more Night brother, I'm gonna punch one of them.

"Can none of you actually answer questions in a straightforward manner? Is it part of your curse, to be so annoyingly vague?"

He grunts at that. "We shouldn't have to explain this world to you. You should already be part of it. I don't know how you saw the ad or got this job, but it's a giant mistake."

That stings, but I try not to let it show. "Well, as it happens, I did see the ad and I did get the job. So now I need you guys to actually answer my questions and tell me shit or it's going to be hella hard to do my damn job."

We are walking across the muddy cemetery towards a mausoleum. It's a massive structure, far larger than I would have expected. The towering gothic building casts a long shadow over the dead with its clustered columns, sharply pointed spires and flying buttresses. The stained-glass windows give added color to the Dragon's Breath in a magical display as we approach the entrance.

Sebastian pauses between the two intricately carved stone gargoyles guarding the door.

I wait, unsure of what we're doing. "Are we going in or...?"

"We will. In a moment. Once we have permission." Sebastian clears his throat and says something in a language I don't recognize.

It kinda sounds like, "*oobolacky jambonick kay*." But really, I'm totally guessing about that.

At his strange words, a sound like grinding stone startles a pair of birds perched on one of the leafless trees near us. And then the gargoyles blink!

I blink as well, thinking maybe I imagined it. But no, the stone gargoyles are definitely moving. One yawns, its mouth opening and stretching, revealing dozens of large stone teeth.

My flash is blinking in my mind, but it doesn't feel like a danger warning as much as something auspicious I'm being alerted to.

"What does the Son of Night seek in the place of the dead?" one of the gargoyles asks, its voice like gravel.

"Greetings, Akuro. We seek the wisdom of the Infrits in our investigation of a wrongful death," Sebastian replies.

The second gargoyle then leaps down from its pedestal, wings spread, tail wrapping around itself as it lands before me. It's at least twelve feet tall with a fierce face full of sharp teeth. It's nearly identical to the other gargoyle, with only subtle differences that most would miss on a casual glance. It bends its head down to sniff me.

I inhale sharply, and the scents of stone and earth and air mixed with cedar hit me.

"I know she is human, but she is under my protection," Sebastian says. "She works for The Night Firm."

At his words, both gargoyles begin to shake and make a sound that resembles rocks being thrown at a boulder. It takes me a moment to realize that they're laughing!

Sebastian frowns, clearly perplexed by their reaction.

"The Sons of Night have much to learn," the gargoyle in front of me says. This one's voice is lighter, more feminine.

Each of the gargoyles' eyes are the size of my head, and I have a hard time knowing which one to look into as it lowers itself further to make eye contact with me.

"Tell me what you know," she commands.

Somehow, I know it's a she.

I'm about to say I don't know what she's talking about, that I don't know anything, when her mouth gently rests on my forehead and a vision overtakes me. I am no longer in the cemetery, but on the highest imaginable mountain. At the peak, the two gargoyles are together, and the one that spoke to me shoots into the air, flying higher, higher, higher. She screams as something within her pushes out, and a baby gargoyle slips into the wind, falling into the other gargoyle's arms.

I see the baby gargoyle, feel into it, and then the vision disappears as quickly as it came. I fall, my legs too weak to sustain myself, and feel strong arms catch me before the earth does.

"What did you do to her?" Sebastian demands, drawing closer and reaching for me.

I place a tempering hand on his arm. "I'm fine."

With his help I stand, leaning against him for balance, as I look into the eyes—or at least into one of the eyes—of the female gargoyle before me. Sebastian gasps as I place a hand on the gargoyle's face gently. "Your child will be born atop a mountain, and she will be healthy and safe and beautiful."

The gargoyle nods, huffing into my face. "Thank you, Wise One, for that blessing."

With that, the gargoyles return to their posts and resume their stone-like slumber as the door before us swings open.

"What was that all about?" I ask, my heart jack-rabbiting in my chest.

"I do not know," he says, casting a suspicious glance at the gargoyles before leading us into the darkened hall of the mausoleum. "Akuro and Okura have been guardians of the dead for as long as I can remember. But they've never behaved that way before." He looks at me with wonder and confusion. "How did you know she was pregnant? Gargoyles rarely breed. It hasn't happened in thousands of years, that I know of."

I shrug. "When she asked me, I saw a vision and I knew. I've always had hunches about things, and sometimes I have ideas that I write about, but never anything so clear, or about someone other than myself. I always assumed I was just making them up." My mind flashes to the vision of the brothers defending me against the evil forest. I assumed that was just a fantasy, but what if it wasn't?

"Who are you, Eve Oliver?" he asks, his arm still around my waist in case I collapse again.

I shrug again, feeling stupid. "I don't know how to answer that. I'm just me."

"Indeed," he says, skeptically.

"Indeed," I repeat, with an edge to my voice. "Do you think I'm lying to you?"

"No. But I do think there's more to you than is immediately evident."

"Isn't that true of everyone?" I ask. "None of us are what we first appear. We all have layers, depth, secret pains and hidden desires that subtly shape who we are. Why would you ever presume to know someone with so little effort?"

I step away from him and suck in a breath of air. "I can walk now. Shall we?" I say, before he has a chance to respond. I'm still shaken with what just happened and I don't really want to talk about it with skeptical Sebastian, at least not until I have a chance to think on things.

He's still eyeing me strangely as we walk into the darkened halls. It smells of death and dust and old flowers and cold marble, and every step we take echoes in the large, sparse space.

Even our breathing sounds too loud as I walk beside him. He seems to know where he's going, so I stick close as I look around, trying to take it all in. The walls, ceiling and floor are all made of white marble. There are no pictures, no furniture, nothing but arched doorways with heavy doors appearing every so often. "Where do the doors lead?" I ask.

"Various places. Examining rooms. Storage. Broom closet."

I do a double take to see if Sebastian is actually making a joke, but I can't tell. His face is stoic. And they probably do need broom closets here. So he might have just been being very literal. But do I perhaps notice a corner of his mouth twitching ever so slightly?

The man is maddening.

We stop before a large arched double door and Sebastian reaches for it very cautiously. "Stay behind me," he says softly, as he opens the door.

I do as I'm told because I am not stupid and my survival instincts are alive and well.

The door swings open, and I feel the flames before I see them. Warm and dancing on the edges of the marble, casting golden light everywhere.

Sebastian clears his throat and the fire dies down, though the room is still uncommonly warm as we enter, and sweat beads on my skin, sliding down my spine uncomfortably.

My eyes widen. In some ways it looks like a standard morgue, with bodies lying on tables, but that's where the resemblance ends. The rest of the place looks like something out of a mad scientist's laboratory, with seemingly miles of glass tubing connecting beakers of bubbling liquid and a strange apparatus who's purpose I can't immediately discern. Specimen jars line the shelves of multiple cabinets and here and there I think I can see something moving inside them.

But they're not the most remarkable nor eye-catching part of the room, not by a long shot.

No, that honor is reserved for the two men on fire standing in front of us.

They are both leaning over a table, the body of something that looks like a cross between a stag and man before them, its chest cut open as the two flaming men probe and poke and pull things out of the cavity they've created.

I squint and realize they aren't on fire; they are literally made from fire. It's a part of them. It is them. One of the men glances over at us, his eyes like small fireballs burning brightly in his face of flames. "Oh, how rude of us!" he says with a chuckle and a wave of his hand.

Immediately, the flames encasing both of them die out, and, as I blink, they turn into normal-ish looking men.

Normal-ish because their exposed skin is still a burnt orange-red in color and their eyes still glow like fire. They both have red hair, but one man is bigger, more muscular than the other, who is shorter and leaner. They're dressed in identical white lab coats.

The shorter one walks over to us and holds out a hand to shake mine. When I hesitate, he glances at his hand and only then realizes that it's covered in blood and guts. "Sorry about that, truly. It's been *a week.*"

He saunters over to the sink and washes his hands. "Elal, tell them about the week it has *been!*" His words are over-enunciated and exaggerated and he shakes his hips for emphasis.

The big one, Elal, covers the body on his table with a sheet and removes his coat, revealing the white shirt and pants he's wearing beneath. Miraculously, and unlike his lab coat, his clothing is free of bloodstains. "It has been a week, as Ifi said. The werewolves have a problem on their hands. One of their own has been leaving unauthorized half-eaten corpses both in the mundane world and Otherworld. The dragons are in a fit for us to wrap this up. The vampires, are, of course, loving this. No offense," he says, glancing at Sebastian.

Sebastian nods. "None taken. Everyone knows there's no love lost between our kinds."

"Indeed," Elal says, with a nod.

Ifi joins the three of us, sans lab coat, and there's not a speck of blood on him either. He wraps one arm around Elal's waist, while holding out a hand to shake mine. "Let's try this again, shall we? I am Ifi, Ifrit of the High Kingdom of Furor, Lord of the Flaming Backlands, son of the Great Flame herself."

I raise an eyebrow and accept his hand, which is hot to the touch. "I'm Eve Oliver, Managing Director at The Night Firm."

Elal and I then shake hands. "I'm Elal," he says, simply.

"No other titles?" I tease.

Elal laughs. "Ifi made those up. He likes how it sounds to strangers."

Ifi pouts and bumps Elal with his hips. "It's not as fun when you tell them. And besides, I am the son of the Great Flame herself."

Elal rolls his eyes. "As is every Ifirit born of the Flame. That's hardly noteworthy." But then Elal glances down at who I assume is his romantic partner, and his face softens. "But you are the flame of my heart, and always will be. You are the only one who can claim that title in all the worlds."

Ifi's frown turns into a beatific smile and the two share a moment, and a kiss, until Sebastian, the party pooper, clears his throat.

"Sorry to break up the foreplay, boys, but you've done the autopsy on Mary Dracule, Vlad Dracule's wife, yes?"

The two Ifrits glance at each other, frowning. Ifi answers first. "Yes. We did. Her and her child."

I flinch at the memory of the crime scene projection. So gruesome and senseless.

"We need to know everything you found," Sebastian says.

They nod, and Elal points at the door of a refrigeration unit on the other side of the room, which pops open at his command and disgorges an exam table, complete with a cloth-covered form, that rolls swiftly to his side without a sound. Together the two morticians reach down and pull back the sheet, revealing the body of Mary and her newborn baby. I'm stunned to see that the pair have been put back together in the wake of the autopsy with precise care. It's impossible to even see where they were cut into.

"The child was killed first, while she watched, most likely," Elal says, soberly.

"The child's head was ripped off and his blood drained," Ifi says, continuing. "Mary was then drained of her blood and left for dead."

My eyebrow shoots up at that. "So the killer might have left before she died?"

Sebastian looks at me and gives an imperceptible nod. Oh, did I finally do something to maybe impress him?

"Or the killer watched her die slowly," Elal says. "But the creature who killed her didn't drain her entirely. They left enough so she could bleed out on her own, holding the pieces of her dead child in her arms as she did."

Vomit burns the back of my throat and I swallow it down. This is heinous. "You said 'creature'. So it's not necessarily a vampire?" I ask.

"A vampire would be the most likely culprit, but there are some unusual inconsistencies," Elal says.

"Like what?" Sebastian asks.

"Her blood not being entirely drained, for one. It would take a lot of self-control for a vampire to leave her alive like that," Ifi says. "And the bite wounds were slashed, so it's hard to tell exactly what killed her."

"And what of paternity?" Sebastian asks. "Have you been able to confirm whether the child is Vlad's?"

Elal shakes his head. "That test will take longer, I'm afraid. We will turn those results over to both you and the prosecution as soon as we have them."

Sebastian doesn't look happy about that, but what can he do?

"Were you able to extract her dying wish?" Sebastian asks, as if this is a totally normal and common request.

"Dying wish?" I ask, when it seems clear no one is going to offer an explanation.

"We are Ifrit," Elal says.

"And?" I ask.

Ifi grins and sashays over to me. "Oh darling, you're so new it's almost painful, in a delightful kind of way. We are Ifrits. Genies of the fire. Elal and I have the special gift of discovering the dying wish of the recently deceased."

"What do you do with their wishes?" I ask, imagining the massive problems that could occur if every person's dying wish was granted.

Ifi shrugs. "Usually nothing. Most beings are entirely uncreative and boring. Sometimes we pass it on to the authorities and let them handle things. And sometimes," he says, with a gleam in his eyes, "sometimes, if it's interesting enough, we grant them."

"All legally, of course," Sebastian says gruffly.

"Of course, Mr. Night," Ifi says, moving closer to Sebastian seductively. "Always legal."

Ifi tweaks Sebastian's nose like a schoolboy then laughs and returns to Elal's side.

"Alright, enough monkey housing," Elal says. "Show them the wish."

Ifi sighs dramatically. "Fine, fine. Step back a moment. Wouldn't want to hurt anyone. Humans and vampires are so delicate when it comes to fire."

Sebastian stiffens by my side and pulls me back as Ifi bursts into flames.

The fire burns around us, and I sweat profusely, the air hot and heavy in my lungs.

Ifi begins chanting in a language I've never heard. His voice seems powered with magic. It becomes layered with other voices, the vibration of them shaking the room. I clutch Sebastian's arm to avoid falling over, and he braces me as everything rattles. I worry the building will cave in on top of us. I glance at the vampire by my side with frantic eyes, but he looks calm, collected, like this is par for the course.

I take a breath and calm myself. A loud screeching fills the air. Flames dance against the marble walls and ceilings. And then the body of Mary Dracule begins to shake as flames flow into her, animating her from within.

She sits up and turns to us, color filling her cheeks, light and soul filling her eyes. She locks her gaze with mine, a plea on her face as she clutches her dead baby to her chest.

"Save them. Save my babies. Please! Save them!"

And with that, she drops back down to the table with a

loud thunk. The fire leaves her body, flowing back into Ifi, who staggers to the side and is in turn caught by Elal. Ifi returns to his more human form and the temperature in the room drops about thirty degrees, though I'm still sweating profusely. I'm dizzy, too, though whether that's from the heat, the fire, or the dead woman coming back to life, I can't rightly say.

With everything going on, it takes a moment for Mary's last words to register.

"Are dying wishes considered reliable?" I ask.

Elal nods. "Generally. We can tell if someone's spirit is too broken to make sense. Why do you ask?"

"Because Mary only has one child. So why was her wish that her babies—plural—be saved?"

THE CRIME SCENE

He who dares not grasp the thorn should never crave the rose. ~ Anne Bronte

THE COLD AIR of the rainy evening hits me as we exit the mausoleum. The gargoyles, Okura and Akuro, do not come to life to greet us again, but I feel Okura's eyes on me as we walk away, and I swear she winks at me.

"What do you think it means?" I ask, referring to the final wish of Mary Dracule.

Sebastian shrugs. "Perhaps she had a child in the past no one knew about? We'll have to look into it. Maybe something at the crime scene will give us a clue."

Lily greets us with a cheery smile when we return to the carriage. "Aren't they amazing?" she says, gushingly.

"The gargoyles or the Ifrits?" I ask.

She considers. "Well, both, but mostly I meant the Ifrits. The gargoyles don't talk much."

"I've never met an Ifrit before," I say, which is true of

all of them actually. First dryad, vampire, Ifrit and gargoyle. And whatever Matilda is.

"They're fun. You should come clubbing with us sometime. They know the best spots for partying."

Sebastian huffs at that, and this time I'm on the side of the boring vampire. "That's probably not my scene," I say, diplomatically.

We climb into the carriage and Lily takes us through town towards Dracula's place.

The tightly packed town becomes more spread out the longer we drive, turning into farmland and then larger estates.

The carriage comes to a stop, and I look out the window and see a Spanish-style villa sprawled out over acres of beautiful land with a view to kill for. "This is incredible," I say. "Clearly Dracula lives on the right side of the tracks."

"Tracks?" Sebastian asks.

"It's an expression. He's rich."

"Vampires get very good at acquiring wealth," he says.

"I assume that applies to you as well?" I say, thinking about their freaking castle and cars and all the things.

"Yes," he says, simply.

"Then why do you still work as lawyers? You could just retire on your wealth, couldn't you?"

"We could. But even vampires need purpose. Being immortal is a long time to live, and for that life to have meaning, we need work that fulfills us and makes a difference."

"That makes sense," I say. "But why law? Specifically, why defense?"

"The paranormal legal system can be finicky. Dragons

are generally decent judges, since they are considered wise and long-lived even by our community standards. But their perspective can get skewed as a result and they can be overly harsh in their judgements. It's our job to make sure our clients get a fair trial. That they aren't unnecessarily punished beyond what is reasonable for the crime they committed, or, if innocent, that they are not punished at all."

"And Dracula? Do you really believe he's innocent?" I ask.

He shrugs. "I don't know. I don't think he would kill Mary, but then again, I can't be sure I'm being impartial when it comes to him. As I'm sure you've gathered, our history with him is complicated."

"Yeah, that is pretty clear."

Lily opens my door and I slide out, with Sebastian following. I notice a ruined cathedral opposite of Dracula's manor. A mighty structure of gray stone, its two twin towers almost reaching the Dragon's Breath. Half of its roof is caved in, and chipped Gargoyles perch on what remains, their gazes old and tired.

Sebastian follows my eyes. "The place has been in disrepair for so long, most call it the Broken Cathedral now," he says.

"What was it called before?"

He shrugs. "I don't partake much in religion."

Somehow that doesn't surprise me. "And what sort of religions exist in the Otherworld?"

"The same as in the mundane world. The cathedrals are open to all faiths carried over into this place."

I nod, and we make our way to the villa. It's even more stunning up close. There's a beautiful garden in the courtyard we pass, and Lily squeals at the flowers blooming under the shifting lights of the Dragon's Breath. "This place is amazing," she says, clearly delighted.

"Remember, we're here to investigate a murder, not to have afternoon tea," Sebastian says.

I frown at him. He really needs to learn to lighten up sometimes.

Lilly doesn't take any offense. "I know, Uncle Seb. I just think it's pretty here. That's all."

Yellow eyes peer at us from behind a bush, and I kneel and make a clicking sound, luring a beautiful Egyptian Mau out of hiding. The cat hisses at Sebastian but nuzzles against me purring. I give the sweet thing some love and then stand when someone comes out to greet us.

The butler Dracula mentioned. "You must be from the Night Firm?" he asks.

We nod.

"The Count said to expect you. Please, follow me."

The cat scurries away as the butler leads us through an open living room, and upstairs into a master suite larger than some apartments I've lived in. It would be a gorgeous room if not for the bloodstains soaking the bed and staining the white silk sheets.

"This is where the mistress and her child were killed," the man says quietly.

"What's your name?" I ask.

He looks up in surprise. "Leonard," he replies.

"Thank you, Leonard. Would it be possible to get some tea and blood? Lily can help you."

He looks at me with an expression of relief. "Of course. Yes. I can do that. Will you two be okay here?"

I nod, smiling, and he leaves Sebastian and I alone in

the bloody bedroom with a look of relief. Lily follows him out.

"We are going to need to Memory Catch him," Sebastian says, once they are gone.

"He's human?"

"No, so it can't be used in court, but it can give us useful information regardless. Even if his memory's been tampered with, that in itself can be a clue."

"Can you tell if he's messed with it?"

"We can, yes. Usually. Someone has to be really skilled at memory manipulation to deceive us. We've been doing this a very long time."

I nod and study the room, imagining Mary's final moments of life, bleeding out on the bed, her dead baby in her arms. Who did this?

"Are there no surveillance cameras?" I ask.

"No, we don't use technology of that type here. That's why I said you wouldn't be needing a new phone. The Otherworld is... slow to change. Technology is frowned upon. There are no cell towers or electricity. Everything is powered by magic."

"Huh. Wow. Do you prefer it here?" I ask.

He shrugs. "There are advantages and disadvantages. Certain technology is useful and is considered contraband here. You can get into legal trouble for owning so much as an electric toothbrush. But, here I am not subject to the whims of the sun, and I do not have to hide who and what I am."

"Good thing you have a magic castle that can go anywhere, then."

He smirks. "Yes, good thing."

I scan around the room, refocusing on our task. "So, what are we looking for?"

"Anything that might give us a hint into Mary's life. Did she have other lovers? Other children? Enemies? Any letters? Journals?"

I nod. "Do I need to wear gloves or avoid touching anything?"

"No. The area's already been examined by the Enforcers."

I head to her closet as Sebastian checks the dresser and bedside tables.

Everything in this room and in the closet appears to belong to her. "Did Dracula sleep somewhere else?"

"Yes. They had separate rooms. We can look there next."

I shiver at the thought of going through the personal items of *the* Dracula. That's just so wild my head can't fully comprehend it. And yet, it's astonishing how quickly we can adapt to new life circumstances, no matter how outlandish they might be. We are remarkable at survival, for a species with so little physical protection.

Mary has a lot of fancy dresses that show little to no wear, indicating that they were rarely used. Same with the shoes and hats I find. It's not until I get down to the bottom drawer of her dresser that I find the clothes she preferred. More casual clothing. Cotton pants and blouses. Comfortable clothes that aren't stylish, or appropriate for the Otherworld from what I've seen.

"Did Mary like living here? Being with a vampire?" I ask, coming back into the bedroom holding jeans and a Grateful Dead band shirt.

"I don't know. She and I weren't close. But she

wouldn't have been allowed to wear those in public." He glances away, and I leave it at that for now.

We continue searching her room for a few more hours. We find nothing and are about to give up when a flash gives me pause. I walk to the fireplace and run my hand over the stones, feeling for something but not sure what. So far nothing. Frustrated, I push a sitting chair over and stand on it, balancing myself against the wall as I feel the along the stones I couldn't reach on my own.

"What in the blazes are you doing, woman?" Sebastian says, grabbing my hips and nearly causing me to topple from the chair.

"I'm checking something."

I ignore the warmth of his hands on my hips, his fingers digging into my flesh, as I strain to reach the top stones. Finally, my persistence pays off. One of the stones is loose. I struggle to pull it out and then reach into the dark hole and smile as my hand touches a box. I take it and replace the stone.

Sebastian helps me down, and still has his hands on my waist as I hold up the box to show him. "She was hiding this. Let's find out why."

It doesn't take us long to realize Mary was hiding a secret.

I hold up a letter and read:

MY DEAREST LOVE,

It pains me to stay away for so long, to not hold you or caress you or see your face every day.

When can we be together again?

. . .

148

Yours,

L

We read through a few more, and they are similar. None are dated. None are signed with anything other than an L.

"Who's L?" I ask, putting the letters back into the box.

"I don't know," Sebastian says, frowning. "Given we don't know when these were written, they might not mean much."

"Is there a way to determine how old they are? Science or magic or..." I shrug, still so new to this world that I don't know the right questions to ask yet. In the absence of knowing what is possible, I choose to believe nothing is impossible. It keeps more options open that way.

"Elijah might have a contact that can help. We can check after we're done here."

Having exhausted all options in Mary's room, we move to Dracula's. Despite there being less blood, I'm suddenly anxious about entering his space.

His room is lighter than I expect, with grey and white the dominant color scheme, amidst splashes of turquoise. "I expected his go-to color would be red," I say.

Sebastian chuckles. "That is the vibe he gives off."

There are a few surprises in Dracula's room.

First, we find a stack of romance novels by the bed. I raise an eyebrow. "Unusual reading preference for the most famous vampire in the world," I say.

Sebastian shrugs. "He always did have a taste for the romantic. It would explain his success with women."

We also find a journal written in his hand. I glance

through it, then hold it up. "This could prove insightful," I say.

Sebastian nods in response.

Other than those two things, however, we find little else of note.

Sebastian glances around one last time and seems to come to the same conclusion I have. "Time for the butler."

I have to admit I've been morbidly looking forward to this part of the investigation. How does a Memory Catcher work? What does it do? I've seen the final result, but I'm looking forward to learning the rest.

We find Leonard in the kitchen with Lily, where the two of them are chatting over tea.

He jumps up when we enter, his face paling. "Pardon me. I was just about to bring you refreshments," he says, wringing his hands, clearly stretching the truth as there are no refreshments prepared.

I step forward. "I'm feeling a bit sick to my stomach after being in that room. I couldn't eat a thing. But thank you for your kindness."

He smiles in relief, and the stress in the room palpably lowers as he sighs.

"It has been hard living here since her death," he admits. "She was a fair and kind mistress. What happened to her is an abomination."

Sebastian pulls a gold chain out his pocket. A clear crystal set in a base of gold hangs from it and I can see intricate designs etched into its various faces. "I assume you won't mind sharing your memories in hopes it will help us find who did this?" Sebastian says to Leonard.

The butler nods. "Of course not. You may have everything in me. Though I don't know that it will prove useful.

I wish I knew something helpful, but I'm useless. Absolutely useless." He wrings his hands again, his face crinkling in despair.

I reach a hand out and place it on his. "You never know what little clue might lead to something. It might not even be a memory you realize is important. Don't give up hope. The light shall reveal the truth. *In lumen et lumen*."

My words seem to soothe him and his agitation stills as he stands straighter. "I'm ready," he says, with as much bravery as he can seemingly muster.

Sebastian places the crystal in front of George and steps back, then utters the word *revelare*.

The crystal begins to glow, casting rainbow shards against the polished tile floor and countertops, and then an image appears before us, like the one I saw earlier. It's the perspective of the butler as he goes about his day, cleaning, acquiring blood, cooking and caring for Mary. It's startling to see her alive, to see her laughing and smiling and hear her voice through his mind and memories. It makes the memory of her corpse that much more tragic.

Seeing Mary through the butler's eyes makes one thing very clear.

He adored her. Worshipped her. You can feel it in every look he gives her. It's nearly stifling. He would do anything for her. That much is clear. What I want to know is would he do anything *to* her? If his affections were rejected? His name does start with an L.

Sebastian says "*ante*" and the scenes speed up, like fast-forward. We watch through it all, and I work to catch as many details as I can, but I see nothing out of the ordinary. Leonard was right; he didn't see anything helpful, at least not that I can tell.

"Thank you, Leonard," I say when Sebastian removes the crystal and pockets it. "This was extremely useful."

His eyes brighten at that. "It was?"

"Of course. Mary would be proud."

He smiles.

"Just one more thing," I say. "Would you mind giving us a writing sample? We're asking everyone to supply them just in case we have need of them later."

"No, of course not. What do you want me to write?" he asks, retrieving a note page and pen from a nearby utility drawer.

"Oh, I don't know. How about 'I love being on vacation but hate being away from home so long'?" I suggest, thinking about the note from earlier and trying to get some of the words to match without making it too obvious.

Leonard doesn't question the line at all, just dashes it off with a quick flourish and hands the paper over without a word.

We leave him with a tear in his eye and a heavy heart. Is it just grief that weighs on him? Or does he also carry guilt? Is he the man behind the letters?

Once outside, Sebastian pauses to look at me. "His memories weren't helpful."

"I know," I say.

"Then why did you tell him they were?"

"One, because he needed to hear it. And two, because you can't determine the worth of something so quickly. There are many ways to ascertain something—or some-one's—worth." I glare at him pointedly. "In this case, his willingness to give up his memories helped us, even if the memories themselves didn't."

"How so?" Sebastian asks.

"Because he was clearly obsessed with Mary. He could have written those letters. That's why I asked him for the writing sample, just to be sure. He could have killed her in a jealous rage. But unless his memories have been tampered with, he was willing to let us pry into his mind. He probably didn't do it. That's useful information and further narrows our suspect pool, doesn't it?"

He nods. "That's impressive thinking, Eve. And you're right. If his memories haven't been tampered with, then he's most likely eliminated himself as a suspect. Though it doesn't mean he didn't write the letters."

"True. What kind of information can we get about them?" I ask.

"That's Elijah's department. He's got a contact, but they'll only work with him."

Something interrupts my attention, darting past the peripheral of my vision, and I spot the cat I saw earlier, slinking behind a bush. I put a hand on Sebastian's chest to pause him, not taking my eyes off the feline, an idea percolating.

"Those Memory Catcher things. Do they work on animals?"

"They can work on any living thing," Sebastian says. "Except plants. We tried that once. A plant witnessed a murder and we thought we could catch a memory. It... didn't go well."

That sounds like a story for another time, so I press on. "The cat we saw earlier is still here. Which likely means it hangs around the villa a lot. What if we catch its memory and see what it knows?"

Sebastian cocks his head. "That's bloody brilliant. If you keep it still long enough. Cats don't typically like vampires very much."

"Why's that?" I ask, remembering his brother said the same thing when I found Moon.

"Maybe they remember how we fed on them when humans were scarce. Especially during times of plague and famine."

"Ew. Gross." I shift and squat to my knees. "Stay away then. Give me a minute. And give me the memory catcher."

"You don't know how to use it."

"Do I need magic?" I ask.

"No," he says.

I hold out my hand, palm up. "Then I know how to use it."

He sighs and places the crystal in my hand. I wait for him to move away and then creep forward, making clicking sounds with my tongue. "Hey kitty. Come say hi."

The cat peeks out of the bushes and then saunters forward. I hold out my hand and let it come to me. It rubs against my hand, then my arm.

Soon the cat is in my lap purring happily as I scratch its chin and make cooing sounds.

Slowly I set the Memory Catcher in front of it and repeat the word Sebastian used earlier. Once again the crystal glows, then images begin to appear. The perspective of a cat is harder to sift through. They aren't interested in the things we would be, and so I get a lot of small dark spaces and some rats. I whisper "*ante*" and the images speed up, but still show nothing interesting. As the cat's vision pans another set of feet, I'm about to call it a night when Sebastian steps forward.

"*Prohibere!*" he says, freezing the memory.

"What is it?" I ask.

He points to the image, which show a pair of feet in expensive shoes. "We've seen Mary's, Leonard's and Dracula's feet so far. These feet don't belong to any of them."

Upon closer inspection I see that he's right, though I hadn't noticed it before. "Then who's feet are they?" I ask.

"I recognize the shoes," Sebastian says, turning his head toward me. "They belong to Liam."

THE CONFRONTATION

He that shuts love out, in turn shall be shut out from love, and on her threshold lie, howling in the darkness. ~ Alfred Lord Tennyson

I ASSUME we're heading back to the castle, but Sebastian has Lily stop at a pub on the corner with a wooden sign hanging outside that reads "The Naked Dwarf." He opens the door for me and I step into a smoke-filled dark din full of raucous laughter.

The pub itself is decorated in dark wood-paneled walls and black onyx flooring with dim red lighting giving it an eerie vibe. Sebastian finds us a seat in the back corner near the large fire pit that does a decent job of keeping the place warm despite the slightly damp and mildew-smelling seats. It is as private as we can be in such a place.

"I assumed you might be hungry," he says, as he slides into the booth.

I sit across from him, enjoying the warmth and the smell of freshly baked bread coming from the kitchen. My stomach rumbles and he smiles at the confirmation.

A man comes by to take our order and I have to school my face to not drop my jaw. He's human from the waist up, but from the waist down he's all horse. As I live and breathe, it's a centaur.

"What can I get the two of you?" He eyes Sebastian a moment and says, "Blood?"

Sebastian nods, then they both look to me.

We never got menus, though, and I have no idea what they serve. "Um, what do you suggest?" I ask.

"The stew is good. Vegetable or meat. With fresh bread."

I'm about to order the meat, but Sebastian shakes his head. "Get the vegetable," he says.

"Okay, I'll take the vegetable stew and bread, and some water, please."

"Not water. We'll both have a glass of Elf Juice," Sebastian says, causing the centaur to raise an eyebrow and smile.

"Coming right up."

When he leaves, I face Sebastian. "Why not the meat?" I ask.

"They often use meat sources that humans would find unfavorable," he says.

"Oh. Um. Okay. Such as?"

"All manner of animal. As long as it doesn't talk or shift, it's fair game," he says. "Cats, dogs, horses, pigs, goats, cows, chicken. They're all the same here."

My stomach turns and that delicious smell now inspires a wave of vomit to climb up into my throat. "In theory, I get it. Pigs are smarter than dogs. So why do we eat one and not the other? But in practice, it's too ingrained. I can't."

He nods. "You humans become quite attached to your domesticated animals. But inconsistently so."

"It's true. Looks like I'm becoming vegetarian while we're here."

The centaur returns with bread and two blue fizzy drinks.

"What's Elf Juice?" I ask, studying my glass goblet.

"An incredible and rare concoction made by the Woodland Elves from a hard-to-grow berry found in the highest mountains. This is the only tavern in town that's allowed to serve it," he says.

I take a small sip first, then sigh in pleasure and drink more deeply. It is a perfect blend of sweet and tart and it makes my vision swim just enough to enjoy. "This is the best thing I've ever tasted," I say, with a more relaxed smile than I've had all day.

Sebastian returns the smile, sipping his own drink, which is the same blue, but as he drinks it begins to turn purple as it mixes with a red at the center. "Does yours have blood in it?" I ask, enjoying the swirl of color in his glass despite myself.

"It does." He says.

I nod. "It makes a cool color."

He raises an eyebrow and continues drinking as I look around, studying the other diners.

There's a couple who look like they're on a first date. Rough choice of place, dude. She doesn't look happy. She catches my eye and we share a knowing look and rueful smile. I'm only slightly surprised when I look more closely and notice her eyes aren't human, but rather more like those of a fish. Then I notice the sheen to her skin isn't a trick of light, but a reflection off of the iridescent scales on her skin.

"Is that... " I ask Sebastian, my words training off.

"A mermaid? Yes. Though she won't be able to remain on land too long."

"What is the guy she's with?" I ask.

"Werewolf," he says with distaste. "Odd match. I doubt it'll last."

I snort at that. "I agree, but not because of their species difference. He's not impressing her at all."

"Not surprising. He is a werewolf, after all. They're a rather brutish bunch."

The centaur arrives with my food, and I poke my spoon at the thick stew. "You sure this is safe?" I ask.

"I'm sure."

"And these are normal vegetables? Nothing strange or sentient?" I feel like a real lawyer, finding the loopholes in everything.

"Yes, normal vegetables. You have my word." He's got an amused glint in his eyes and I squint at him in distrust, but then decide to take him at his word. I take a small bite, teasing it with my teeth and tongue. "It's quite chewy," I say, when I can finally swallow. "Like a tire."

Sebastian laughs. "So not a fan, then."

I push the bowl away. "Not so much."

I study the man across from me as we drink our Elf Juice and I nibble on bread. His green eyes are intense, his body full of energy.

"Why would Liam be visiting Dracula?" I ask, refocusing our attention back onto the case.

"He wouldn't," Sebastian says, gritting his teeth and clenching his fist.

"You don't think... you don't think Liam is the letter writer, do you?" I ask.

"I do not know. For the sake of this case, my brother, and everyone involved, I certainly hope to gods not."

It's a tense drive back once we've finished our drinks, and Sebastian stalks into the castle. I brace myself for the confrontation I know is about to happen.

We find Liam in his personal quarters, head bent over his desk as he writes in a journal. He slams it shut when we enter, then curses as he knocks over a vial of ink onto a stack of papers. "What do you want?" he growls, avoiding eye contact with me.

Sebastian doesn't say anything, but instead pulls out the crystal and projects the memory of the cat. "Those are your shoes," he says, pointing to Liam's feet. Sure enough, the shoes match.

"So?" he asks.

"So, this memory occurred inside Mary Dracule's bedroom. What the hell were you thinking, Liam? Were you having an affair with our sire's wife?"

Liam stiffens, then stands. I step back, not wanting to get in between two vampire brothers, but not wanting to miss anything important either. A flash tingles in my mind and flows down my body like electricity. Something is happening.

"What I do is my business, not yours," Liam hisses, his face inches away from his brother's.

Sebastian laughs mockingly. "Really? Because this sure as hell looks like it's all our business now!"

"What's all our business?" Derek asks, walking in with Elijah by his side.

"Private meeting. Go away," says Liam.

"Is that any way to greet your brother?" Derek asks with a charming smile, not the least bit put off by Liam's attitude. "I came to find out if you tracked down anything about who might have it in for our beloved sire, but it seems I've walked into something much juicier. Pray tell."

Liam jerks his head at Elijah. "And what are you doing here?" he asks, ignoring Derek's question.

Elijah holds up a journal. "Research. I needed to borrow a book and happened to arrive at the same time as Derek."

"How convenient," he says, then glares at me as if it's my fault. "What did you do?"

"Me? Nothing. What *could* I do?" I ask.

He scoffs. "As if you don't know."

Now everyone in the room is confused. "What are you talking about?"

"Did you think you could hide the truth from us?" Liam asks.

He shifts positions and stalks to me. The other brothers step closer, presumably to protect me if hothead here loses his shit again.

Sebastian glances at me, then grabs Liam's arm. "Stop trying to change the subject. It's just as well everyone is here so I don't have to repeat it." He turns to address Derek and Elijah. "Liam, here, has been paying visits to Mary behind Vlad's back. We also found love letters she had hidden, signed by the letter L. I'm trying to determine if he was having an affair with her."

"I wasn't," Liam says.

"But you were visiting her?" Derek asks, crossing his arms over his chest.

There's a long pause, and it's clear Liam is debating how much of the truth to tell us.

"Let me remind you," Sebastian says, "we have evidence you were at their house."

"What kind of evidence?" Derek asks.

"A memory," Sebastian says.

Liam scoffs. "Those are easily tampered with and you know it."

"It was the memory of a cat," I say, speaking for the first time. "Unless cats on this world are something quite newsworthy, I doubt it's been tampered with."

"Show me," Derek says, frowning and glancing suspiciously at Liam.

Sebastian plays the memory, pausing at Liam's shoes.

Derek and Elijah lean in, studying the frozen projection.

"Your penchant for custom clothing might be your undoing after all," Elijah says dryly to his fuming brother.

Liam finally nods curtly. "Yes, I was there. Okay? I was there. But not for the reasons you think."

"Why, then?" Derek asks. "What could possibly justify you going against our sire like that?"

Liam steps back and paces in front of his fireplace. "It's not what it looks like. Mary reached out to me. She needed help and didn't know who else to ask."

"What did she need help with?" I ask.

Liam glares at me again. "Her baby. She was worried about her pregnancy and needed a healer. So she called me."

"You're a healer?" I ask, the astonishment clear in my voice.

"I was," he says. "Before the curse. She thought that since I'm a vampire who was a healer, I could help her. She was very sick and worried she wouldn't make it through the pregnancy alive."

A pause descends on the room as the brothers take each other's measures.

"Why risk it?" Elijah asks. "Why risk everything for Vlad's wife?"

"I took an oath, before the sacred groves of our ancestors." His voice is plaintive, broken. "I vowed to provide healing to those in need. How could I refuse her?"

"Who else knows?" Derek asks, and I can see his mind working, trying to sort out how best to contain this in the midst of the trial.

"No one," Liam says. "We were beyond careful."

"Why meet at her house?" I ask. "Why not somewhere else, where you were less likely to get caught?"

"This isn't your business," Liam hisses at me.

Derek opens his mouth, but I beat him to the punch. "Actually, it is. I work here. I'm working on the defense team. That makes it my business whether you like it or not."

Derek's mouth snaps closed, and Sebastian smiles despite himself. Elijah raises an eyebrow and gives a brief nod of his head in encouragement.

Liam, seeing no one else will be coming to his defense, relents. "Vlad had her house-bound. He claimed it was for the safety of her and their unborn child, but he was just jealous and paranoid."

"Seems he was justified in his paranoia, assuming he's as innocent as he claims," Sebastian says.

Liam just grunts at that.

"What about the letters?" I ask.

Liam frowns. "What letters?"

Sebastian pulls the missives out of his leather satchel and hands them to his brother, who studies them. "I have no idea what these are," Liam says with what appears to be genuine confusion.

"You didn't write them?" I ask.

"No, I didn't write them. Why would you think I had?"

I roll my eyes. "Really? Because you were there. In secret. They are signed with an L. And you're acting awfully defensive."

He shoves the papers back into Sebastian's hands. "I didn't write them. I've never seen them before."

I cock my head and study him. I don't know if he's telling the whole truth, but I don't think he's lying about the letters. "Do you have any idea who might have written them?" I ask.

He shakes his head. "I can't even imagine who might have. She was pretty isolated."

Great. A dead end.

"We need to contain this," Elijah says. "If the prosecution gets ahold of this information, it's going to make our defense a hell of a lot more complicated."

Sebastian nods. "Agreed. I'll put the Memory Catcher in our safe. It's immaterial at any rate. But we still need to have these letters analyzed. We need to figure out who wrote them and when."

Elijah steps forward. "Then you'll be needing my assistance."

Sebastian hands them to his brother. Elijah glances at them, then looks at me. "It is too late in the evening for a visit to my contact. But Eve, would you like to join me tomorrow night? It could be educational for you."

"Yes, I would love that, if I'm not needed elsewhere?" I look around, not entirely sure who I'm supposed to get permission or direction from.

Derek speaks first. "That's an excellent idea. You should spend time with each of us, in order to get a complete picture of what we do and what the Otherworld is like. For now, let us all make our way to dinner and then prepare for a good day's rest."

"Where's Dracula?" I ask, as I follow the brothers to the dining room.

"Did he not meet you at his house?" Derek asks.

"No," Sebastian says. "It was just the butler."

"And the cat," I say, with a smile.

Sebastian holds my gaze a moment, then smiles. "And the cat. Eve has quite a way with the felines it seems."

"Speaking of cats," Lily says, coming down the hall towards us, "this little guy has been missing you."

I squeal and hold out my hands for Moon, who nuzzles against me, purring the moment I have him in hand.

"You're not going to bring him to dinner, are you?" Elijah asks, with a frown.

"He needs to eat, too, don't you, little guy?" I say, nuzzling his nose. "Besides, he misses me."

Dinner is a quiet affair. Only Lily, Matilda, and I eat food. The brothers, of course, feast on blood, and Moon enjoys his cat food on a small plate by my feet. No one is much in the mood for talking, though Liam keeps casting suspicions glances at me, for reasons I do not understood. I'm relieved when dinner ends and I retire quickly to my room, exhausted and with much weighing on my mind.

Moon curls up on my lap as I sit in front of the fire with my eyes closed. The heat warms my face and hands, which are perpetually cold from the drafts in the castle. In the distance, I hear the music of a violin playing a haunting melody. My skin buzzes with my flash as the music slides into me, calling me.

Even my kitten takes notice, jumping off my lap and stalking to the door in curiosity.

I stand, wrapping myself in the knit blanket from my chair, and follow the notes through the halls. I feel a presence behind me and turn, expecting to see Lily or Matilda, but no one is there.

I keep walking, and again, I feel like I'm being watched, or followed. I turn again and catch the hint of a white dress turning the corner. I follow it, calling out, but when I look, no one is there.

Perplexed, I resume my hunt for the beautiful music and find myself before a heavy door that is slightly ajar. I knock softly, though I am loathe to interrupt the masterful playing.

The door creaks open just enough for me to see inside.

I am stunned to see the man behind the magical music is none other than the hot-headed Liam Night, bane of my existence and perpetual pain in my neck...literally.

Emotions of irritation and admiration war in me as his music sucks me in. His body sways in time to the melody, his eyes are closed, his concentration solely on his instrument. He is naked and his muscular upper body glints in the silver light of the Dragon's Breath shining through the large window that he is silhouetted against. He works his violin like a true master, coaxing each note out like a lover bringing his partner to climax.

I want to turn away and leave, to put as much distance between me and this arrogant bastard as possible, but his music has paralyzed me. I feel rooted in place, transfixed by the complex emotions this unfamiliar piece evokes.

When the song ends, the silence comes slowly as the last notes fades into nothing. I'm brought back to myself and flush a scarlet red as I turn to leave, but I am not fast enough.

He opens his eyes and sees me before I can make my escape.

"Stop. Why are you here?" he growls, holding his violin in his left hand, the bow in his right, as he stalks over to me. He seems unconcerned with his nudity, but I don't know where to let my eyes land.

I know where they *want* to land.

"I heard someone playing and wanted to be closer to the music," I say, hating how dwarfed I feel by him.

He doesn't seem to know what to do with that answer, so he turns away.

That just gives me another enticing view I shouldn't be noticing.

"What piece was that?" I ask, not sure why I want to continue this conversation as I force my eyes to stay on his upper back and no lower.

"Something I wrote," he says reluctantly, and my heart thumps loudly in my chest at this unexpected tenderness that arises in him when he plays.

"It's beautiful," I tell him honestly. "I'm sorry to bother you. I'll leave you be."

"Wait," he says, turning. He frowns, staring at me. "Do you really not know?"

"Not know what?" I ask.

"What you are?"

I gulp, unhappy with the direction this conversation is taking. "I'm human. A mundane, as you call it. Haven't I been reminded of that often enough?"

"But you aren't really, are you? At least not fully. You could read our ad."

"Yes. That's been established."

He puts his violin on its stand and hangs the bow, then turns and walks towards me. My kitten meows and hides behind my legs as Liam comes so close I can feel his breath on my face. His body emanates heat and his eyes burn with barely contained passions, though for pleasure or pain it's hard to tell. I've only experienced pain from him thus far.

"You could not have read our ad as a mundane. I do not know why you smell like one," he says, leaning in to inhale my neck, his mouth a hair's width from the vein pulsing in my neck. "But I have tasted you, Eve Oliver. You are no human. There is power in you. Deep and dark and wild. You are dangerous," he says, his voice a low growl. "Who sent you?"

"Who sent me?" I ask, repeating his question. "No one. You did. I don't know. Fate, if you will."

He steps back, his eyes narrowing on me suspiciously. "You confound me. And I do not like to be confounded."

"I don't like to be bitten against my will. I guess life is just rough sometimes, isn't it?" The sass is back in my voice, naturally. Because that's never made a problem worse.

"You are guileless. Which makes you innocent of your own heritage. Or extremely well-trained in the art of subterfuge." His golden eyes bore into mine as if trying to read my soul.

"Um, I'm gonna go with guileless, I think. That seems the safest bet." I bite my lip as something comes to me. "How do you know I'm not mundane? Because you drank me? How did that tell you anything? What do you think I am, if you don't believe me?"

"You are nothing I have tasted before, so I cannot give you a name. But I know power when I taste it. I have been feeling it within me since that moment. And it is showing no signs of fading. If other vampires knew what effect you could have on them, you would be served up as the appetizer and main course at an all-you-can-eat vampire buffet. There wouldn't be enough left of you to identify."

His words send shivers up my spine, and I steel myself against the implied threat, but he's not finished yet.

"You need to figure out who you are before someone else figures it out first. The Otherworld isn't a safe place for someone who tastes like you. Watch your back."

"Yeah, well, thanks for the warning, I guess. I'll be sure to keep an eye out for hordes of vampires wanting to drain me. I'm sure that heads up will be all I need to rise victorious over beings that much stronger, faster and more powerful than me." The sarcasm drips from my voice, and though I am grateful for the warning and knowledge, I'm annoyed at how useless it is. If vampires want me, at the end of the day—or night, rather—there's not much I can do to stop them.

At least...nothing I know of. But what if there are more things I don't know? Because that's absolutely true.

There's a shit ton I don't know and that lack of knowledge could get me killed.

I know who I have to talk to.

Liam has already turned his back on me as he picks up his violin and prepares to play again—still naked as the day he was born. Vampires clearly have no modesty. Or this one doesn't, at any rate.

I avert my eyes and slink out of the room closing the door firmly behind me before his music pulls me back.

I search deep within myself for a pulse or flash of some kind to help me figure out where I can find Grand-mother Matilda. But it turns out, I don't need a flash. Moon is already on the trail, and so I follow the tiny thing until we reach the old woman's suite. I knock once and the door opens of its own will.

Matilda is leaning over the fire, stirring something in an iron pot. "Come in, and close the door, my dear. The hallways are always so drafty. I keep telling the boys to upgrade the ventilation system, but they are always too busy."

She speaks as she stirs, and Moon and I walk over to her. "I'm sorry to bother so late, but—"

"You have questions," she says, standing and turning, wiping her hands on a black apron around her waist. "So many questions, buzzing around in your mind like a swarm of wasps."

She gets two soup bowls with handles and fills them both, handing one to me. I sniff it and smile. "Apple cider?"

She nods and sits in one of the chairs before the fire, gesturing for me to do the same.

Her suite is one very large room, where her desk,

bookshelves, work shelves, bed, wardrobe, small dining table and chairs all share space.

"Take a seat, dear. It's time we talked."

I do as I'm instructed and sip on the cider, enjoying the sweet, earthy taste of it.

"When Liam bit me, he said he could tell that I'm not entirely human, but he doesn't know what I am. Do you?"

Matilda stares into the fire, as if it holds the answers to all the questions. The fire makes me think of Liam, of the warmth of his body, the way his muscles moved as he played his violin in an almost feverish trance.

When she speaks again, it is with a different voice. Matilda but not Matilda. A prophetic voice. A voice that gives me chills. A voice I know will haunt my dreams.

Her eyes are alight with the flames of the fires as she says, "Beneath the silence of the golden bell the wolf will hunt the lamb and the stones will feed on the blood that freely flows."

THE EX

like a black rose, her darkness was beautifully fatal.
  ~ *e. corona*

MATILDA and I sit in silence, drinking our cider, for a long while. I think over her words but cannot put voice to the many questions running through me. I'm too tired. Too weary of the way everyone speaks in puzzles. I'm not even sure they realize they're doing it. To them, this is how one communicates. To me, it's utterly maddening.

When I return to my room, I intend to go straight to sleep, but the image of Liam playing the violin has me enthralled. Blood rises to my cheeks as I remember him as he looked, standing against the lights of the Dragon's Breath, his full body on display.

I can't get him out of my head, so I pull out my sketchbook and begin to draw.

I use shading and smudging to capture the contoured muscles of his chest and the movement of his body as he allows the music to consume him. I draw with intricate detail, with thought to motion and sound. His power, his rage, his fire and passion, all captured in the intensity of his expression and the way he holds his instrument, as if speaking through his music, pouring parts of himself into it.

I study it once it's complete, sucking in my breath. I can practically hear his music as I look at the drawing.

Once the image is out of my system, I crash into bed and sleep restlessly, haunted by dreams and visions and voices of doom. I rise several hours later with bags under my eyes and knots in my hair from tossing and turning.

There is a hot bath drawn for me when I rise, filled with the same scented oils I used before. Once again, I'm perplexed. I locked my door. No one could have gotten in.

This castle is starting to creep me out.

I'm not hungry, so instead of going to the kitchen after bathing, I head to the library and retrieve the letters we found in Mary's room. We never asked Dracula about them and going on a gut instinct and a bit of my flash, I decide it's best I talk to him alone.

His relationship with the brothers is too complicated. None of them are seeing each other clearly.

I remember the suite Matilda was preparing for Dracula's arrival, and I head there, my hands sweating from nerves.

I find the legendary vampire sitting before a grand piano, his long, tapered fingers gliding over the keys, playing a sad, melancholy song in a minor key. It's haunting, and I pause, not wanting to disturb him. When he finishes, his shoulders slump forward and he seems lost in his own grief. I knock gently, and he turns sharply, all signs of sadness gone. In its place is a cold curiosity as he studies me.

"Miss Oliver, do come in. I had hoped we would have a moment alone together at some point."

I pause, momentarily regretting my impulsiveness in coming here alone. But then I force myself to step forward. After Jerry, I vowed to myself I'd never let another man intimidate me again.

That includes Dracula.

Smiling, I take a seat in a comfortable chair by the fire. He sits across from me and pours himself a goblet of blood. "I would offer you something to drink, but... "

"I'm good," I say, wrinkling my nose. "I just had a question for you, if you don't mind."

"By all means," he says, leaning back elegantly as he sips at his drink.

He has a regal stillness about him that sets my nerves on edge. I pull out the letters and place them before him. "Have you ever seen these?" I ask.

He takes them and studies them, frowning as he does. "No. Why? Where did you get them?"

I gulp, nervous about his response. "From Mary's room."

He sets the papers down and stares into the fire, saying nothing, offering nothing.

"Do you think Mary was cheating on you?" I ask outright.

His response surprises me. "I am not an easy man to love. I know this. Especially for one such as Mary."

"What do you mean, one such as her? A human?"

He steers his gaze towards me. "Yes. Being human is part of it. Humans have a different moral compass than those of us who are immortal. Life has a different flavor when it only lasts a few short years. To us, time is immaterial. But more than that, Mary was a sensitive soul. She could not always handle the peril inherent in the Otherworld."

"Did you never think to turn her?" I ask.

"Of course. She was the love of my life. But we wanted a child together," he says. "If she were vampire, we would not be able to have one. I was going to turn her after our son was born. We would have spent eternity together."

His voice cracks at the end of that, and he turns away, schooling his face into something unreadable.

"I'm so sorry for your loss," I say, standing. "I'll leave you in peace. Thank you for answering my questions."

He doesn't speak again as I leave the room and head downstairs in search of Elijah. We're meant to see his contact tonight about the letters. Hopefully they can shed more light on the mystery or at least turn us towards another potential suspect. Reasonable doubt. Even in the Otherworld, that's all we need.

Derek joins me as I look over the other paperwork we have on the case.

"Anything come to you?" he asks.

I tell him about my conversation with Dracula and he frowns. "That was risky, but brave. And useful, I suppose. He doesn't talk very openly to us."

Matilda comes in, interrupting us. "You have a visitor. The prosecution is here with a settlement offer. In the sitting room."

My heart thumps against my chest as I follow Derek down the hall.

I haven't heard anything about the prosecution yet,

and I have no idea what to expect. Another type creature I've yet to meet?

I'm imagining all manner of creature. Gnomes. Giants. Sprites and fairies.

I'm not expecting a beautiful tall blond woman. Her hair is perfectly kept; not a single strand out of place. So, too, is the rest of her; from her makeup to her nails to her perfectly schooled expression of irritation for the job she's come to do. Unlike most women that I've seen in the Otherworld, she's wearing a style more suited to the men. Trousers and a cloak. She nods to Derek and then glances at me with a frown.

"Moira, this is Eve Oliver, our Managing Director. Eve, this is Moira Van Helsing, lead prosecutor on Vlad's case," Derek says, by way of introduction.

"Van Helsing?" I say. "As in *the* Van Helsings?"

"Yes," Moira says, with such force it feels like a slap. "Now, if we can get onto business? Derek, I come with an offer. A generous one, I might add," she says, with clear distaste.

"I take it this wasn't your idea," Derek replies, with a chuckle.

She glares at him. "You know it wasn't. But I'm forced to make the offer. If Dracula pleads guilty and surrenders his holdings to the council, his punishment will be reduced to ten thousand years underground rather than all of eternity."

Derek laughs sarcastically. "*Only* ten thousand years. How truly generous. You know my client will never agree to it."

"I hope he doesn't," she says, "because we've got him by the balls and I'd personally like to see him pay."

"I'll relay the offer at any rate," Derek says, ignoring her last comment. "Is there anything else?"

"No, that was all. You have until tomorrow to accept."

"Duly noted," he says. "May I escort you out?"

"I can find my own way," she says, stalking out of the sitting room and heading straight for the front door.

Once she's gone, I turn to face Derek as we head back to the library. "Maybe we should advise him to take it," I say reluctantly.

He raises an eyebrow. "You don't think we can win?"

"With what we currently have? I'm not confident."

He smiles. "Maybe this will boost your confidence, then. We've received word from Vlad's ex-wife. She's agreed to meet with us. Vlad is sure she'll be an excellent character witness."

"When?"

"Right now," he says.

Dracula enters the library and pauses when he hears what we're discussing. "Lilith and I had a special bond," Dracula says, and it takes a moment for the name to register.

"Lilith?" I ask. "*The* Lilith?"

Dracula nods. "I was human when we met and fell in love. She, of course, was the first of our kind, created by the Night herself, when a moonbeam hit a rare black rose at just the right moment, and that rose turned into a beautiful woman, pale as moonlight, lips red as blood, hair black as the night herself, teeth sharp as thorns. The first vampire. And the first woman, before Eve. Adam's true love."

He has us spellbound with his words, with his voice, so hypnotic and melodious. "But Adam betrayed her, and she left him in the garden alone while she roamed the earth in search of others like herself. When she found none, and as humans began to populate the world, she realized she would have to turn them herself, to create her own family. And so she did. First Able, when he was left for dead by his jealous brother. They were lovers for many centuries. Then many after. Until me. But alas, we wanted different things in life. I wanted children, and so we divorced, and I met Mary and gave her what was left of my cold, undead heart."

So Lilith is the mother of all vampires. And I'm about to meet her.

* * *

ONCE THE DECISION is made to visit Lilith, we don't waste any time. Derek and I climb into the carriage and Lily gets us underway without a moment to lose.

I stare out the window as we leave the lowlands behind and climb high into the mountains to the east. The road is narrow, with a staggeringly steep cliff falling away to one side as we make our way into the dark peaks ahead of us, and I'm suddenly thankful that our trusted steeds have an extra pair of legs each to keep their footing secure as Lily drives them onward.

After what feels like forever – at least, to my height-addled nerves – we pass through a narrow canyon and emerge into a wind-swept valley high in the mountains. A Mediterranean-style villa sprawls across the lawn ahead of us, lights beckoning from its windows like a thousand sparkling fires. Dozens of servants work the grounds, tending to roses and lavender, trimming shrubbery into the shapes of dragons and horses. The tail end of a dark coat catches my eye, then disappears instantly behind a pillar of white stone. I wouldn't be surprised if we're being watched. Our movements accounted for. After all, a manor like this must have security.

Lily stops the carriage in front of a grand red door, and soon Derek and I are seated in a spacious gathering room inside the main building as Lilith's servants bring us drinks. Everything is gold-crusted or rimmed or framed, and I feel a bit like I've been transported inside an Oscar statue.

Lilith herself is nothing short of divine. Her long black hair is worn in tight curls beaded with gold stretching down her back. Gold powder on her eyelids brings out the gold in her tiger-like eyes, and gold lipstick shines against her pale skin. Her gown is a matching gold, flowing down her slim frame like a waterfall of sunlight. To look upon her is to look upon something sacred.

"He was a terrible husband," Lilith says frankly of Dracula, to the disappointment of Derek and myself. "He had an unparalleled thirst, which is my fault, really. I knew the kind of man he was in war, the blood of his enemies flowed in his veins. I just overestimated my ability to control him. He was violent, prone to flashes of temper that required me to use compulsion on him. He could never harm me, of course, but by the gods he tried." Lilith takes a delicate sip of blood from a gold-rimmed wine goblet before continuing. "I'm convinced he killed his wife and child."

Derek sighs and looks at me. I shrug. We both know what this means. Not only is she not going to be a good witness for us, she'll be a great witness for them.

Then she grins. "Is that what you fear I'll say, when the prosecution calls me to the stand?"

Derek blinks and I narrow my eyes. She's playing with us.

"I could say that," she says, leaning back gracefully and crossing one leg over the other. "There is truth in my words. We all carry within us shades of dark and light. What fun would this drab world be without it?" She glances at my fingers. "You know, my dear, do you not? An artist, more than anyone, appreciates the shades of gray."

I glance at my fingers, but I can't see any visible charcoal smudges on them. "How—"

"You have the eyes and the hands of an artist," she says, leaning forward. She reaches for a parchment and hands it to Derek. "The Van Helsings are out for blood. They want me to say what I just told you. With as much emotion and wringing of the hands as I can muster."

I wondered when I'd see the corruption creeping in. You can't have a legal system without corruption. It's partly why I chose business over law. Both are corrupt, but at least business doesn't try to pretend it's upholding something sacred.

"What did you tell them?" I ask.

"I haven't decided," she says. "There are so many sides to the man you call Dracula. Who am I to say what's the truth?"

"What's the other side?" I ask.

She winks. "All in good time. First, tell me, what are you?" Her gaze is locked onto mine and I hold it, playing this game of wills with the oldest vampire in the world.

Lilith smiles at me like a cat playing with a mouse and

she walks over, sliding up against me in the couch, draping her arm around my shoulders. "You are a curious creature, are you not?" She slides a finger down my cheek so gently I almost don't feel it, then licks her finger, closing her eyes.

"Curious. You are a tasty little mystery, aren't you, my dear? What I wouldn't give for just one true taste, to know for certain—"

Derek stands and pulls me against him, leaving Lilith on the couch alone. "That's enough. You know the rules, Lilith."

She licks her finger one more time and stands, sighing. "I wasn't going to hurt her, Derek. Not without consent. You Night brothers are all far too serious."

"However," she continues, turning to us with another mischievous smile. "I will make a deal with you. Give me a taste of your blood willingly, my dear, and I will tell the court the story of a loyal and kind man who was the love of my life. But for his desire to have children I could not give him, we would have spent eternity together. But I loved him too much to tear him from his fate of father-hood and so I set him free. He will make a strong and yet tender father, just as he did a husband. I will have the jury and judge alike eating out of my hands. What say you?"

"Which story is the truth?" I ask. They are both entirely too compelling.

She laughs. "The truth? Why, all of them. And none of them. We are each a truth unto ourselves."

I realize I'm willing to say yes, despite the warning Liam gave me, despite my own revulsion to the idea, despite the fact that I don't know what game she's playing. I'm willing to do it, if it helps our case. Because her testimony could make or break us. And if it breaks us, the Night brothers will be forever tormented.

Derek must see how close I am to offering myself up, because he stands between us once again and shakes his head. "No deal. You know I can't allow that."

I tug at his sleeve. "But we need—"

"No deal." His eyes are hard.

I nod.

Lilith pouts and reclines back to the couch. "Pity. See you in court then."

* * *

WE SIT in the carriage in silence. I'm breathing heavily. Everything feels surreal.

"Why didn't you let me do it?" I ask.

"It's too risky. You could have died. You could have become her obsession, in which case we couldn't protect you. She'd turn you and you'd have no say. Also, it's not ethical. It would be considered buying a testimony. We could be disbarred."

"Those are a lot of good reasons," I say, breathlessly. And I'm an idiot, I add silently. I clearly have no self-preservation instincts. What the hell is wrong with me?

When we get back to the castle, I excuse myself to my suite to collect my thoughts. And to sketch.

I first draw Lilith, the way her neck curves in just such a way, and the way her large cat-like eyes take everything in. She misses nothing in the going-ons around her, and I suspect she's always several steps ahead. Her and Dracula must have been quite the potent power couple.

And then I draw Derek the way he looked when he

was refusing Lilith to protect me. My hands fly across the page as I capture his stance, the strength in his frame as he stands between us, a living barrier to whatever mischief Lilith had planned for me should I have agreed to her offer. I don't think I could have imagined any of the Nights as white knights, but something in the way he holds himself brings that image to mind, and I know there is more to all of them than I have yet imagined. I know he gave the argument of being disbarred as a reason for turning down Lilith's offer, but their legal standing isn't going to matter much if they lose and become tormented until insanity by their sire. He was protecting me, at the cost of everything, possibly.

The trial is starting soon and our case isn't yet strong enough to guarantee a win. We need more.

When I finish Derek's drawing, I admire the determination in his eyes, the slope of his nose, the way his jaw tightens when he's serious.

Pulling out of my self-induced trance I realize it's time to find Elijah and head to his contact to study the letters.

I'm putting a lot of unearned hope that this will be the clue that breaks the case.

And hopefully in our favor.

THE GRAPHOLOGIST

She's mad but she's magic. There's no lie in her fire. ~ Charles Bukowski

I FIND Elijah in his study, surrounded by books, which is not surprising.

His pale blond head is bent over a large leather-bound tome, and he mumbles under his breath as he reads something in Latin.

"Not summoning any demons, I hope?" I ask jokingly, and then I realize we are in a world that likely has demons and all manner of other creatures, and suddenly my little joke isn't so funny.

"Not at the moment," he says, in all seriousness. "That requires more candles. And a virgin sacrifice."

It takes me a beat to realize he's joking. He winks at me, and I exhale and then laugh awkwardly. "Ah, the classic virgin sacrifice joke. Good one!" I clumsily punch him in the arm, then step back and screw my mouth shut and plaster my arms to my side, because I am being entirely too weird.

"It was a joke, yes?" I ask after a moment.

"Yes," he says with a softer smile. "We don't use virgins anymore. Too hard to find." I frown at that, and he tugs at one of my braids. "Don't take it all so seriously or you'll make yourself crazy."

"Right. So, where are we off to today?" I ask, as he grabs a cloak and drapes it over his shoulders.

"I have a contact. She's a graphologist—of sorts—and will be able to tell us about the letters. When they were written. How old they are. Possibly who wrote them."

"That reminds me," I say, pulling a piece of paper from my satchel. "Here is a writing sample from the butler. As far as we can tell, Dracula, Liam, and the butler, Leonard, were the only three men who came in contact with Mary in the months leading up to her death. But the author of the letters may not have seen her in person, so that might not be very helpful."

"Any new information is helpful," he says, taking the paper from me. "It all gives us information with which to narrow down our defense."

"And what is the defense going to be for Dracula?" I ask, as we walk through the castle and out the front door, into a cold evening still damp from rain.

I shiver and pull my cloak more tightly around my shoulders when I realize we won't be taking a carriage this time but will be walking instead.

"Lily is taking Derek and Sebastian to the courthouse tonight, so we will be on foot. I hope that's okay?"

I nod. "I could use the exercise. Is it always so cold here though?" As I ask, flakes of snow form in the sky, landing on my skin and dissolving into tiny puddles. I can feel the cold in the back of my throat and I inhale a deep breath.

"Winter is nearly upon us," Elijah says, as we walk briskly down the cobbled path to town, tall trees lining each side and reaching towards each other above us form a living tunnel through which we walk. "It's only going to get colder. Soon we will have the Midwinter Festival. You'll enjoy that. There's all manner of food, live music, dancing and huge bonfires as we welcome winter. It's traditionally a gift-giving time in our world as well."

"Sounds like Christmas," I say. "Without the dogma."

We make it into town, and despite the snow, booths are set up and there are many townsfolk shopping and going about their evening. "Is the town this busy during daylight hours as well?" I ask.

"There's no real distinction between night and day here, so we all keep whatever schedule suits us. Since most creatures don't have the same sleep needs as humans, the town is bustling at all times."

I pay attention to the people as we walk. There are all manner of beings; some with horns, some with skin like dyed leather, some with body parts that aren't human.

Elijah takes us through an alley and as we pass, someone throws out their bodily waste through the window, creating a trail of odor that has me gagging.

Elijah sighs, and with a flick of his hand, the wind picks up, carrying the scent in the opposite direction and clearing the air for us. "We have more efficient sanitation systems in place now—and that took a lifetime to get the council to vote in—but some creatures are entirely too stubborn for their own good and refuse to leave the medieval era behind where it belongs. Thus we are forced to endure their filth as they cling to the old ways."

"How unpleasant," I say, glancing back at the brown puddle left behind.

"Indeed."

I look at Elijah, wondering about him. "Can I ask you a question?"

He nods. "Of course."

"You're air, yes? That's the element that's part of your curse?"

His lips tighten together. "Yes."

"Well, I can see how Liam's fire makes him hot-headed. And Sebastian is stubborn as an old goat."

Elijah snorts at that.

"But what downside is there to air?"

He frowns, considering. "I have always been more in my head than my brothers. More lost in ideas. In thoughts. In books. But it was always balanced by my love of people. By my desire to bring new ideas to the world. After the curse, and then once I was turned, I found it hard to…" He stops walking and turns to face me. "I found it hard to connect. To care. Ideas have become their own end goal. Books are a world unto themselves. I struggle to find the passion I once had to help others. It has made me cold. Vacant, if you ask my brothers. Aloof."

"You seem very self-aware. That's a good step," I say, surprised by his honesty.

He nods his head. "We have had many years to become such. Even Liam, were you to gain his trust, would admit to his own shortcomings. We all know, but we struggle to do anything about it. We are stuck in this inertia, unable to move forward. It's maddening, particularly when our

Druidic Order focused on spiritual and personal growth in order to be of service to all. Our curse has put us in direct odds with our oath. Our purpose. It has left us rudderless at sea. At the whims of our egos, rather than guided by our higher nature."

"Are there other Druids still around?" I ask.

His face darkens. "We are the last of our kind. Our Order was killed."

He turns sharply and continues walking, clearly uninterested in continuing the conversation.

When we reach a black door hidden in shadows in the crook of a winding alley, he stops. "We are here."

The door is plain, with an eyehole in the shape of an actual eye in the center.

Elijah knocks sharply three times, and to my astonishment, the eye opens, revealing an obsidian eyeball that flits between the two of us, taking our measure.

"Tell Kana that Elijah Night is in need of her assistance."

The eye blinks once, then closes.

"Magic?" I ask.

Elijah's lips curl up in a small smile. "Yes."

The door opens a moment later revealing a beautiful woman in a red kimono with a glowing ball around her neck as a pendant. Her glossy black hair is pulled up in an elaborate bun and her voice is soft and trickling, like tiny bells. "Elijah, so good to see you again. Please, come in. Both of you."

We enter through a hall decorated with simple ink drawings of lotus flowers and into a spacious room. To the right is a desk with piles of scrolls covering it. In the center of the room are tatami mats for sitting, with a sunken hearth in the floor between the mats and a fire below that is meant to heat tea during a Japanese tea ceremony. I participated in one during a trip to San Francisco years ago for work and recognize some of the elements.

Kana guides us to sit on the mats as she lowers herself onto one across from us. She places some aromatic wood on the fire and then begins to mix a green powder, creating the base for our tea.

We sit in silence as she works with measured movements. Her body flows with such grace and elegance that I'm mesmerized by her. I've never seen anyone move like her, and I wonder at it, realizing she is likely not human, given where we are. She sits the cups before us, but Elijah places his hand over my cup before I can drink.

"Pardon the interruption, Kana," Elijah says, "but will this be safe for my associate, who is thought to be mundane?"

He removes his hand, and I frown at the tea as I realize something is moving within the delicate porcelain cup. A tiny sea creature of sorts, long and slim like a worm but with green scales and tiny black eyes. I shiver as it splashes in the green liquid.

Kana sips her tea, swallowing deeply, then looks to me and with a wink says, "She may drink."

That seems to be enough for Elijah, and he takes a long drink from his cup. His eyes encourage me to do the same. I have so many questions, but it's clear this is expected before we can do business, so I say a silent prayer to any gods that may be listening, and I drink.

Whatever little creature was in my cup is now slithering down my throat, and I nearly gag and vomit it back up when Elijah's hand comes to rest gently on mine. The touch sends a cool breeze through me, calming my throat reflexes and allowing the tea—and mini sea creature—to stay put. For now, at least.

My face flushes and my skin begins to tingle, but this isn't a flash. It's something else entirely.

As I blink, the room changes. As if a new lens has been added to my sight. I see things that weren't there before. Furry creatures scurrying around books. Paintings that move and shift and change designs. A room that looks more like a den or cave, and pillows that are now furs. When my gaze lands on Kana, she is no longer a beautiful woman in a kimono. Or she is, but she is also a fox, beautiful and white, with several tails splayed behind her and large eyes that stare deeply into mine.

"Kana is a Kitsune," Elijah says, "a magical fox who often takes the shape of a beautiful woman. She only shows her true form to a rare few."

I nod my head to Kana. "Thank you for the honor," I say, my skin buzzing again, this time with a flash.

"And you as well," Kana says, with a nod towards me. "It is not everyday we have one such as yourself to visit here."

I glance at Elijah, wondering what she means. But he's already digging through his satchel to pull out the letters. "We were hoping you could help with these," he says, handing her the stack of letters. "We need to know everything you can decipher about them."

She closes her eyes and holds them in her hands/paws, then sighs and opens them. "I fear you will not like the answers. But I will provide them nonetheless. Do you have my payment?"

Elijah nods and reaches into his bag again, this time handing her a vial of blood.

My eyes widen. "Who's blood is that?" I ask.

"Mine," Elijah says. "It is the cost of doing business with Kana."

She slips the blood into a mysterious gap in her kimono, the image of her fox form still superimposed over her female form. I remind myself to ask about this later. What does she do with the blood? In the normal course of affairs, this would be odd enough? But in this realm? With magic and mystery the norm? Here, I'd be extra worried.

Kana takes the papers over to her desk, which with the second sight looks like a stone boulder with runes carved into it. She works quietly, studying the papers, turning them over, examining them from all sides and comparing them to each other. She frowns, then takes a pouch and pinches a bit of black granules that she blows onto the papers. A spark of light ignites in the air above them, then fizzles out into a dark cloud of dust.

The entire process takes quite a long time. Maybe hours. Elijah and I sit silently for so long my feet go numb. I try to discreetly wake them back up with subtle shifts of weight, frowning as pins and needles overtake the numbness.

Elijah smirks at me like he knows what's going on and finds it amusing.

When she finally brings us the letters back, she looks tired. "They were written over the last year. They do not match any of the handwriting samples you brought me. The author is old. Powerful. Ancient. And dangerous."

She hands Elijah the letters. "I cannot give you a name

but I know that this isn't a person to trifle with or to take lightly."

"What other man could she have been in contact with?" I ask, looking at Elijah.

He shrugs. "She was fairly isolated. I can't imagine many people had access to her."

"I should clarify," Kana says. "The writer of the letters wasn't male."

We turn and look at her, surprise on both of our faces. "So the writer was female?" I ask.

"Yes. A powerful female."

"Is there anything else you can tell us?" I ask.

"Like what?" she asks with a wry grin.

I shrug. "I don't know. Like, who might have read them?"

She cocks her head. "Curious question. The emotional imprints are few. The writer of the letter, clearly. Several from your firm. And...a woman. A pregnant human woman."

"Can you tell if Dracula read them?" I ask. "Earlier. Not recently."

"He hasn't, no," she says. "Will there be anything else?"

Elijah and I stand and bow. "Thank you," he says.

As we leave, she slips something into my hand. I look down and see a crystal pendant with a fox carved into. "For protection. You are going to need it, one thought to be mundane. Watch yourself," she says, then closes the door behind us.

When we step outside, the cold slaps me in the face. The office, or den, was so warm, that I'd forgotten about the impending winter awaiting us. My nose burns with the cold as we walk quickly through the streets. It's snowing more harshly outside, and neither of us speak right away as we bundle against the cold. I slip the pendant around my neck, studying the craftsmanship.

We walk in silence for a few moments before I turn to Elijah. "If the writer was female, maybe Mary wasn't the intended recipient. Or she had a female lover."

"Those were my thoughts as well," he says. "But I do have a suspicion. The letters are signed with an L. Written by a powerful, ancient woman. Who do we know who is involved with this case and fits those criteria?"

And then it all clicks. "Lilith."

* * *

ELIJAH ISN'T EXPECTING it when I suggest that I go see Lilith alone.

To be honest, I'm a bit surprised by it myself. I'd nearly succumbed to her entreaty once before, and here I am volunteering to put myself back into harm's way without one of the Nights to protect me this time?

My companion must have been thinking the same thing.

"Not a chance," he tells me, without even a glance.

But I'm not content to leave it at that. I reach out, grab his arm, and pull him to a stop.

"It is our best option and you know it. She'll have her guard up if you or one of your brothers shows up on her doorstep full of questions and we won't get anything out of her. But if I go alone, she'll be too intrigued to worry about what I'm actually doing there. She's underestimated me – everyone does – and that will give us out best chance to get the information we need from her."

"Eve..." Elijah begins, but I cut him off.

"You know I'm right. There's no sense in arguing about it."

He looks off into the distance, an expression of exasperation on his face, and I know in that moment that I've got him.

Which is how I ended up sitting in Lilith's living room a few hours later, waiting for her to join me, my hands sweating from budding anxiety. My nerves are a bit rattled, and I'm starting to regret volunteering myself like this, but it's too late to turn back now.

I stand as she glides into the room, resplendent in her gown—today a blood red floor-length design that hugs her body like she's been dipped into it, with matching lips, and long hair shimmering down her back like an inky waterfall. She raises an eyebrow when she sees that I'm alone.

"No Night brother to guard you against my dangerous appetites?" she asks, with a mischievous spark in her eyes.

"Should I be scared?" I ask in reply, in what I hope is a confident-totally-not-scared-at-all attitude.

"Not of me," she says, sliding gracefully into the chair across from me.

She sips at a wine glass full of blood as red as her dress and then smiles at me. "What can I do for you, Eve?"

She says my name slowly and with meaning, and given who she is, I wonder about her life. Her adventures. Her history.

"I had a few more questions I was hoping you could help me with," I say, pulling out the letters.

I had a whole speech planned, but under her intense gaze, my mind is a bit tongue-tied, as it were.

When she sees the letters, her eyes widen a fraction and she sets her glass down. "May I?" she asks, holding out her hand.

I give her the stack of parchment and study her as she flips through them.

"Where did you find these?" she asks.

"Mary Dracule's bedroom," I say.

She raises an eyebrow. "I underestimated her."

"So you don't deny that you wrote these?" I ask.

"No. I don't. But they were meant for Vlad. How did Mary get them?" she asks, but the question is clearly rhetorical.

"Dracula never saw them," I say, wondering if I'm telling her too much.

"How can you be sure?" she asks.

"He denied knowing what they were," I say, "and we had a third party test them."

"That explains so much," she says, looking almost relieved.

"Like what?"

"Like why he never contacted me, even to tell me to bugger off. It's not like him to ignore me so entirely."

"Why did you send these?" I ask, cocking my head to the side slightly as I study this enigmatic mystery before me.

"I missed him. I still miss him. Vlad is my match in every way. He is the love of my many lives. He is my personal sun, the light and warmth I thought I would never experience the joy of...that's what he has always been for me." Her expression is that of one lost in memory, blind to what is in front of her, trapped in the past.

"If that's true...why did you break up then?" I ask, curious about her side of the story.

"I knew he wanted a child of his own blood more than anything. Maybe even more than me. But he would not betray me in that way. He could not. Not with our sire bond. So..."

A single tear slides down her perfect cheek and she makes no move to dry it as she continues. "I ended things between us and freed him to find a human with which to procreate. Something, despite all my years on this earth, I will never be able to do. A vampire's womb is full of death. It is too barren to carry a child to term."

She leans forward and slips a hand under the cushion of her chair and pulls out a box of cigarettes and a lighter. Noticing the surprise on my face, she shrugs. "Don't tell the brothers. They'd frown at my flagrant use of contraband. Not that I give a single shit about their fragile boy feelings, but I'm not in the market for trouble at the moment."

She pauses to light a cigarette, and takes a deep puff, closing her eyes, a look of sublime joy passing across her face before she exhales and then refocuses her gaze upon me. "I'm sure you've wondered about this world, and why any of us would spend time amongst mundanes, given the limitations of the sun, the risk of being discovered?"

I nod. "Yes, that's true. I have wondered." I'm not surprised she surmised this about me. Given her lifespan and clear intelligence, I imagine she is quite the master manipulator, which means she has a keen insight into others. And the tragic irony isn't lost on me. Eve was the mother of humanity, but also blamed for the fall of humanity. The creator and the destroyer. The savior and the villain. Lilith was the mother of all vampires, but never a mother herself. For some, that could be a great and painful burden to bear for so many lifetimes.

"There are perks to your world," she says, taking another hit from her cigarette. "These, for instance." She smiles. "Technology, sanitation, style, and comfort of living. The mundane world has it all. Yes, it comes at a price, so those of us with means have homes in both worlds, to move back and forth through them as we like. The best of it all. Sometimes the Otherworld can be frustrating with its artificial limitations of advancement and growth. Its backward ways." She blows smoke and it coalesces into the shape of a dragon storming the sky with billowing fires. "It will soon be time to set the worlds on fire, Eve. I wonder if you'll be ready."

I swallow, shifting uncomfortably on the couch. "Ready for what?"

"For the role you will be asked to play. And for the role you are destined to play. Women with great power make sought-after targets. Men do not like to yield power to anyone, let alone a woman. And women who have chosen to align themselves with the enemy in order to gain favor above their sisters do not like the system they have erroneously chosen to be toppled, so you will have many enemies, even amongst those you think are trustworthy." She snuffs out the cigarette in a crystal ashtray I hadn't noticed before.

"I don't think I am who you think I am," I say. I know I'm different, but I'm definitely not the explosive power-house she's painting me to be.

"You have no idea who you are," she says plainly. "But then, I don't know either. I assume that will be your next question and I'm sorry to say I don't have an answer for you. Though that in itself is its own kind of information. I know much of many beings. But I do not know you."

My heart is beating hard against my chest and I feel heat pulse through my veins. "What does that mean? If you of all people don't know what I am, how can I ever find out?"

A new desperation fills me. This has been eating at me like a cancer, not understanding the core of my own being. Having a sense of something living in me but not understanding what that means and having no one outside of Adam to share that with. And now he's gone and there is no one.

A flash.

Just a blink.

Did I really see it or just imagine it?

Isn't that always the question?

The woman with the silver freckles. The silver horn glowing in the soft swirls of the Dragon's Breath colors.

A cooling of the heat.

A calmness.

Lilith smiles. "So she has visited you. Good. You are not as alone as I had feared. There might be hope for you yet."

THE COURTHOUSE

It is during our darkest moments that we must focus to see the light. ~ Aristotle

WHEN I RETURN, all four brothers are waiting for me.

"Well, did you get anything useful?" Elijah asks, without preamble.

"She confirmed the letters were hers, written to Dracula," I say, giving a recap of the conversation.

Derek paces the library, thinking. "It's risky, but we could cast a shadow of a doubt on her. She has means and motive," he says, with a frown. "But she's a powerful enemy to make."

"She didn't do it," I say. "She was at a ball that night. She gave me a list of individuals who can confirm her presence. It should be easy enough to check."

"Then we've still got nothing," Liam says, with a clench of his jaw. "We still don't know who killed Mary or why."

Derek shrugs. "While it would be useful to identify the

actual killer, it's not necessary for our purposes. We just need to prove Vlad didn't do it. And we don't have much time left, so let's get to work."

* * *

WE SPEND the next few days diving into law books, preparing for Dracula's legal defense. We've sussed out all the evidence we can, and at this point, his guilt or innocence will largely be circumstantial. The final verdict will rely on compelling testimony and closing arguments.

Derek is lead counsel, which is how I find myself alone with him late one night in his office, as he practices in front of me.

"Feel free to speak your mind," he says, after going through his opening statements.

"I don't know your legal system well enough to give helpful feedback," I say, biting my lip.

He cocks his head. "That's rubbish. I can tell you have thoughts. Speak them. You won't offend me." He offers up a charming smile as proof that his feathers won't be ruffled.

Of all the brothers, he's the easiest to be around, I've found. Maybe it's the water element in him, but Derek is less rigid than Sebastian, less volatile than Liam, and less mentally distracted than Elijah. With Derek, I feel I am the center of the universe when he looks at me, like I'm drowning in him, but not unpleasantly. His dimpled chin and ocean blue eyes pull me in, and his charisma is organic, consuming the room and me with it. It's no wonder he's lead counsel. He could charm anyone. He reminds me a lot of my brother, which sends a twinge of pain through my heart.

Adam would have loved it here. He always believed there was more to the world than what we could see. This would have vindicated him and those beliefs.

Being sent from foster home to foster home was tough on both of us, after our dad died, but it was especially tough on him. He didn't keep his ideas about monsters and superheroes to himself, and not all the foster parents appreciated his creative interpretation of the world. He was beaten a lot for his stories. And though I did my best to protect and defend him, it usually just led to both of us getting the belt across our backsides. One time he was hit so hard it split his skin clean open. I had screamed louder than him when I saw what our foster father had done in his drunken rage. Adam couldn't sit for weeks. We were sent to a new home, but it wasn't much better.

I shake my head, ridding it of past memories, and focus on the man before me. "You're trying to make a case for Dracula's innocence, right?"

Derek nods. "Obviously."

"But you're trying to soften him. To paint him as a regular Joe blow who couldn't possibly commit such a heinous crime."

"Well, yes," Derek says, scratching the dimple on his chin.

"I assume Dracula's reputation proceeds him, even here?"

Derek chuckles. "You could say that."

"Then it won't work. The jury, the judge, they're already going to have ideas about Dracula. They may have even decided he's guilty. I don't know how impartial the system is here, but in my world it's pretty corrupt."

Derek narrows his eyes but doesn't challenge me. "What would you suggest?"

"Play up his reputation. Lay it all on the table. The prosecution goes first, yes? They're going to paint him as a monster. So let them. Encourage it. Bring out the monster in him."

He begins pacing again. "How will that help win the case?"

"Because you'll be showing the jury and the judge you know the truth of your client. You'll be creating a bond of trust. Then, you show Dracula's intelligence. His cunning. His ability to plan and implement acts of cruelty." The ideas are coming to me quickly, as I consider his best defense.

"Okay... " Derek says slowly.

I stand from the chair I've been curled up in and pace the room as Derek pauses to watch and listen. "And once you've done all that, you show how this crime, this crime scene, is sloppy. It's messy. It's lazy. It's not the crime of a genius monster like Dracula. It's a bad frame job that's too poorly done to be him at all. Prove that Dracula is too evil, too monstrous, too good at his killing to have done this crime. Then, you can use the Ifrit's testimony to cast doubt on whether a vampire committed the crime, and argue that he wanted a child more than anything and would never have killed his."

Derek's eyes widen, and in two long strides he is by my side pulling me into an embrace and kissing my fore-head. "That's genius, Eve Oliver. Pure genius!"

Our bodies are pressed together, and the light moment

of celebratory breakthrough turns into something else, something that stirs desires in me as once again I am lost in this man's eyes.

I pull away, and his gaze follows me as I take my tea and sit again, trying to ignore the color rushing to my cheeks. "Do you think it'll work?"

Derek is already at his desk rewriting his argument. "I think it's the best chance we have, either way."

I nod, scanning over the notes I've taken at my side. "So much has come to light, and yet we don't really know what happened to Mary. Who killed her? Why? Perhaps we've been running in circles. Perhaps Dracula is guilty all along."

Derek pauses, looking up, his fingers stained black from the ink of his feather pen. "Does it matter? Don't the guilty deserve someone advocating for them?" he asks, in response.

"I guess it depends on what they did," I say.

"What crimes are too heinous to justify a fair trial?" he asks, curious.

"Rape, certain kinds of murder, child abuse and molestation," I say, checking off the big deal breakers for me.

"And what of extenuating circumstances?" he asks.

"That's why I said, certain kinds of murder. There are times it can be justified. But how can you ever justify rape or hurting a child?"

He nods. "We are selective." He shrugs. "Usually. But we do believe everyone deserves to have someone in their corner. We can't always ascertain guilt or innocence. Part of our job is to uncover the truth. The rest is to make sure our client isn't unfairly sentenced, even if they are guilty.

The guilty were all innocent at one point, and many of them became monsters because of what was once done to them."

A voice in the hall interrupts us. "Time to go!" Liam.

I stand, as does Derek. "One more question," I say, laying a hand on his arm before he opens the door. "Would you have taken on Dracula's case if he hadn't compelled you?"

"Yes," Derek says.

"Why?"

"Because the prosecution isn't objective when it comes to him. They have a long vendetta against him. I don't believe he'll get a fair trial in this world, and I believe he deserves one, regardless of who he is."

The door bursts open and Liam is there looking smoking hot in a scarlet cloak and golden vest. "Time to go. Can't be late. We've been assigned Judge Dath'Racul."

"Shit," Derek says, under his breath.

"What's wrong with this judge?" I ask.

"He's the fire dragon. If you think Liam is hot-headed, wait until you meet Dath'Racul."

Liam scowls at Derek at that, but I just smirk. "He's not wrong," I tell the auburn-haired fire Druid.

"Let's just go. We're already on bad footing with him from that Leprechaun case."

"Leprechaun? I'll have to get more details about that later."

The four brothers and I, carrying leather satchels with legal briefs and papers, squeeze into the carriage and Lily drives us to the courthouse. "Where's Dracula?" I ask.

"He's meeting us there," Sebastian says.

This is my first time in this part of the town, but I

know the courthouse the moment I see it. It's the tallest building I have ever seen, dome-shaped, made of gray stone, stained glass windows throughout. You could fit several baseball stadiums and a couple of high-rise buildings into the structure and still have room to spare.

"It's huge!" I say, gasping.

"That's what she said," Derek quips, and I nearly choke on my tongue.

"That's some serious teenage boy humor for an immortal and wise vampire," I say.

He shrugs. "We have to stay relevant and current with the times." He winks at me, and I flush.

Elijah speaks without looking up from the book he's reading. "It has to be this large to accommodate not only the judges, but also all manner of creature who may need to come to court. About 100 years ago the giants petitioned the doors be made larger, because though the dragons can fly in from the top, the giants had a hard time getting in through the regular entrance. It was a whole drama that eventually resulted in the building being remodeled. Now everyone is more or less happy, though some of the flower fairies complain it's too big and they get tired trying to find their way. You can't please everyone it seems."

The carriage is silent as we pull up to the front. The doors are made of stone. Everything is stone. No wood. I assume because of creatures who breathe fire or burst into flames.

Elijah finally looks up and smiles. "It's time."

We pile out and make our way in. I idly wonder who opens and closes these doors each day, but then I see that one of the guards is a an actual giant and my question is answered. He towers over us, easily the size of a tall tree, and I can barely make out the features of his face. "Are you carrying any weapons, magicks or forbidden items?" the giant booms at us.

"No. We are here for the defense," Derek says.

"You may enter."

The space within is just as huge as it seems from without, and has benches of varying sizes, presumably to accommodate all manner of creature.

I try to take it all in as the brothers rush us to our courtroom. We travel through long hallways with impossibly high ceilings until we reach our destination. It's set up more like a throne room than a courthouse, though there are nods to the latter with the defendant's box and jury box.

I already know from my reading that the jury selection is different here. The judge chooses the jury based on a pool of interspecies candidates who have been given legal training and have been vetted for impartiality. The lawyers are stuck with who they get, unless there are no jurors from the defendant's race.

The courtroom is packed already with bystanders who want to see Dracula. It's more of a celebrity spotting than a court of law. The judge's seat is a huge stone platform big enough for a dragon. There is no ceiling, and yet the snow that is starting to fall more heavily outside doesn't enter the chamber. There's some kind of magical field that keeps out the weather but allows a view of the sky and the swirling colors of the Dragon's Breath. We take our place at stone tables and super uncomfortable stone benches. Derek explained to me that court cases here are different than in the mundane world. Here, there are breaks, but court isn't dismissed until the case is complete. Which means we could be here for days. And the accommodations are less than comfortable.

And I'm a human who actually needs a reasonable amount of sleep.

I glance at the prosecution and see two women and a man conferring with each other, their backs to me. One of them is familiar. She came to the house offering the plea. The Van Helsings.

I glance at the jury box and study the thirteen chosen to hear the case. Elijah explains that the three dwarvish-looking fellows with the craggy faces and long beards are druegar, from the diamond mines in the far north. The naga has the upper body of a woman – and a beautiful one at that – but the lower body of a monstrous python, and next to her, in a special tank to accommodate their aquatic nature, are a pair of selkies that the average person would have a hard time differentiating from a couple of seals. I ignore the others and ask the question that's been on my mind since entering the room. "How many vampires do we have?" I ask.

Derek glances over. "Three. That could be to our favor, or not. Dracula has a mixed reputation amongst our kind."

Speak of the devil, Dracula enters the courtroom and everyone falls silent as he makes his way to us, his black cape flowing behind him like a macabre wedding train.

"Cutting it rather close, aren't you?" Liam hisses, as Dracula takes a seat at our table.

"I am here. That is what matters."

"Where have you been? We could have used your help in preparing your defense," Sebastian says.

Dracula glares at the Night brother. "I had business to attend. I trust you made do in my absence."

A very tiny woman comes out of what looks like a hole in one of the walls. She's so small she could fit in the palm of my hand. She must use some kind of magic to amplify her voice, because when she talks, it fills the whole room.

"Hear ye, hear ye. Judge Dath'Racul residing. Court is in session in the matter of the Otherworld vs. Vlad Dracule on two counts of murder, two counts of unlawful draining of blood, and two counts of violating the Non-Violent Vampire Act."

With that, there is a great whooshing sound and the air around us is whipped into a frenzy as a huge red dragon descends from the sky and into the chamber, wings spanning the length of the space as he lands upon the platform, his giant claws digging into the stone as he does.

I gasp and clutch at Sebastian's arm. It's one thing to imagine a dragon, it's quite another to see one up close and in person. His scales shimmer like gemstones and his large ebony eyes scan the courtroom.

"Rise," the dragon says with a deep, thunderous voice, a puff of fire spurting from his nose.

We rise, my legs still wobbly from being in the presence of an actual freaking dragon!

"Who stands for the defendant?" the dragon asks.

"The Night Firm," Derek says.

The judge nods his giant head. "And who stands for the Otherworld?"

"The Van Helsings," one of the women says. "Moira, Anna and Able."

"Very well, begin with your opening arguments."

The Van Helsing woman steps forward, and the tiny woman who is now seated at the side of the dragon waves her hand and an iridescent cloud appears above us. When the prosecutor speaks, her voice is also amplified.

"Your Greatness, we intend to show that Vlad Dracule, also known as Dracula, has a history of violent and bloody crimes against others. That he was abusive to his wife, and when he found out she was having an affair, he killed her and her child in a most brutal fashion."

Derek stiffens and the brothers look at each other.

Dracula's eyes narrow. His nails scrape at the stone bench, leaving grooves in their wake.

I lean in toward the Count, speaking softly. "They'll need proof of an affair. Otherwise, it's just speculation."

He nods. His hands clenched.

Moira calls her first witness. "We call Lilith to the stand," she says.

The courtroom door opens and Lilith walks in like a celebrity on the red carpet. Her dress is white silk and has a long train that trails behind her. She looks like a bride, innocent and virginal. Dracula stiffens, his eyes glued to her.

Liam hisses. "I thought she wasn't going to testify for them?"

Lilith catches my gaze and winks, and I put a steadying hand on Liam's arm. "I don't think she is," I whisper.

Lilith takes the stand and the tiny woman next to the dragon brings a giant book for Lilith to swear on.

"Who is that woman, and what is that book?" I whisper to Sebastian.

"She is a gnome and is the right hand of Judge

Dath'Racul. And the book is an ancient book of magic that is said to hold the secrets of the dead. Everyone swears on it when testifying."

"What is your relationship to the defendant?" Moira asks Lilith.

"I am his sire, and he was my husband for several hundred years," she says, with a bell-like voice that carries through the courtroom.

"And how would you describe your relationship to Dracula when you were married?" Moira asks.

Our entire table holds our collective breath as we wait to see what her answer will be.

"We were as close as two people could be. It was the happiest time of my existence." There's a sad melancholy to her voice and I know this is her truth.

Moira frowns. "Would you describe Mr. Dracule as violent?"

"Objection, Your Honor," Derek says, standing. "Leading the witness."

"Ms. Van Helsing, you know better," the judge says.

"I'll rephrase," she says, turning back to Lilith. "How many people has Vlad killed?"

"I couldn't say. You'd have to ask him."

Moira looks frustrated. "How many did he kill while you were married?"

Lilith's lips twitch. "Again, I couldn't say. I wasn't his keeper. We were equals. Partners."

"How would you describe his temperament?" Moira asks.

"Intriguing, brilliant, thoughtful," she says.

Moira sighs and looks to the judge. "Your Honor, permission to treat Lilith as a hostile witness."

"Granted," the dragon says.

Moira looks back to Lilith, her eyes hard. "Isn't it true that you've claimed Vlad was abusive and volatile?"

"He was never abusive," Lilith says. "And I found him more calculating than volatile. Vlad never let his temper get the best of him."

The rest of her testimony is more of the same. She paints her ex in the best possible light, explaining that they only separated so Dracula could fulfill his desire to have a child.

When Derek stands to cross-examine Lilith, he asks only one question. "Based on what you know of Vlad, do you think he's capable of killing his wife and child?"

"Not in the least," Lilith says. "He wanted a child more than anything. He would never have harmed Mary or their baby."

The testimony went better for us than expected and the prosecution doesn't look happy.

Moira looks through her notes, then speaks. "We call Jerome Van Helsing to the stand."

Derek stands. "Objection, your honor, this witness is not on the list provided to us."

"Your honor, new evidence only recently came to light. Jerome is being called as an expert witness to testify to the defendant's frame of mind surrounding this new information."

"I will allow it," the dragon says.

The courtroom doors open and I turn, studying the man called Jerome Van Helsing.

My blood runs cold.

My hands tremble.

My breathing becomes rapid. My vision blurs with the burning of tears.

I'm sitting between Sebastian and Derek, and both of them notice my body tense and shake.

"What is it?" Sebastian asks, his lip glancing against my ear.

"It's him," I say. "It's Jerry. My ex."

THE PAIN

Submit to you—
   is that what you advise?
   The way the ripples do
   whenever ill winds arise?

~ Ono no Komachi, *loose translation by Michael R. Burch*

"How?" asks Derek, eyes wide.

I shake my head, a rising panic flooding my senses. "I don't know. But that's Jerry."

I would know him anywhere. The dark eyes and black hair that's always perfectly coifed. The long, brown coat he always wears. The cruel glint in his eyes.

Sebastian curses under his breath. "I heard he had a practice in the mundane world, but I never imagined the two of you had met. It can't be coincidence."

"What do you mean?" I ask. "He sought me out as a client?"

"Or perhaps Matilda's ad sought you out because of him. I'm not sure." His eyes look dark. His brow furrowed in worry.

Before we can say more, Jerome—Jerry—Van Helsing passes us by, smiling and winking at me. All four brothers stand and call for an objection at the same time.

"Your honor," Derek says, as the other brothers sit, "this is highly unusual. This man has never met with my client professionally and has a history of violence against women. He's unsuitable to be their expert witness."

At the words "violence against women" I shrink into myself, my mind clouding with the unreality of it all. What's he doing here? How is this happening?

Sebastian reaches for my hand under the table and squeezes it. The touch, the strength in it, soothes some of the frantic fear out of me, but I'm still left perplexed by the situation I now find myself in.

Moira Van Helsing stands, glancing at me before she speaks to the judge. "Your honor, my brother is an expert in the field of psychology, has given professional testimony in this court before, and is more than capable of studying Count Dracula's file and giving his expert opinion on the accused."

"Objection overruled," the dragon bellows. "You may continue."

Derek frowns and sits, his hands clenched into fists at his side.

Moira smiles and nods to the judge. "Thank you, Your Greatness."

She faces Jerry with a flourish. "Dr. Van Helsing, please recount your qualifications for the record."

My head fills with the sound of whooshing water and I feel like I'm going to vomit as Jerry stares at me while elaborating on his skill and training, including pack therapist for the Van Helsing werewolf clan.

My ex is a werewolf?

He then goes on to testify about Dracula, that he's hot headed, dangerous, abusive, feels himself above the law. All the expected attacks that we prepared for.

But we didn't prepare for what happens next.

First, the courtroom door opens and Elal, the coroner, comes in and hands a slip of paper to Derek and to Moira. He looks apologetically at us, then slinks away.

Moira's eyes widen when she reads it, and her smile is damning.

Derek looks it over and swears.

Moira admits into evidence a Memory Catcher. The crystal looks familiar.

Derek objects but is overruled again, and Moira hands the stone to Jerry, who proceeds to show the image.

"This is the memory of a cat," Jerry says. "One who lives on Count Dracule's property." Jerry speeds through until he gets to the part where Liam's shoes are clearly visible. "And these are the shoes of Mr. Liam Night, for the defense. He was there, with Mary, while Dracula was away."

The court goes wild. But the gnome woman screams for everyone to settle down, and Moira, before she loses momentum, submits the paper Elal brought in as evidence.

"And can you tell the court what this document says?" Moira asks Jerry.

Jerry smirks. "It says the child wasn't Dracula's. Which means Mary was having an affair."

Dracula stands and flips over a stone table in sheer, uncontrollable rage. He dashes to Liam and pins him to the floor, stepping on him with his boot. "How dare you betray me this way, after everything I've done for you!"

Liam thrashes under the weight of his sire. The dragon bellows fire into the air with a loud screech, and the tiny woman with the big voice walks over and grabs Dracula by the cuff of his pants. It's all she can reach. But I watch, wide-eyed, as she yanks and Dracula is pulled into the air and smashed against the marble flooring with a loud thud.

"There will be silence in the court," the little woman screeches to a stunned audience.

Dracula stands, dusting himself off, and nods to her, showing a deference I've never seen in him. He stands quietly, holding his rage tightly around him like a cloak against the winter winds.

Liam climbs to his feet, backing away from Dracula, a sneer on his face. "I wasn't having an affair with Mary."

"Silence!" the woman screams. "Court is adjourned for fifteen minutes. Counselors, the judge will see you in his chambers. Only one from each side."

Moira follows the gnome towards the dragon, and Derek steps forward, telling us all to behave until he's back. His jaw is locked in anger.

Elijah has retreated to his book, Liam looks ready to murder everyone, and so it is left to me to reprimand Dracula himself. I stand and face him, eye to eye. "You need to chill your shit immediately. If this case wasn't already damned by their testimony, your outburst was surely the nail in the coffin. Unless you want to spend the rest of eternity underground, calm the hell down now."

His teeth elongate, and he eyes my neck like it will be his dinner, but I don't back away. "Calm. The. Hell. Down."

Finally, Dracula nods. "You are right. This display has not helped us. I will save my anger for later." And with a flourish of his cape, Dracula strides out of the courtroom without another word.

We follow him into the main hall and find a few benches tucked away in a corner, hoping for smidgen of privacy. Liam, Elijah, Sebastian, Lily and I sit on one bench. Dracula alone on the other.

"Let Liam explain," I say to the Count, then glance at the red-haired vampire. For once, he almost looks grateful.

"I was her healer," Liam says calmly. "She was worried about the baby and didn't want to worry you, so she asked for my help. We were not having an affair, and I had no idea the baby wasn't yours."

The rage on Dracula's face evaporates into grief so deeply profound and heartrending I have to look away. The sobs shake his body as all the pain of this loss consumes him.

It's too much. No one moves to offer him comfort, so I do.

I take a seat by his side and put an arm around his broad shoulders. With a soft, soothing voice, I give him what solace I can. "The grief will destroy you if you let it," I say. "I know how hard this is, and I'm truly sorry for the loss you bear."

I ignore the brothers. I even ignore my own wariness about this man—this vampire. Instead, I connect with the part of him that is in all of us. The heart and soul, the pain and sorrow. In this we are the same.

In this, Dracula and I share the same unsealing wound.

When he looks up and into my eyes, there is new understanding there. We are now kindred, bound by pain, through pain. Bound in the darkness of grief.

Bound.

"Thank you," he says softly.

I nod and step back, giving him space, and take a seat between Sebastian and Liam to discuss strategy. "That crystal looked awfully familiar," I say.

Sebastian nods. "Indeed." He motions to Lily. "Return to the castle. Check the safe."

She nods and sprints away, disappearing down the hallway.

I lower my voice. "You don't think the prosecution stole it, do you?"

Sebastian grits his teeth. "We shall see. But in my experience, the Van Helsings will do almost anything to punish Dracula. He caused much pain to their family, back in the days when we were not governed by laws."

I look to the Count, but he says nothing, his eyes fixed on a fireplace crackling amongst the gray stone.

"If the baby wasn't Dracula's, then who was Mary involved with?" I ask aloud, though no one answers.

Dracula just clenches his fist.

Liam looks ready to set the building on fire.

Elijah and Sebastian have no more answers than I do.

Derek steps around the corner, looking drained of all life—even for the undead. "It's not good," he says, speaking to all of us. "If another outburst occurs, we will each be fined. Heavily. And..." he pauses, looking uneasy.

"And?" asks Sebastian. "Spit it out, brother."

Derek takes a deep breath. "And for the remainder of the trial, due to his entanglement in the case, Liam isn't allowed in the courtroom."

"What?" roars the fire Druid. "I've done nothing wrong."

"Be that as it may," says Derek coolly, "the judge believes things will proceed more...smoothly...if you are not present."

Liam leaps to his feet, pacing next to the fireplace and sparking the flames with his fingers. "Fine. Go and protect this monster," he says, gesturing to Dracula. "I took this case for Mary. And we don't even know who actually killed her yet. So go. Go play lawyer. And while you do, I'll be here focusing on what really matters. Finding the truth!"

He clenches his jaw, and the fire roars at his back, casting him in crimson light. Steam mixes with his breath.

"Perhaps," Elijah says plainly, "if you had been honest with us from the start, we could have avoided this problem."

"It wasn't that simple," hisses Liam.

"Listen," I say, looking at everyone calmly. "We could argue all day, but that's exactly what the prosecution wants. Dracula's outburst set us back profoundly, as did the paternity test. We need a new plan. We need..." I swallow, this next part hard for me to say. "We need to discredit their expert witness. I have to take the stand, to testify to what Jerry did to me."

My words have the intended effect, and all their fury at each other seems forgotten.

"No!" Sebastian says roughly. "We aren't putting you through that."

"We can find another way," Derek says.

Elijah shrugs. "If she's willing, I say we let her."

"You would say that," Liam spits. "All head and no heart."

I can see the wound his words create in Elijah, though I suspect no one else can. It's covered up so quickly.

"Then what do you suggest?" Elijah asks Liam, who has no response other than to glare and turn away.

"It's the only way," I say. "If you want to win. And…I can do this. I need to do this. And not just for the case."

One by one they seem to understand what I'm not saying. That this is my way of fighting what he did to me. This is my way of standing up for myself.

Each of them nods at me in turn.

Then Lily returns, breathless, her suit stained with sweat around the collar, pink hair disheveled. "The crystal wasn't there," she says between heavy gasps. "It's gone."

"Shit," curses Sebastian. "How did they get past our security?"

"Perhaps they didn't," says Dracula, his voice defeated. "Perhaps the Van Helsings aren't the only ones who wish to see me imprisoned."

Liam's eyes narrow at Elijah. "You," says the fire Druid. "You gave them the crystal." He sounds more shocked than angry.

"Why would I do such a thing?" Elijah asks, his voice cold and calculating. "What would be the reason?"

"Because you are no longer committed to our oath,"

Liam says. "You would rather see us lose, see us forever bound to Dracula, than find us released from our compulsion."

Elijah looks at me worriedly, then back at Liam. "It's true that I have reservations about a plan we made so very long ago, under wildly different circumstances." He clenches his hands and frowns. "But I would never betray our firm. You must know that. It wasn't me."

Liam scoffs. "I've read your journals. Your misgivings."

"Those were private—"

"You betray our oath."

"Never."

This isn't the first time I've heard them talk of oaths, and it makes my stomach cramp at what I suspect is their intention. But I need to know for sure. "What oath?" I ask through trembling lips.

Elijah looks to me, compassion in his eyes. "When we were cursed—"

"Shut the hell up, Elijah," Sebastian says, with a warning.

"She deserves to know. Isn't this why she was hired? To help with the last piece?" Elijah casts a challenging gaze at each of his brothers, and an understanding passes between them. The passion in their eyes drifts away, replaced by a quiet resignation.

He looks back at me, his voice thin and morose. "When we were cursed, the power consumed us. Made us crazy. We lost ourselves in the excess of our gifts, in the excess of each element. It turned us cruel. Monstrous."

Elijah looks away, gazing at the fire, his words far away. "There are many sins laid at our feet from those days. We set fire to homes, villages, cities. I cannot even count the innocents we killed.

"We couldn't contain our power. Earthquakes erupted wherever we went, uprooting trees that had lived thousands of years. Ravaging towns and collapsing mountains.

"We were the apocalypse incarnate. Flooding followed us, drowning anyone and anything in our path. Destroying livestock and farms. Killing wildlife and humans without discrimination."

Elijah nods in remembrance, his words full of sorrow. "And we brought the winds. They howled and shook the earth, blowing away homes and destroying whatever might be left. We tried to separate, as our collective power was too great, but we just spread our destruction farther. We tried living alone, as far from anyone as we could, but it was no use. We were too strong. Too out of control."

"And so we made an oath," Derek says, cutting in. "A suicide pact. If we could not control the powers we had been cursed with, we would end our lives and spare those around us. But we are not easy to kill. Only a great power can kill one such as us. We had to create a perfect storm, using all the elements, to end our lives."

"And it almost worked," Sebastian says bitterly.

"But Dracula found you," I whisper.

They nod.

"I gave you control," says the count. "I gave you life."

Liam frowns. "You sucked our power away, leaving us shells of our former selves." He holds his palm out and a single flame ignites on it, glowing. "This is all that's left of who I was."

I shake my head, confused. "But then... if vampirism

solved your problem, why do you still want to end your lives?"

Sebastian looks over to me, his eyes heavy with too many lifetimes of grief.

They say nothing. But I think I understand.

Some sins are too much for anyone to bear. Some crimes too heinous to forget.

I understand.

But I don't agree.

"So you plan to die when this trial is over?" I ask, my voice cracking. "And I'm supposed to help you somehow?"

"You're supposed to help us win this case," Derek says, not making eye contact with me. "That is why Matilda's magic chose you. Perhaps because of your relationship with Jerome, or perhaps because of some yet unknown reason, you are critical to the outcome of these proceedings. You will help us win. Then Dracula will free us from the sire bond, and we will handle the rest."

"The rest? As in killing yourselves?"

They stay quiet, avoiding my gaze.

"I won't do it," I say, standing up, my entire body shaking with fear and anger and sadness. "I won't help you. If you lose this case, Dracula won't release you, and you won't be able to cause any harm to yourselves."

Derek shakes his head, finally meeting my eyes with his own. "If we lose, Dracula will be tortured for all time. The sire bond will remain, and we will feel his pain as our own. We will go mad from an eternity of torment. No. Whatever your wishes, it will be done by midwinter."

I look to the count, my eyes pleading.

"They are not wrong," says Dracula.

"Please," I beg. "Please. Even if we lose, don't make them suffer."

"Why not?" he says, staring at his own hands, his long sharp nails. "Have I not suffered? Have I not lost all I hold dear?" He closes his eyes, a single tear falling down his cheek. "Even so, it does not matter. If the sire bond remains, they will feel what I feel. And if I free them, then they will carry out their oath. As you can see, Miss Oliver, the Night Brothers have chosen their fate."

There's only one way then. We have to win the case. But before we do, I must convince the Night brothers to abandon their plan.

"It's time we return to the courtroom," I say simply, checking the giant copper clock at the end of the hall. I take the lead, my stride quick as the others lag behind. Someone walks up beside me, and I'm surprised to see Matilda, dressed in a green gown, beads in her hair, keeping pace with me. "I thought you were staying at the castle?" I ask.

She nods. "I was."

"Then what changed?"

"I was needed here," she says, a kindly smile on her face. Then her features turn grim. "You understand now, what my boys intend to do."

"We have to stop them. You have to stop them. They'll listen to you," I say, firm determination in my voice.

"I have talked to them, and in most things, they do listen. But not in this. Their pain has been too great. Their losses too deep. They cannot fathom a life of eternal darkness. They've yet to see how light can still live within them, even if they cannot live within the light."

"*In lumen et lumen*," I whisper.

Matilda nods. "You are their light. You are the only person who can change their hearts in this matter. That's why the spell called to you above all others."

"Wait a second." I raise an eyebrow. "Derek said the ad chose me to help win the case."

The old woman waves her hand dismissively. "Oh, that is what they all think, yes. That is what I told them. But they are wrong, Eve Oliver. I made a spell to find the one who can save the Night brothers. The one who can remind them of who they truly are." She winks mischievously and steps back, chatting with Lily.

Somehow, the woman's words always manage to cheer me up, and I walk a bit straighter then. As I near the door to the courtroom, a man cuts me off, his brown trench coat old and rugged. Jerry. He wears a wolfish grin.

"How nice to see you again, Eve," he says smoothly, as if we were old friends. "How have you been?"

His easy manner makes me boil with rage, but I keep my anger below the surface. "Better and better since I stopped going to therapy," I say, crossing my arms,

"Glad I could help."

I nod, my voice sincere. "You were a prime example of what not to do."

A hint of a frown on his lips. Quickly gone. He gestures behind me. "I see the Night brothers have roped you into their little game. No doubt to tell lies about me. Come now, Eve, I thought you had more integrity than that. Tell me, what did they promise you?"

I shrug. "I don't have to tell you anything." And with that, I walk past him and into the courtroom.

THE WILD

You may shoot me with your words,
   You may cut me with your eyes,
   You may kill me with your hatefulness,
   But still, like air, I'll rise.
   ~ Maya Angelou

WE ALL RETURN to our seats, with the exception of Liam, who remains out in the hall. The other Night brothers crowd around me protectively.

"Are you alright?" Derek asks gently. His eyes shift to Jerry for a moment, then back at me. "I heard what he said."

"I'm fine," I say, though my gut is buzzing like angry bees. "And I don't care about what he said."

"He will never harm you again," Derek says, sincerely.

"He will die if he tries," adds Sebastian.

I can't help but smile at their determination to keep

me safe. "I'll be okay. Don't go losing your law license over me."

"Our actions would be of a noble nature," says Elijah. "Besides, it's not as if we don't know any lawyers to bail us out."

We all chuckle lightly.

"I can sneak into Jerry's house if you'd like," whispers Lily. "Summon moths to eat through his clothing. Cause his garden to wither. Make his food go rotten."

"Wouldn't that be nice," I say, sarcastically.

She grins devilishly.

"Wait," I add. "You know I was joking, right?"

"Right." She winks.

Before I can say anything else, the judge returns, and the prosecution resumes their case.

They spend what feels like a thousand years parading witness after witness to talk about all the bad things Dracula has ever done.

It's…a lot.

And makes me sick to my stomach.

But just because he did all those things, doesn't mean he killed Mary and the baby.

The baby that wasn't his.

Considering his outburst, I doubt he even knew the true paternity at the time of the murder.

When the prosecution finally closes their case, my palms are sweating and I'm close to having a panic attack.

I'll be the first witness Derek calls.

I will have to tell everyone in this courtroom the details of my abuse at Jerry's hands.

And pray it will be enough to discredit him.

When Derek makes his opening statement, he is

mesmerizing. He owns the courtroom with his confidence and charisma, and I am pulled into his powerful presence.

To take my mind off what's to come, I pull out my sketchbook and begin to draw him in his element. Talking to the jury, making his case, explaining how this crime is too sloppy for the likes of Vlad Dracule.

I draw his eyes, full of intelligence and cunning, and the strong slope of his nose and jawline. The dimpled chin that deepens when he smiles. With shading I create the solidness of his body, the way he fills a space.

He says something funny and the jury laughs. They are putty in his hands. So am I.

And then it comes time for me to testify.

I take the stand with wobbly legs.

Jerry stays in the courtroom, watching. Studying me.

It's unnerving, and Derek lays a hand on mine as I pass him. "Just keep your eyes on me," he says.

I nod, swallowing through a dry mouth.

I'm sworn in by the small gnome woman and then Derek begins his questioning. "How do you know Jerome Van Helsing?" he asks.

"He was my therapist in the mundane world," I say.

And then I explain how Jerry seduced me during the most painful part of my life. How he used our relationship in therapy to become my lover. And how he abused me.

"The first time it happened he was drunk," I say. "He came over to my apartment and demanded to be let in. He accused me of cheating on him and began choking me until I nearly passed out."

I can still feel his hands on my throat. The panic as I couldn't breathe. The belief that I might die.

"The abuse escalated from there," I say. "In another instance he broke my finger when I got angry at him for driving erratically."

It had healed, eventually.

I recount more instances of abuse, my eyes locked on Derek's.

But the real panic doesn't hit until Moira stands to cross-examine me.

"If the abuse was so bad, why didn't you report it?" she asks.

"I was scared," I say. "I also wanted to believe him when he said it wouldn't happen again. I didn't want him to get in trouble."

My excuses sound weak. Lame. But it's so messy when you're in the middle of it. So complicated. It's not as easy to walk away as people think.

"So he was awful and abusive, but you didn't want him to get into trouble? That's odd, don't you think?"

"Objection," Derek says, standing.

"Sustained," the dragon says. "Keep the questions relevant."

"Apologies, your honor," Moira says, refocusing on me. "Why didn't you leave?"

"I did," I say through clenched teeth.

"Why didn't you leave earlier?" she clarifies.

"My brother was dying of cancer. I had no one else to turn to. I was scared, alone, and heartbroken."

"It sounds to me like it wasn't that bad at all," she says, through Derek's objection. Moira smiles. "Withdrawn."

"Jerry didn't just abuse me," I say. "He continued to stalk me after I broke up with him."

Moira cocks her head. "Do you have proof of this?"

"Yes," I say. "I saved screenshots on my phone."

"Can you produce this phone? I'm sure the judge will allow contraband for the purposes of evidence."

Shit. "No, the phone broke," I say.

"How convenient. One final question, Miss Oliver. Isn't it true you're making this up to help your new bosses with their case? That my brother actually broke up with you, and this is your attempt to get revenge for a broken heart?"

"No, that is not true at all," I say, my rage simmering. "Jerry abused his position as my therapist and abused me before I finally broke up with him just before my brother died. Then he continued to stalk me."

I'm shaking. Tears are streaming down my face. I can't breathe as I'm excused from the witness stand and rejoin the Nights at their table.

Sebastian takes my hand the moment I sit, squeezing it reassuringly. His face is hard, his jaw locked as he glares at Jerry and the other Van Helsings.

Derek now presents our case.

We debated about having Dracula testify, but decided against the idea. It could too easily turn against us. Or the count could have another outburst. Instead, Derek calls Liam to testify that he wasn't having an affair with Mary but was actually the doctor helping with her delivery. He calls Elal, the coroner, to testify that it might not have been a vampire who killed her. He calls Leonard to testify that the Dracules had a good marriage, that Dracula was excited about his baby and in love with Mary.

And then he pulls the arguments together. He talks about how this crime was too messy to have been orchestrated by the great Vlad Dracule. How the Van Helsings hold a grudge against the count going back centuries.

He is both persuasive and powerful in his presentation, but the jury doesn't look swayed. In fact, they seem to sneer at Dracula more and more. When the time comes to make a verdict, I suspect they will be driven by emotion rather than logic.

Derek wraps up his speech, and we receive a short five-minute break before closing arguments begin. Each side is allocated thirty minutes. Finally, the end is in sight. Though I dread it more and more. If we lose, and I don't see how we won't, Dracula and the Night brothers will suffer for all eternity.

The prosecution goes first. Moira summarizes the facts of the case, reaffirms Dracula's cruel reputation, and replays the memory from the cat. She fast forwards to the relevant part of Liam's shoes, and as she does, something catches my eye. Something I hadn't notice before. As the feline scrambles up an ancient stone gargoyle, I see a speck in the distance, a crop of twigs in the abandoned cathedral opposite of Dracula's manor. The image lasts less than a second, and the picture is a muddy blur, but I'm sure of what I saw. Someone else was nearby that day. Someone may have seen what happened.

"I need to check on something," I say quickly, getting to my feet.

"Is something wrong?" Sebastian asks.

"No. It's about the case. It might be nothing. Or it might help us."

"I'll come with you." He starts to stand, but I gesture for him to stop.

"Stay here." I look at all three brothers and Lily. "Work

together on the closing argument. And...buy me time. Make a commotion if you need to. Liam will come with me."

They each nod in unison, though they don't look too happy as they return to their notes.

I rush out of the courtroom, in the most polite-yet-quick walk I can manage, and find Liam pacing by the fireplace. "What's happened?" he asks, red-hair disheveled, as if he's been running his hand through it over and over again. "Is the trial over?"

"Not yet." I grab his hand and pull him toward the exit. "Come on."

I'VE LOST track of how long it's been since the trial began. Since I was last outside. Since I had any sleep. At least a few days. And when I step out onto the stone square of the courthouse, a storm greets me. Winter has come in earnest, it seems, and brought with it all the pent-up energy of waiting for fall to end. The wind lashes at my face, causing my eyes to tear. Ice, thin and sharp, falls from the sky, beating across my skin. I wrap my arms around myself, shaking, my breath a fog before my eyes. Liam yanks off his cloak and throws it over my head like a hood, then pulls me close, shielding me with his figure. An unnatural warmth radiates from his body and the chill inside me fades away. Liam is so close, his scent overtakes me. Charcoal and wood and the feeling of coming home to a roaring fire. Other feelings begin to rise in me as well, but we don't have time for those right now.

"Quickly," I yell over the wind. "To the carriage. We need to get to the Broken Cathedral."

Liam nods, leading me to a grand stable, fit for fifty horses, opposite the courthouse. Over the last three days, Lily took breaks from the trial to feed her steeds and take them out for rides. There are stable hands in service to the court who do that as well, she told me, but she prefers to do it herself.

Once in the stable, we're offered some respite from the cold, but it doesn't last long. The smell of straw and manure fill my nose as Liam quickly finds our carriage and opens the door for me. I shake my head, pointing to the driver's seat. "We need to be able to talk."

He nods, and together we take Lily's usual place behind the horses. A part of me wishes I had asked her to come with me, so I could sit cozy in the back with Liam, but when it comes to delaying the court with a distraction, I have more faith in Lily than anyone else. She's not a lawyer. She doesn't have as much to lose due to bad behavior. And from what I've heard, she's good at mayhem.

I just hope all of this is worth it.

Liam yanks on the reins and we're off, rushing down the cobbled streets of the Otherworld, the harsh winds piercing even the warm protection the fire Druid provides.

"What's going on?" asks Liam. "What happened?"

"I...saw...something," I say, teeth chattering, making my words stilted and broken. "In the memory. There... might be another witness. Someone who saw the truth. But I'll need your help. I'll need you...to catch them."

* * *

WE ARRIVE at the Broken Cathedral, the Otherworld sky darker than I have ever seen before, the storm clouds blocking out the Dragon's Breath, and no lanterns to light our way. I nearly trip climbing off the carriage, and Liam raises his hand, his palm lighting with a soft flame, illuminating our near surroundings. "Thanks," I say. "I'm surprised you didn't do that earlier. How could you even see the roads?"

"I can see better in the dark than I once did," he replies quickly. And I remember what Sebastian once told me, that vampires are creatures of shadow.

"What are we looking for?" asks Liam, holding his blazing hand up higher.

"A gargoyle. I'll know it when I see it."

He nods, and together we run into the cathedral ruins. In the main hall, half of the roof is gone, making way for snow and ice, and I walk carefully to avoid slipping. "Are the gargoyle's here alive? Like in the mausoleum?" I ask, as we keep searching.

"They were once," Liam says somberly. "But when the earthquake that brought this building to ruin came, the gargoyles gave their life so that some of the cathedral could remain standing. They are just stone now."

I shake my head. "That's terrible. Why die to protect a building?"

He sighs. "It is what gargoyles do. And they saved many lives that day. You see, the cathedral was still in use at the time."

I pause, studying a gargoyle near a broken window. It's

not the one I seek, but I take a quick moment to thank it silently, before continuing on.

"It is said," Liam continues, "that when the cathedral is restored, the gargoyles may return to life."

I raise an eyebrow. "Is that possible?"

He shrugs. "Such things have happened before."

We climb higher, searching for the ancient gargoyle in the memory. My heart nearly stops when I see it, perched at the edge of one of the great towers, looking out at the world below. We are near the top of the cathedral now, surrounded by the stone pillars that hold up a solid ceiling. They are spaced far apart, making the area open to the wind and sky, to the dark clouds swirling above. We are so high up, I feel I can almost touch them, these thick rolling masses of thunder and ice.

Here the wind comes swiftly and harshly and leaves just as quickly. Snow has piled on in tall mounds near the pillars. Thick ropes fall from pulley systems built into the ceiling, coiling at our feet, and a golden church bell hangs over our heads, engraved with runes, wider than three horses, so enormous not even the storm can sway it.

I run to the gargoyle, pulling myself up on its wings, much like the cat had done in its memory.

"This is madness," says Liam. "You'll fall."

But I don't. I stay steady as I climb up over the head of the ancient statue.

And there, at the top, I see it.

A coil of branches and twigs, nestled safely against the crook of a stone wing.

A nest.

Filled with speckled eggs.

Liam climbs up behind me, wrapping his arm protectively around my waist. His hand is no longer on fire, but it's easier to see this close to the Dragon's Breath. "What are you doing?" he asks. "Have you gone—" He freezes, his eyes landing on the nest. "You don't think—"

"There's a bird nearby," I say, my breath heaving, the cold in me burned away by adrenaline. "And maybe, just maybe, it saw what happened." I look up, and there, amidst a swirl of dark cloud, I see a raven descending to protect its home. "Your babies are safe," I say softly. "We mean no harm." I turn to Liam. "Catch it. But be gentle."

He nods, and in a flash, he runs up the stone pillar, three steps straight up a horizontal wall, and leaps into the air, catching the bird and holding it like a precious gem. He lands across from me, balanced on the gargoyle's wing, a space only three inches wide. He sits down on the heels of his feet, steady as a rock, and lowers his hands in front of me. The bird, held firmly between his palms, meets my eyes, curiosity in its gaze. It stays still, quietly content, and not thrashing about as I imagined. There is an ease between us I can't quite understand.

I pull out the memory catcher Sebastian gave me and say the necessary words, praying to see something useful. There are many memories, of flying above Dracula's manor, of hunting for worms in the dirt, but I feel something inside me, a flash, guiding me to what matters most. There. The memory.

It is dark. The Dragon's Breath dim in the sky.

The bird sits perched on a tree near Dracula's front entryway. The door opens, spilling golden light into the shadows, and the Count himself steps out, wrapped in black. But before leaving, he turns back, holding up a gentle hand, and putting it to a woman's face. Mary. She stands in the doorway, dressed in a white gown, belly large, dark hair messy but beautiful all the same. She looks happy and radiant and a woman ready to bring joy and life into the world. She laughs at something Dracula says, then stands up on her toes and kisses him on the lips. With a final smile, she closes the door, and the Count walks away. The moment is intimate and peaceful, and it will never happen again.

The bird takes flight. It drifts through the quiet air, returning to its nest, studying its eggs. *No*, I think. *That can't be it. There must be something more.*

Something.

To save Dracula.

To save the Night brothers.

But there is nothing. The bird doesn't leave the nest.

I sigh, my energy dissipating, the cold creeping back into me.

"I'm sorry," I say, lowering the memory catcher, my eyes blurry as I look at Liam. "I thought I could save you. I thought—"

In the memory, the bird turns toward the manor, and I gasp with astonishment. Somehow, the image of the Dracula's home, though at least a mile away, is crystal clear.

"Photoreceptive cones," I mumble, laughing to myself, my eyes filling with tears.

"What are you going on about?" asks Liam.

"Photoreceptive cones in the retina," I repeat, louder, the strength back in my voice. "Birds have far more than humans. Some can see four or five times further. I read it once."

Liam smirks.

And the memory continues.

A figure walks toward the Manor, moving briskly. They wear a long brown coat. Their hair is a mess of dark curls.

It can't be...

And yet, Jerome Van Helsing enters the Dracule Manor on the night of the murder. Several moments later he steps out, his clothing soaked in blood.

My hands shake at the sight, and I almost drop the crystal. Instead, I lose my balance and Liam catches me, steadying me, and gently lowers the bird to the ground. It jumps into its nest, sitting calmly near its eggs.

"We need to get this back to the courthouse." I turn, looking over the snow-covered fields below, and a stone sinks in my throat. It will take a long time to climb back down the cathedral and even longer to ride back to the courthouse. There's no way we'll make it back before the trial is over. No way, unless...

"Go," I say, pushing the Memory Catcher into Liam's hand. "You're faster than me."

He pauses, still holding me with his other hand. I expect him to argue, to spew warnings about my safety. Instead, he meets my eyes, a fierce determination in his gaze, and nods once slowly.

And then, he leaps off the cathedral.

* * *

THE EARTH CRACKS where Liam lands, kicking up dust and snow, and leaving veins of black in the stone. He bends his knees to absorb the impact, and stands up without hesitation, red hair wild in the storm. He doesn't take the carriage. He just runs, faster than I have seen anyone run before.

I turn away from the dizzying sight and crouch, staying low as I climb back down the statue and make my way under the great bell, looking for the stairs. Without Liam's fire to guide me, it's near pitch-black inside. I almost reach the stairs when a warm orange glow spills out from their depths. For a second, I freeze, bewildered, and then I realize someone is coming, carrying light.

My first thought is Sebastian must have come looking for us. But then I see the man step onto my floor, blazing-torch in hand. The man from my nightmares.

"You found something, didn't you," says Jerry, his face half in shadow, the other half cast in red angry light. "A memory." These are not questions. Just statements.

"I need to return to the courthouse," I say, trying to step around him.

He blocks the path, the heat from his torch too close to my face, too hot on my skin.

"I can explain," he says, brown coat billowing in the wind. "I received a letter. Signed by Mary. She asked for my help. That's why I was there that night."

I take a deep breath, trying to keep my emotions in check. Though I find it hard to look at him, I meet his eyes, looking for sincerity. For kindness. He does not have these things.

"Where is this special letter then?" I ask.

He bows his head. "Not here."

"Then go get it."

"I can't. It's gone. Went missing."

I snicker, unable to contain my sneer. "Well that's very convenient for you, isn't it?"

"It's the truth," he says, and for once, he looks broken, weak and fragile and human like I have never seen him before. But that doesn't mean he's earnest.

"Then prove it to the court," I say, pushing past him.

He grabs my arm, hard enough to bruise. "They'll never believe me. Not after your testimony. You need to withdraw your statement. Say you were manipulated. Say you were confused. I don't care. Say you were wrong." He growls, and the sound from his mouth is nothing human.

"I wasn't wrong," I say. "The things you did to me were horrific. And you will never do them to anyone else again."

He snarls, grabbing me by the neck and yanking me close, so close the stench of his breath is on my face, and I see his teeth are sharper than before. Mouth dripping with saliva.

"Say you were wrong," he repeats, his voice low and guttural and beastly. "Or I will squeeze the life out of you." His grip tightens. Nails that were once short and neat now dig deep into my flesh like claws.

"You're a monster." I spit in his face. And knee him between the legs.

He yelps, letting me go for an instant, and I rush away toward the stairs. A shadow flies across the floor, and Jerry lands in my way, clothing stretched tight over bulging muscles too large to be human, long claws sprouting from thin veiny hands. He must have dropped the torch and jumped over me, all before I could take three steps.

Words flow out of me, quicker than thought. "If you kill me, the Night brothers will make sure you suffer for all eternity. You will stain your family name. You will—"

"Where's the crystal?" he roars.

"Not here. But I can get it." I'd never give it to him, but I need to make him think I will as I work out a plan to escape.

"He has it," says Jerry. "The one with red-hair. I saw the both of you leave together."

"Yes, but—"

"Then it's too late. He's at the courthouse by now." Jerry bows his head, defeated. He talks slowly. "Do you know, Eve, the greatest pleasure a werewolf can feel?"

I shake my head rapidly, my entire body vibrating with fear.

"It is the hunt," he says. "The chase of prey. Digging your teeth into a ripe, plump, juicy neck. Feeling the blood spraying into your mouth. Feeling the pulse of your query slow. Feeling the life leave them." He looks up, eyes mad and hungry. "If this is to be my last day of freedom, then I shall feel the hunt once again."

He pulls his head back and roars, muscles ripping out of his clothing, skin turning dark and matted with fur. All the charm of his face is torn away, replaced by a wet snout and purple lips, long ragged ears and too many barred teeth. He turns into the monster I know him to be.

And then I run.

A howl on the wind.

A beast on my heels.

* * *

I TAKE THE STAIRS. Not down, as I would have liked, for Jerry blocked that path. But up.

The torch, left at the base of the room, is dimming

241

now and provides me little light as I climb. The staircase, which has railings but isn't surrounded by walls, zigzags toward the ceiling, and I realize I will soon reach the roof with nowhere else to run. That won't do. So I look out to my side, to the beams and pulleys holding up the church bell. Below, a shadow moves to the base of the stairs. He is taking his time, creeping in the darkness.

I carefully climb onto the railing, reaching out for a rope. My arms aren't long enough. I'll need to jump. And quietly, because I need Jerry to still think I'm on the stairs.

Gritting my teeth, I take one slow breath, and leap forward, hands fumbling clumsily in front of me. They find purchase, but slip, the coarse rope burning my skin as I tighten my grip to stop from falling. My descent slows and I hang near the ceiling, biting my lips shut though my entire body needs to scream.

The rope steadies. I allow myself one more breath. Slow. Quiet.

Then I pull myself higher and clasp one of the wooden beams holding up the church bell. My muscles straining, cold and restless, I climb up onto the beam, and lie flat as I crawl forward toward a rope at the other end. Then I can slide down and take the stairs.

One breath. Two.

I'm almost there.

The stairs behind me creak.

And I know he's standing where I stood a moment ago.

Keep moving, Jerry. Just keep going up.

He doesn't.

A sniff.

Another.

Like a hungry dog locked onto a scent.

I climb forward.

The torch is below me.

The rope within my reach.

I climb forward.

And something digs into my arm. Hot and sharp. A piece of splintered wood I hadn't seen. I suck in my breath, burying all the pain blooming under my skin, and reach forward, my hand slick with blood, and grab hold of the rope.

Silence.

The quiet before the storm.

The moment before the predator's leap.

I let myself fall, sliding down the rope, skin tearing from my palms in my haste.

The beast flies over me.

Landing where I was just a moment ago.

I made it, I think, for one ludicrous second.

And the wooden beam cracks under his weight.

The rope goes slack in my hands.

And we both fall to the ground.

I land with a crunch, my head hitting stone, my body collapsing near the burning torch. Spots blur my vision. Nausea fills my gut.

Two sets of claws land before me.

I am laying at the beast's heels.

Broken and weak. And suddenly, I am taken back to another time, another me, one who was beaten and choked. One who was left alone to weep on the floor and wonder what she did wrong. But that is me no longer.

The pain leaves me, burned away by a surge of strength. My mind is clear and light. My skin has forgotten the cold. And I stand, feet steady as rock, and I look the monster in the eye.

"You will never hurt me again," I say. "Know that. Even if you kill me now. Even if you rip me apart. I will feel nothing for you. Not anger. Not sadness. Not fear. Nothing." I take a breath. "I am not afraid."

The beast tilts his head, as if he hears something I do not. And then he charges.

One bite.

Deep into my neck.

My throat closes shut with blood.

My eyes twitch.

All I think is…

Nothing.

The beast rears its head. Letting me go. And I fly across the room. Past the pillars. Out into the sky.

I am falling, and yet I know, I will not fall.

I know it with a certainty I have always had. A certainty for things yet to come.

And a flash overtakes me.

More powerful than I have ever felt.

I don't fight it. Not as I have before.

And as the energy courses through my body, I realize, it is not just visions I have. Not just a feeling of what will happen. It is power. Raw, uncontrolled power.

It takes hold of me.

And I do not fall.

I fly.

I AM ME, and yet I am not. There are things I do, and things done through me. My voice is mine, and not my own.

. . .

"I AM the woman in the wild!" I scream into the shrieking wind. As I speak, lightning flashes, the fire of the torch blazes, and the clouds swirl around me. The pendant from the kitsune blazes at my throat. I am suspended in mid-air. My skin and clothes glow white, smooth and clear of any blemish, illuminating the dark sky. Illuminating the werewolf, who stands at the edge of the cathedral, jaw slack with wonder.

"I am the blood sister of the moon! I am the call of the night and her secrets. The radiance left from a star. I am all that you need and more than you know. I am the hidden that shall now be found. I am the magic that you seek. I am the wild!"

The wind thrashes at my words, so hard it pushes the beast backwards. He growls, barring his teeth. He bends his knees, preparing to leap.

"Do not move," I warn. "Do not try."

He howls one last time.

And jumps.

He swipes his claws forward mid-air, aiming for my neck.

He is nearly at me, when I raise my arm, and a gale of wind strikes down from above, so fierce and quick, it draws the clouds toward it like a tornado, and sends the beast falling down.

He does not land smoothly.

One might say, he does not land at all.

His body hits the tip of a gargoyle wing.

And the stone pierces his flesh, bursting from his chest.

I don't recall the gargoyle wing being there. It wasn't there last I looked.

But perhaps I'm wrong. I'm not myself right now.

I am the radiance of a star, burning away. And as the energy fades, I glide back toward the tower. The power is gone before I find my footing, and I collapse, not quite on solid ground. I reach to grab the edge.

Someone grabs me first.

Strong arms pull me close.

"I'm here," he says, his warmth seeping into my body. "I'm here."

And I drift away.

And dream of nothing.

THE FIRE

Through love, burning fire becomes pleasant light. ~ Rumi

My consciousness comes and goes in waves. I'm aware only of strong arms carrying me through the streets of the Otherworld, of Liam's voice alternating between chastising me for my foolishness, cursing himself for leaving me, and offering words of comfort. All of this comes in fragments, until it's as if I'm with a different man altogether each time I awake.

Liam is a man at war within himself.

There is no winner in a war against yourself.

The storm around us grows in fury and hail the size of snowballs falls from the sky, the temperature dropping dangerously fast.

I shiver, my body convulsing without guidance from me in its attempt to warm itself.

Liam curses and a warmth spreads through me,

blazing through his skin and into mine, fighting the chill that's settling into my frigid body.

When darkness overtakes me once more, I see Jerry's face, his anger and hatred, his desire to see me suffer even at his own demise.

And when I open my eyes again, I see the golden eyes of Liam studying me thoughtfully, his expression unreadable.

This time I feel more-clear headed, better in control of myself. Like I can actually keep my eyes open for longer than a few second, despite the pounding in my skull.

"Where are we?" I ask, trying to sit up and failing miserably.

"Move slowly," he says. "You've been through a lot."

He offers the support of his arm to prop me up, and I see we are in his bedchamber. A fire warms the space, dancing in shadows off the walls.

A familiar purr brings a smile to my face as Moon nudges against my leg and then curls up next to my lap. I pet the fur ball. "You're a sight for sore eyes," I tell my cat.

Liam snorts. "The beast wouldn't shut up. Howled outside my door for hours on end until I finally let him in. He can't stand me, but he wouldn't leave your side."

I give Moon extra love for that level of loyalty and devotion.

"What happened?" I ask, my mouth dry and thick.

Liam hands me a goblet of water and I sip it gratefully. He's sitting on the bed next to me, his arm still supporting me, our bodies pressed closely together, the heat between us tugging at my gut, sending a tingle up my spine.

Our fingers brush against each other on the bed, and his pinkie covers mine. We both studiously avoid looking at our fingers, but my every nerve is focused on how his finger feels brushing against mine.

"What happened?" he asks.

I search my memories, but it's all a bit fuzzy. "Jerry. He... he tried to kill me."

Liam's jaw clenches, and he nods. "He must have followed us from the courthouse."

"He's dead," I say. It's not a question. I remember the sound he made, a last, thin exhale as life left him. The last sound he'll ever make.

"Yes." Liam brushes hair out of my eyes and examines my face with one hand, while keeping the other on the bed touching mine. "How do you feel? Something... something happened to you. I came at the end, but for a moment I saw. You glowed like the moon." He looks almost frightened.

"I don't know," I say. "I still can't entirely remember." And then I suck in my breath as more details come back to me. "What happened in court? Did the judge see the memory of Jerry covered in blood?"

My heart beats frantically against my chest as I realize we need to get back, to tell the others what happened. But Liam moves his hand to cover mine, our fingers intertwining, the heat between us growing—and this time it has nothing to do with his Druid powers.

"The trial is over," he says. "The jury has reached a verdict and my brothers are at court now to hear it. I gave them the Memory Catcher in time." His lips curls in a smile. "Though apparently there had been a delay. Something about a dryad running naked through the courtroom. She got away though, her face unseen."

I chuckle lightly, but it hurts my ribs and turns into a groan.

Liam stiffens at the sound of my pain. "I came back for you as soon as I could," he says. "I brought you home, and Matilda sent word to the court of your altercation with Jerry. She explained, in great detail, how you acted in self-defense."

I pause. "But if you only arrived at the end, how could you know what happened?"

A playful smile crosses his lips. "I may have told the enforcers I saw the entire attack. With your previous testimony, and the memory of Jerry covered in blood, it was not hard to convince them of your innocence. You will, however, have to answer some questions eventually. The Enforcers will need your first-hand account."

I nod. "So the court saw the memory?"

Liam nods. "They know everything."

"So they have to find Dracula innocent, right?"

"It does seem likely, though you never know until the end. It's just the way of things." He shrugs like it doesn't matter, but I know it does. It matters in so many ways.

"What will you do?" I ask. "When the sire bond is broken?" I hold my breath, waiting for his reply.

"I do not know," he says, turning away from my gaze. "There is much we need to consider."

Is he thinking of me, I wonder? But his eyes are far away. Fixated on the fire. There is someone else tugging at his heart. And I think back, to all the things Liam has said these past months. *I took this case for Mary. I was her healer.*

"You were more, weren't you?" I ask hesitantly.

"What do you mean?"

"More than her healer." I place a hand on his face and pull it back to me gently. "The baby. He was yours, wasn't he? You weren't just helping Mary deliver her baby. You were helping her deliver *your* baby."

His eyes glisten with unshed emotion and he nods. "Babies," he says, in such a whisper I almost don't hear him.

"Babies?" I ask, sucking in a breath, thinking of Mary's last wish. That her babies would be protected. "There was more than one?"

He nods. "Twins. I… "

He pulls away from me and stands, pacing back and forth nervously. Cold rushes in where his warmth once existed and I find myself missing having him close.

I take another sip of water and place my goblet down, then slowly rise, pacing myself so as not to pass out. I take a step towards him, then another, until I have reached him.

"Liam. What happened?" I keep my voice soothing and calm, like I would if talking to a wild animal. He has that power in him, that wild, untamed madness that all the Night brothers have so much of.

"I was too late," he says, his voice breaking. "I knew something was wrong, but I didn't know what. When I showed up, she was already dead, covered in blood, the baby killed. It was a massacre. It took me a moment to realize…" he sucks in his breath, then lets it out in one long, slow exhale before continuing. Each word costs him a piece of his soul to say. "She was still in labor."

It's my turn to suck in my breath. I had several theories, but this wasn't one of them. I reach for his hand, taking it in mine, my icy fingers thawing at his touch, as our fingers once again intertwine. I stay still and silent, creating the space he needs to tell his story.

"She was pregnant with twins. She didn't want anyone to know. Didn't want to jinx it. She said she'd had nightmares that one of the babies died. So she refused to speak about the children to anyone but me." He pauses. "We weren't close, Mary and I. Not really. Our time together was one of passion, but little else, and each time I regretted it. Still, for some reason she trusted me. Trusted me with the truth above all others." With his free hand he runs his fingers roughly through his wild auburn hair. "I... I delivered my daughter into the gore of her mother and brother's deathbed. And then I ran. Like a coward, I took her and I ran, telling no one."

His grief breaks him, and I pull him into a fierce embrace. His arms wind around my waist as mine wrap around his neck, and he presses his body into me, his face buried in the crook of my neck, his tears drenching my shoulder as his sobs tear free from him.

The pain he's been holding in and using to feed his rage pours out of him, and I catch it all, staying strong enough for the both of us so that he can break, just for a moment.

I don't speak again until his body stills and his breathing returns to normal. Then I ask the burning question on my tongue. "Liam, where's the other baby now? Where's your daughter?"

"She's somewhere safe," he says, pulling back from me to wipe his eyes and compose himself. "Somewhere Dracula wouldn't find her. She is being cared for well. Better than I ever could." His face hardens, and he looks at me. "If Dracula ever finds out about her, he'll kill her."

I swallow, believing him. "We will keep her safe." I say, knowing it's presumptuous to assume he wants or needs my help in this matter. But also knowing it's the right thing to say. The necessary and true thing to say. However it happened, whatever it might mean, the Night family has become my family. I will not abandon them to the darkness that lurks so closely at their heels.

"Liam," I say with all the tenderness in my heart, "you must know you were not a coward. No man should ever be put in the position you were in, and yet you delivered your daughter, you saved her and kept her safe. You did what Mary would have wanted. You were brave. You were your daughter's hero."

He flinches at my words. "I am a danger to her. She's better off without me." He moves to turn away from me, but I stop him.

"She's not," I say. "I promise you, she's not. You have so much to offer her. To teach her. To give her. Starting with your love. She needs her father. Trust me. This comes from a girl who would give anything to have her own father back, even for a day."

This softens him, but it's not enough. I know I need to show him the truth of himself. "You're so deeply enmeshed in your own self-hatred you can't see past it. But you're only seeing the shadows, not the light. There is light in you, Liam. In all four of you. And yes, there is darkness, too. But that's true of everyone. We all carry within us the entirety of existence. The light and the dark. The noble and the ignoble. Sometimes we have to walk in the shadows, but we must always strive to come back to the other side. Your daughter needs you to find your way back. Your brothers need you." I pause, hesitating, assessing my own feelings, and then I speak, knowing it is the truth. "And *I* need you."

Our faces are inches apart. My right hand is in his, my left hand now resting on his chest. Our fingers are intertwined and I'm suddenly keenly aware of the contact, of flesh on flesh, of his breath mingling with mine, of all my senses responding to his.

"What are you, Eve Oliver?" he asks, sliding a finger down my cheek.

"I don't know," I say honestly. "I just know that everyone deserves a fair trial and a strong defense. So I'm fighting for you and Sebastian and Derek and Elijah. Even if you won't fight for yourselves."

The mood in the room has shifted. The tension between us is visceral.

Every nerve in my body is on fire as he moves closer to me, his head bending down, his lips brushing against mine.

The kiss starts softly, gently, a teasing only. When I move in closer, I surprise us both.

My arms wind back around his neck and he pulls me against him, his hard chest pressed against my breasts, his nails digging into my back as his lips claim mine again, this time with all the heat and power of a Druid turned vampire.

He tastes of warmth and honey and my body responds to his with all the desire that's been pent up in me since starting this job.

I moan into his mouth as I feel his body further harden against me, in clear evidence of his excitement.

My mind clouds with the passion and I know where this is leading. And still, I don't pull away. I have fought against my own desires for so long, out of fear. Fear of being hurt. Fear of losing another person I love. Fear of getting too close.

I can't live in fear any longer.

Liam gazes deeply into my eyes. "You look oceans away," he says softly, his lips so close to mine I can feel them moving, our foreheads pressed together.

"I was just thinking about the nature of love," I say, and then I kiss him again.

Our passion moves us across the room, where he presses me against the wall and moves his mouth down my neck, his teeth gliding against my pulsing vein, my pains and aches forgotten for the moment.

My breath hitches, and I can't tell if what I'm feeling is fear or excitement as pleasure wars with past memories of a violent Liam tearing into my neck.

He pauses, lips brushing against the flesh of my ear. "Is this okay?" He asks breathlessly. "Tell me to stop."

"Don't. Stop." I say.

And he wouldn't have, had Matilda not come to the door at that precise moment.

THE OATH

We can easily forgive a child who is afraid of the dark; the real tragedy of life is when men are afraid of the light. ~ *Plato*

LIAM and I pull away from each other like guilty teenagers caught making out in the basement.

Matilda gives us both knowing looks and smiles. "It's good to see you two getting along with one another at last," she says, in the understatement of the year.

Liam coughs and I hide a smile, my body still buzzing with need for him. It's almost painful to not be touching him right now.

"I came to tell you the verdict." She pauses dramatically, letting us both compose ourselves. "Dracula was found innocent of all charges."

Liam and I both exhale at the same moment, smiles playing across our lips.

Matilda continues, looking directly at me. "Eve, the

Van Helsings are beyond mad with anger and grief. I expect Moira will want to see you punished for Jerry's death, but the law is on our side in this matter. You have nothing to fear in this regard." She says it in that way she has about her. As if she knows things the rest of us don't.

She turns to Liam. "Your brothers had a final meeting with Dracula at the courthouse. They should return shortly."

He nods, and her lips curl in a smile. "Very well then. I shall leave the two of you to your...celebration." And with that she walks out the door, Moon meowing as she does, then winding around my legs and purring. As soon as we are alone again, Liam steps closer, pulling me back into his arms, a wide grin on his face. "I can hardly believe it," he says. "We won. We...we could never have done this without you, Eve. I hope you know that."

"I know." I lean in to kiss him once more.

Then suddenly, Liam does something I have never seen him do before. He loses his balance.

And topples towards me, and I catch him as best I can, both of us falling into the wall.

"Are you okay?" I ask. "What happened?"

He raises his head, rubbing his forehead with his hand, when the door bursts open, and the rest of the Night brothers rush in, still dressed in the fine suits and vests they wore to the courthouse, but looking rather disheveled. "Have you felt it too, brother?" asks Sebastian.

Liam nods, his eyes widening in awe. "He's released the sire bond." He smiles at me, the broadest smile I've ever seen on his face. "We're free!"

Elation wars with fear in my gut, and I hold Liam close

and look to all of the brothers. "Does this mean you will…" I can barely say the words. "Does this mean you will go through with your plans? Will you—"

Sebastian rushes towards me and grabs my arms gently with his rough hands, studying me with his forest-green eyes. "Are you well? I would have stayed at your side, but Liam vowed to look after you while I was needed at court."

"I'm fine."

Before I can add more, Derek stands in front of me, his five o'clock shadow a little more beard and a little less shadow than usual over his dimpled chin. "I'm so sorry," he says. "We swore to protect you from that monster, and yet we failed."

"I kept myself safe," I say.

"Indeed," agrees Elijah, running a hand through his blonde hair, joining his brothers around me. "The evidence you procured also won the trial. We are in your debt, Miss Oliver." He bows dramatically, with a flourish of his silver cape.

I chuckle despite myself, then sober quickly. "So… what about your oath?"

Liam looks to each of his brothers, an understanding passing between them. Then he turns to me with his amber eyes and runs a hand softly across my cheek. "There are more important things now," he whispers. Finally, he lets me go, standing straight and speaking to all his brothers. "We have all done heinous things. And we all carry that pain differently. But I think the time has come to stop seeking an end to our lives and to instead search for ways to atone for our sins."

They all nod somberly.

All except Elijah, who lifts up one finger thoughtfully. "So what you're all saying is...you agree with me? And I was right all along?"

A contagious laughter takes us all.

* * *

As day-time approaches, we are all tired beyond imagining and yet none of us feel inclined to be alone.

An idea sparks in my mind, and it's so silly and stupid that I love it instantly. "Let's do a sleepover," I say.

We've all relocated to the library and are sitting on plush red chairs talking. The four of them look at me as if I've gone mad.

"Hear me out," I say. "We'll pull some furs over to the main hearth, light the fire, grab some of that whiskey Derek keeps hidden in his desk," I wink at him and his shocked expression, "and we'll tell stories until we fall asleep."

Liam grunts. "Fine, but there will be no braiding of hair."

I nearly choke on my own laughter, and I tug at a long strand of his auburn mane. "But you'd look very fashionable in a fishtail," I say.

Now Derek is laughing, and that giddiness spreads to us all. Elijah nearly falls off his chair, chuckling so hard he's holding his stomach.

Matilda and Lily come in just as we're settling down, bearing a plate of food for me and goblets of blood for the boys. The old woman is all smiles as she hands me a dish full of baked greens and ripe cheeses, then gives a hug to each of her grandsons.

Lily places a hand on my shoulder, beaming proudly. "I knew you could do it," she says.

"Save the trial?" I ask in between bites, feeling ravenous after such a long and grueling night.

"Save my uncles," she says, her eyes a tad watery as she looks at the Night brothers. Then she wraps me in a tight hug and I almost drop my plate, putting it down beside me.

"I couldn't have done it without you," I say. "Your delay of the court proceedings was perfect."

She shrugs, and when she pulls away, Matilda takes her place. She hugs me long and hard. "You did it my girl. I knew you would. You brought light back into my boys."

"In lumen et lumen," I whisper.

I feel wet tears on my neck and then she stands to leave, wiping her face with her hand. I invite them both to the slumber party, but they graciously decline. Lily will sleep in her tree as usual and Matilda says she is too old for such ways, but I think she secretly wants me to spend more time with the boys alone. She's a crafty one, that old lady.

It doesn't take us long to set up everything, and Sebastian surprises me with two gifts. "Tomorrow is the Midwinter Festival," he says. "And...well, here."

The gifts are both wrapped in gold and purple ribbon and I open the first, finding a book of poetry within. My eyes light up. "You remembered."

He nods. "You aren't the only one with a good memory," he says with a shy smile.

The second box contains my heart's desire. Gourmet chocolates.

I throw myself into his arms. "Thank you. This is perfect."

He holds me tightly, and I rest my head on his shoulder, enjoying the solidness of him, the assurance of having him in my life. He is my rock. My mountain. I know he will have my back no matter what.

There's so much to explore with him. With each of them. I'm rather overwhelmed by it all, but there's time.

Now that they've decided to stay, to give life a second chance, there's time for it all.

* * *

DEREK IS TELLING a story about a great serpent that wraps around the entire world when sleep takes me. My dreams are not easy things. A wolf devours a lamb, spraying blood on the golden bell of the Broken Cathedral. And the wolf has a face I would rather forget.

When I wake, it is with a gasp, my body covered in sweat.

And I find four men on the alert, ready to comfort me, to hold me, to let me cry.

"It's not your fault," Sebastian assures me, pulling me back into his arms as Liam uses his power to give a fresh blaze to the fire.

The flames steal the chill from the air, and I scoot back under the furs, enjoying the feel of Sebastian and Liam close to me, with Elijah and Derek on either side of them. I could stay like this forever. Perhaps I will.

Something moves at the corner of my eye. A fire iron

poking at the fireplace, igniting the wood into brighter flames. But no one else is here, The fire iron moves mid-air on its own. I freeze, clutching Liam's hand.

"What's that?" I ask, pointing at the fire-iron. "More of your magic?"

Liam follows my gaze. "What, them? They're just the castle ghosts."

"Ghosts? You mean, there's ghosts in the castle?"

"Yeah, who do you think cleans and cooks and does all the work around here?" He says it so casually; I can't help but laugh.

"I had wondered about it," I say. "But this wasn't what I was expecting. Who are they?"

"These two are called Mable and Cili," says Liam.

Derek rolls his eyes. "You call all of them Mable and Cili."

"True, but only because we don't have a great way to communicate. We can share general ideas, but not specifics."

Elijah sighs, elaborating. "They are ancient beings. Ones who worked for this castle for centuries before we took residence. It would have been rude to kick them out, so instead we made a deal. They keep the castle tidy, and in exchange we maintain their unmarked graves on the grounds. As well as light candles for their souls once a year when the veil is thinnest, allowing them to join the living for a night and celebrate the pleasures of the flesh, as it were."

"Wow," I say simply. Sometimes simple words are best.

We lie quietly then, all of us bundled up together, gazing into the fire, none of us ready to leave. After a while, I feel Liam tensing beside me, something painful building within. His voice is fraught with nerves when he speaks. "I have something to tell you all. Something you should know about me and Mary."

The truth is hard for Liam to admit, especially to his brothers, but to their credit they remain quiet as he tells his story. "By the time we found out she was pregnant, we were no longer having an affair," he says. "But I had to stand by her to the end. And now, I must stay and stand by my daughter, whatever might come."

"So you're a father," Derek says, with a small smile. "Imagine that."

"Who is taking care of the babe now?" asks Sebastian.

"The Ifrits," says Liam. "Ifi and Elal."

Of course, I realize. *They're granting Mary's last wish.*

* * *

Eventually, the natural urges of waking take effect, and I excuse myself to use the bathroom, and we all begin our day. I'm pretty sure it would be night in the mundane world at this hour. But here, in the Otherworld, the schedule of the sun matters little and I've lost all sense of that rhythm. I'm finding a new rhythm in the Otherworld.

As I finish freshening up, Lily bounces into my room, insisting we go shopping for new dresses for the Midwinter festival. I agree, and we make plans to meet the Night brothers at the festivities. Four am sharp.

Lily offers to take me in the carriage, but I insist she refrain from driving people around on the holiday. Besides, the weather is lovely today. Though snow covers the roads, the air is gentle and warm, the Dragon's Breath burning bright in the sky.

Lily guides me to a nearby market full of odd trinkets and food. Together, we find a deep blue gown with tiny rhinestones sewn in around the collar and cuffs. "This," she says eagerly. "This is perfect. You'll look like the sky at twilight."

I smile and buy the dress, using Otherworld money my job at the Night Firm provides. Gold and silver and copper coins.

Lily buys a dress for herself as well. A leaf-green gown adorned with white flowers. She guides me to the changing room where we can both dress ourselves and then we head out to the center of town.

We can hear the festivities before we see them. Live music filling the streets. Fireworks filling the sky. The smell of freshly baked treats in the air. There are carts and stalls set up along both sides of the street, a hundred different merchants with wares for sale, and I'm practically overwhelmed by all the choices that confront me. We move from stall to stall, taking in the dazzling displays before moving quickly on to the next. My cheeks hurt from so much grinning as I pull Lily ahead faster, excited to let off some steam and party like it's 1699.

We arrive earlier than planned, and the brothers are nowhere to be seen as Lily walks off to grab us drinks. I do notice some familiar faces though.

"Look who we have here," Ifi says. "If it isn't the little mundane who isn't."

Ifi and Elal walk over hand in hand, sipping on purple drinks, their skin aflame with golden fire that they let fade into nothing as they approach.

"I was worried I wouldn't know anyone," I say. "It's so good to see you."

"Elal here thought you'd be long gone by now, but I assured him you're here to stay, isn't that right?" He winks at me.

Elal huffs at that. "I said nothing of the sort. Stop your nonsense, love, and just play nice."

I chuckle at them both. "I am here to stay it seems," I say.

"Consider us your first friends in the Otherworld then," Ifi says, but he's interrupted by another voice, this one low and booming and coming from the sky.

"I believe that title belongs to me." Okura descends from the sky, her stone body massive compared to ours. And near her belly, in a solid pouch that wasn't there before, sits a baby gargoyle. Her mate lands beside her, while Ifi and Elal stare at the youngling, jaws hanging wide open.

"She's beautiful," I tell the doting parents, who are clearly smitten with their creation.

"Thank you for your blessing on her," Okura says.

I still don't know what exactly I did, but I nod and smile, glad it could help them at any rate.

Ifi turns back to look at me. "You're quite full of surprises, Miss Oliver. Working with you will no doubt be entertaining." With that, he takes Elal's hand, and the two of them wonder off to refill their drinks. The gargoyles depart as well, walking to admire the great glowing tree at the center of the square.

I look up, checking the massive iron clock that hangs on a nearby tower. It's four am now. The brothers should arrive any second.

Lily returns with cups of golden liquid, and the drink tastes like warm honey with a touch of brandy. We explore the festival, watching as a group of gnomes participate in a challenge of strength, smashing a hammer into a golden disk for points. Five minutes pass. Still the brothers do not arrive.

"They're late," I say.

Lily shrugs. "Liam probably just saw a pair of shoes he couldn't resist."

I nod, and we continue, walking past an Ifrit, burning brightly, sitting above a tank of water, as human-looking girls throw balls at a red target connected to a mechanism which would make him fall.

"Are they young werewolves?" I ask.

Lily shakes her head. "Young dryads."

A light rain begins to fall, and another five minutes pass with no sign of the brothers. I start to get irritated. Then worried. "Do you know where they went?" I ask.

Lily shakes her head. "No. But Uncle Liam did mention they had something important to do. I suppose he was a bit more secretive than usual."

Something important to do.

My gut twists into a knot, but I tell myself I have nothing to fear. I'm just being silly. The Night brothers are safe and well.

Another five minutes pass. The rain falls down harder, so much so that we buy cloaks off a vendor at the festival to keep ourselves dry. A chill enters the air and I find my teeth rattling.

Several more minutes pass and the knot in my gut is now a storm of worry. I wonder at where they could be, and I remember something I had forgotten. Something Derek had said at the trial.

It will be done by midwinter.

There is a pain in my chest, and my stomach burns like acid. I have felt like this once before. When my brother left me his final note.

"What's wrong?" asks Lily.

But I have no words in reply, my mind a flurry of doubt. Had they gone through with it? I wonder. Had the smiles and laughter been easier for them than telling me the truth? Had the sleepover been a way of saying goodbye?

I notice a familiar face in the distance. Matilda, wearing her cloak tight around her against the heavy rain. Matilda, who said she was too old for such parties. Matilda, who is coming toward us all the same, her face dark and grim.

A sob begins to break from my lips.

And just as it does…

I hear them.

"What's wrong, Eve?"

"How can we help?"

"What happened?"

"I swear, if someone hurt you…"

I turn around, seeing the four Night brothers crowding around me. And my heart breaks open with tears of happiness.

"Perhaps she's just upset we're late," says Elijah.

"Sorry about that, Eve," says Derek. "We had a bit of an emergency. You see…" He gestures to his brother.

And Liam moves aside his cloak, revealing a little baby girl, hair red as flame.

"She's beautiful," I say, the tears subsiding. "May I hold her?"

"Of course," says Liam, handing me the baby.

"We picked the little thing up from Ifi and Elal an hour ago," says Derek. "And we would have been on time, if Liam hadn't—"

"If Liam hadn't seen a bit of poop and thought she was dying," says Sebastian.

The fire druid shrugs. "What? It was an unordinary amount of excrement. And such a strange color. That can't be normal."

"We had to pick up diapers," concludes Elijah. "And console poor Liam's soul."

I laugh, holding the baby close in the crook of my arm, playing with her little fingers. "Does she have a name yet?"

Liam glances down, looking slightly embarrassed. "I'm naming her Alina. It's Greek for light."

I look down at the cherubic face and smile. "It's perfect. She's perfect." I look at Liam. "Does this mean we're keeping her?"

He nods. "I think it does. She needs her father, after all."

"What about Dracula?" I ask.

"We will keep her safe," Liam says fiercely, and I know this little girl will be the most loved child in any world.

"You look incredible, by the way," says Derek.

"Thank you," I say, with a grin. With my worries subsided, I take a moment to admire the Night brothers properly.

Elijah sports a look I haven't seen on him before. A black coat with purple buttons, a top hat covering his blonde hair, a silver cane in his hand. He looks every bit the sophisticated gentlemen, pulled straight from the Victorian era.

Derek has shaved since I last saw him, and wears a finely tailored suit, a red scarf wrapped around his neck.

Sebastian is a little more rough around the edges. His jacket and boots are black leather. Simple. Sturdy. But he does sport an elegant pink tie at his neck.

Liam is dressed as he often is, but not any less impressive. Custom designed shoes with fine embroidery. An emerald green cloak that compliments his auburn hair perfectly.

I hand the babe back to Liam as Matilda comes to join us. We exchange greetings, while Elijah and Sebastian begin discussing the finer points of Otherworld law. I link arms with them both and laugh. "You guys, it's a party. No work today. Let's enjoy our victory and our evening, shall we?"

Derek smiles. "Right you are, Eve. Right you are. I for one plan on drinking my body weight in liquor. Who's game to join me?"

"I think that might kill me," I say. "But I will partake in a drink or two." I look at Matilda. "I'll definitely need your hangover cure tomorrow."

The old woman winks knowingly. "I've already prepared a batch for all of you. Now go have fun, my dears."

We make our way through the festival, and I notice it stopped raining almost as quickly as it started. Lucky for us. But as Sebastian tries his hand at the strength competition, the earth seems to shift under my feet, and the Ifrit above the water tank loses balance and falls in.

"A small earthquake," says Elijah. "Nothing to fear. They happen from time to time."

Everyone seems to resume their activities without a

second thought, and so we do the same. Derek and Lily make a beeline for the bar to grab everyone drinks. Sebastian offers to acquire sustenance of some kind for me. "If that includes chocolate, yes, please," I say with a wink.

Liam sees someone he knows and excuses himself to say hi, handing the baby to Matilda who has been vying for her chance to give the little one love. Elijah sits down by the huge bonfire with a book in hand. I shake my head at that. I'm a book nerd myself, but even I know when to let it go for a night.

From the corner of my eye, I notice a familiar black cloak disappear behind a tree. Interesting. I didn't expect him to see him, not so soon after everything that happened. Curious, I snake away from the celebration and towards the shadows, where I find Dracula waiting.

He holds a hand up before I can speak. "I wanted to say goodbye. I'll be leaving the Otherworld for a while, to let all the gossip die down. But I wanted to thank you. You were instrumental in proving my innocence. That won't be forgotten."

I don't know what to say, so I just nod, relieved he'll be leaving. That should make protecting Alina easier.

His eyes are dark, intense, and locked on mine as he speaks. "My sons have a unique bond with you. I haven't seen them like this with anyone else in their long lives. I hope you know what you've gotten yourself into."

"I know enough," I say, a little tersely.

"Oh, but my dear, there is so much yet to learn. How great is your capacity for forgiveness, I wonder? I suppose we'll find out in time."

Another tremor rocks the world around us, sending waves of movement through the land. Most of the partiers don't notice, too lost in the revelry and booze. But a few do, and this time they look around, alarmed.

A small smile creeps onto Dracula's lips. "It has begun. Guard yourself, Miss Oliver. No one in the Otherworld is truly innocent."

I shrug. "The same can be said of anyone anywhere. I choose faith and love over doubt and fear. It's a happier way to live."

He nods, then lifts my hand to his lips, kissing it softly. "Then I bid thee farewell. May you hold onto that optimism as long as you can."

And with that he disappears into the shadows, and I wonder if we'll ever see him again. I think of Liam's baby daughter and hope we don't. She's safer that way.

I'm about to turn and head back to the party when something in the grass glints in the light of the Dragon's Breath. I bend down to pick it up and see it's a Memory Catcher.

Curious, I activate it.

I see a familiar room before me.

Cream walls.

White carpet.

I appear to be looking at things through a window.

Looking straight into Mary's chambers.

There's a scream, and the image tilts to the side, revealing Mary on the bed, dressed in a white gown, halfway through labor. Alone. Crying, calling out for help.

I know what happens next.

Jerry will come in soon. He will kill her and the baby, though a young girl will live. I am ready to stop the memory, unwilling to see the gruesome sight, when a person comes through the door.

A person who isn't Jerry.

The man wears a long black cloak I have seen before. When he walks, his steps are achingly familiar.

And when I see his face, my entire body shakes.

This is impossible.

It can't be real.

And yet the memory unfolds.

He steps closer to the bed, silent, expression cold, and Mary pulls back, frightened, confused. Racked with pain.

As she delivers her own baby, the man grabs the child and—

I look away.

I can't have that image in my mind forever.

But I hear it.

What he does with the child. What he does to Mary.

And when I look back at the memory, she is dead. They both are.

A few moments later, Jerry arrives, a letter in hand he quickly shoves into his pocket. He runs to Mary's side, screaming, trying to revive her though she is clearly dead. When he finally realizes his efforts are futile, he notices the blood all over his jacket, his hands. And then he runs.

Minutes pass. Minutes that feel like hours.

I see her belly moving after a moment, and then Liam runs into the room, a look of utter horror on his face as he witnesses the devastation.

I stop the memory, not needing to see more. I know the rest.

I fall to my knees, a sob building in my throat. My nails dig into the wet earth as I feel the pain wash in waves through me.

This has to be a trick.

The memory has to be a fake.

Otherwise, everything I have ever known will shatter.

And then I see his feet, dark, mud-caked boots.

Then his legs.

And I pull myself up, my beautiful dress covered in dirt, as I face the man I thought I knew.

The man I thought I could trust.

And I face Mary's real killer.

A scent of cinnamon and honey catches on the wind, and I am racked with sorrow as blue eyes I know better than my own look back at me. And when he holds out his hand, my heart lurches in my chest.

"Hello, sister."

My voice catches in my throat. "Adam?"

~ TO BE CONTINUED~

THE SAGA CONTINUES…

Want book 2, I Am the Storm? Grab it on AMAZON.

Thank you for joining us on this new adventure! If you loved this book, please consider leaving a review. It makes all the difference. And if you want the next book in the series before anyone else, check out our patreon. You get all our work before the rest of the world, and behind the scenes access to all the things, plus other perks. Check it out: Patreon.com/KarpovKinrade

Did you know we also make music? I AM THE WILD has an official fantasy soundtrack that you can find on iTunes, Apple Music, Spotify, Amazon, Google Play and more. We also have soundtracks for OF DREAMS AND DRAGONS and MOONSTONE ACADEMY, as well as vocal music all under Karpov Kinrade.

For even more vampire romance,check out Vampire Girl: A complete USA Today bestselling series with 7 books and 3 spinoffs.

NOTE FROM THE AUTHOR

This novel ended up being very personal to me. It deals with themes of suicide and domestic violence, both of which I (Lux) have experienced. (In the case of suicide, with my brother, much like Eve.)

If you are struggling with thoughts of self-harm or of ending your life, please reach out for help.

And if you are in an abusive relationship, I know how hard it is, but please get help. There are resources for you.

There is hope. There is light.

In lumen et lumen.

~Lux

National Suicide Prevention Lifeline
Call 1-800-273-8255

National Domestic Violence Hotline
800-799-SAFE (800-799-7233)
TTY: 800-787-3224

ABOUT THE AUTHOR

Karpov Kinrade is the pen name for the husband and wife writing duo of USA TODAY bestselling, award-winning authors Lux Karpov-Kinrade and Dmytry Karpov-Kinrade.

Together, they live in Ukiah, California and write fantasy and science fiction novels and screenplays, make music and direct movies.

Look for more from Karpov Kinrade in *Vampire Girl*, *Of Dreams and Dragons*, *The Nightfall Chronicles* and *The*

Forbidden Trilogy. If you're looking for their suspense and romance titles, you'll now find those under Alex Lux.

They live with their three teens who share a genius for all things creative, and seven cats who think they rule the world (spoiler, they do.)

Want their books and music before anyone else? Join them on Patreon at Patreon.com/karpovkinrade

Find them online at KarpovKinrade.com

On Facebook /KarpovKinrade

On Twitter @KarpovKinrade

And subscribe to their newsletter at ReadKK.com for special deals and up-to-date notice of new launches.

~~~~~

If you enjoyed this book, consider supporting the author by leaving a review wherever you purchased this book. Thank you.

Forbidden Mind

Forbidden Fire

Forbidden Life

Our ALEX LUX BOOKS!

The Seduced Saga (paranormal romance with suspense)

Seduced by Innocence

Seduced by Pain

Seduced by Power

Seduced by Lies

Seduced by Darkness

The Call Me Cat Trilogy (romantic suspense)

Call Me Cat

Leave Me Love

Tell Me True

(Standalone romcon with crossover characters)

Hitched

Whipped

Kiss Me in Paris (A standalone romance)

Our Children's Fantasy collection under Kimberly Kinrade

The Three Lost Kids series

Lexie World

Bella World

Maddie World

The Three Lost Kids and Cupid's Capture

The Three Lost Kids and the Death of the Sugar Fairy

The Three Lost Kids and the Christmas Curse

ACKNOWLEDGMENTS

FEATURED POEMS FROM THE KK COVEN inspired by I Am the Wild

by Jennifer Borak
    I am the daughter of the moon
    Part darkness, part light
    One with the stars
    Forged with twilight
    My betrothed, my love
    With whom I'm beguiled
    Beautifully paradoxical
    I am the wild

by Rhena Le Moucheux
    I walk through the darkness but do not fear the light,
    I stare at the sky and the stars so bright,
    I have seen this sky before so many times,
    I can map the stars without a second glance,

for you are my sky my stars so bright
you will always be with me my guiding light.

THANK YOUS...

Thanks to Joe for all the editing and for going above and beyond in all the ways! And Bam for all the awesome graphics and brainstorming and help launching this new series. You two are rockstars!

Special love to the KK Coven for always being our tribe.

And to our patrons for being our rock and support.

We'd like to also thank all those who helped hunt down poems to use for the chapter heads:

Lynn Wright, Kathryn Fothergill, Jillian Falaris, Kimberley Tuong, Allison Woerner, Sharon Lynn Hughes, Melinda Kahler, Jennifer Borak, Darla Stone, Amber Sanders, Alexandra Marie Leith, Rhena Le Moucheux, Billie Cutcher

And finally, to our patrons. We love you all! Every tier, every single one of you is everything. We'd like to especially thank those who are going so far above it all to support us. To Billie Cutcher and Brittany Geary. Holy shit. You two. Wow. And to Sara, Kayla, Brooke, Bunny, Rebecca Silvers <3, Carrie, Ali, Michelle, Christal, Jill, Melodie, Mariana, Laura, Abby, Brandie, Heaven, Mandy, Alexandra, Kala, Kimi, Kira, Meghan, Troi, Sharon, Jenni, Chantelle, Crissy, Jeanette, Allison, Marcie, Jennifer, Shelah, Charity, Sarah, Natalie, Mas, Karen, Kayla, and Kathleen. You are the start of a new kind of magic for us. Thank you.

Love,
   Lux & D

Made in the USA
Monee, IL
04 September 2019